P9-DNT-394

SANDRINE'S CASE

Books by Thomas H. Cook

FICTION

Blood Innocents

The Orchids

Tabernacle

Elena

Sacrificial Ground

Flesh and Blood

Streets of Fire

Night Secrets

The City When It Rains

Evidence of Blood

Mortal Memory

Breakheart Hill

The Chatham School Affair

Instruments of Night

Places in the Dark

The Interrogation

Taken (based on the teleplay by Leslie Boehm)

Moon over Manhattan (with Larry King)

Peril

Into the Web

Red Leaves

The Cloud of Unknowing

Master of the Delta

The Fate of Katherine Carr

The Last Talk with Lola Faye

The Quest for Anna Klein

The Crime of Julian Wells

Sandrine's Case

NONFICTION

Early Graves

Blood Echoes

A Father's Story (as told by Lionel Dahmer)

Best American Crime Writing 2000, 2001 (ed. with Otto Penzler)

Best American Crime Writing 2002 (ed. with Otto Penzler)

Best American Crime Writing 2003 (ed. with Otto Penzler)

Best American Crime Writing 2004 (ed. with Otto Penzler)

Best American Crime Writing 2005 (ed. with Otto Penzler)

Best American Crime Writing 2006 (ed. with Otto Penzler)

Best American Crime Reporting 2007 (ed. with Otto Penzler)

Best American Crime Reporting 2008 (ed. with Otto Penzler)

Best American Crime Reporting 2009 (ed. with Otto Penzler)

Best American Crime Reporting 2010 (ed. with Otto Penzler)

SANDRINE'S CASE

THOMAS H. COOK

The Mysterious Press
an imprint of Grove/Atlantic Inc.
New York

ROUND LAKE AREA
LIBRARY
906 HART ROAD
ROUND LAKE, IL 60073
(847) 546-7060

Copyright © 2013 by Thomas H. Cook

All rights reserved. No part of this book may be reproduced in any form or by any electronic or mechanical means, including information storage and retrieval systems, without permission in writing from the publisher, except by a reviewer, who may quote brief passages in a review. Scanning, uploading, and electronic distribution of this book or the facilitation of such without the permission of the publisher is prohibited. Please purchase only authorized electronic editions, and do not participate in or encourage electronic piracy of copyrighted materials. Your support of the author's rights is appreciated. Any member of educational institutions wishing to photocopy part or all of the work for classroom use, or anthology, should send inquiries to Grove/Atlantic, Inc., 154 West 14th Street, New York, NY 10011 or permissions@groveatlantic.com.

Published simultaneously in Canada
Printed in the United States of America

FIRST EDITION

ISBN-13: 978-0-8021-2608-5

The Mysterious Press
an imprint of Grove/Atlantic, Inc.
154 West 14th Street
New York, NY 10011

Distributed by Publishers Group West

www.groveatlantic.com

13 14 15 16   10 9 8 7 6 5 4 3 2 1

Always, always, for Susan and Justine

Sandrine: a popular French female name. It is derived from Old Greek and is a shortened form of Alexandra, which means helper and defender of mankind.

The Meaning of Names

PART I

The Coburn College community is in mourning today for the untimely death of Sandrine Madison, a much-loved professor of history. Dr. Madison, who earned her advanced degrees from the Sorbonne in Paris, France, had taught at Coburn College for the last twenty-two years. She is survived by her husband, Samuel Madison, also a professor at the college, and their daughter, Alexandria.

Coburn Sentinel
November 16, 2010

DAY ONE

Opening Argument: The Prosecution

Lost hope conceals a rapier in its gown, Sandrine wrote in the margins of her copy of *Julius Caesar*. Strange, but of all the things she'd said or written, this was the line I most wrenchingly recalled on the last day of my trial. Life should fill our ears with warning, I thought as I remembered how she'd penned this little piece of marginalia alongside one of Cassius's melancholy speeches, but it falls silent at our infant cry.

Such was my conclusion as the jury foreman rose to render a verdict in my case, thus the moment when I would either hear, or not hear, the creak of a gallows floor. To some extent, their decision hardly mattered anymore. I knew what I'd done, and how I'd done it, and by what means I had tried to get away with it. Regardless of the verdict, my trial had exposed everything, and from it I'd learned that it is one thing to glance in a mirror, quite another to see what's truly there.

On the first day of my trial, however, I'd been quite beyond so naked an understanding of murder, or of anything else, for that matter. All great revelations are hard won, Sandrine once told me, perhaps as a warning. But until the ordeal of my trial, all my revelations had been small, and none of them had been hard won.

In fact, only one truth had seemed certain to me on the day my trial began: Harold Singleton, the prosecuting attorney, was out to get me.

"You're the proverbial ham sandwich any public prosecutor can indict, Sam," my lawyer, Mordecai "Morty" Salberg, had told me on the day I was charged with Sandrine's murder. Despite certain admittedly incriminating evidence, we'd both been surprised by my indictment, and for a moment, as I'd sat in his paneled office, I'd recalled a moment, weeks before, when Detective Alabrandi had leaned forward, his dark eyes as menacing as his voice, and said to me, You're not going to get away with this.

The result of this grim recollection had been a blinding streak of panic that had actually caused my hands to tremble.

Morty had seen this, and in order to calm me down he'd casually leaned back in his leather chair. "It's a completely circumstantial case, Sam," he said. "And in terms of the so-called physical evidence, there's not one thing the prosecution has uncovered that can't be explained by your wife's suicide."

"But I could have made it look like a suicide," I replied cautiously. "Isn't that what Singleton will try to make the jury believe?"

Morty waved his hand as if to dismiss the entire case against me. "You need to understand one thing, Sam," he said. "This prosecution is not being driven forward by the weight of the evidence."

"By what then?" I asked.

"By Harold Singleton's personal conviction that you killed your wife," Morty said. "He truly believes that you carefully planned the whole thing." He smiled. "He thinks you're one cold fish, Sam," he added. "And I got to tell you, you do come off that way, so before you get before a jury, you should work on your charm skills a little."

At that instant, with my hands now clammy, I'd thought of a moment many months before, the way Sandrine had glanced up from the book she was reading, a study of Iago, of all people, and peered at me quite intently before she'd finally spoken. "Cynics make good murderers," she'd said. I'd thought this remark was about Iago, but later I'd not been so sure. Had Sandrine, in that piercing way of hers, seen that her death was on my mind?

"The real shocker is that Singleton is going for the death penalty," Morty added. "That's the sort of prosecutorial overreaching that can come back to bite you in the ass. Of course he probably threatened you with that in order to pressure you into a confession. Then, once he made the threat, and you didn't confess, he had to go through with it. It's sort of a pissing game, you know, but believe me I can shoot my stream way farther than Harold Singleton." He shrugged as if to dismiss the need for any further discussion. "It'll be a short trial, that's for damn sure," he told me.

Then he rose and escorted me to the door.

"Don't worry, Sam," he said with the iron-clad assurance of his many years of defending with equal skill and success both the innocent and the guilty. "All you need is a good defense, and you've got the smartest Jew lawyer in Coburn County."

Perhaps so, but along with my unfortunate, seal-the-deal novella, there were fingerprints on the glass and emails to April and odd elements in Sandrine's blood, disturbing Internet searches and jarring responses to various questions, a less than sturdy prosecutorial net in which to catch me, as I knew, but a net nonetheless. And there was that coldness, too, of course. I'd need to work on that.

Still it was the location of my trial that had most concerned me as I'd departed Morty's office that day. Coburn County was the problem, it seemed to me, a college town only seventy miles south of Atlanta, a quiet place whose privacy had been violated by the media coverage of Sandrine's death, the subsequent investigation, and, still later, my arrest. Every step in the process had further served to turn the town against me, so that as I'd driven back through Coburn after leaving Morty's office, I'd genuinely feared that no matter what the evidence—or lack of it—its stalwart citizens might well find me guilty at the end of my trial. Sandrine had once said that when she thought of hell, it was as an eternal walk through a shadowy alley. By the time of my trial, I'd come to imagine it as a never-ending fall through a gallows floor.

As the yearlong investigation into Sandrine's death had continued, I'd learned one thing for certain: my initial error had been to underestimate the extent to which little things could trip me up. For example, I'd never expected that first uniformed officer to notice a yellow piece of paper beside my wife's deathbed, ask me about it, then write my response into her notebook. Later I'd realized that she had seen a dead woman lying in a bed, half naked and with no visible marks upon her face or body, and had quite naturally asked herself: How did this woman die? That is to say, she had cared about this death more than I'd expected and had almost immediately begun to look about the room more closely, a focused observation that had eventually settled her eyes on, among other things, that yellow piece of paper.

Thus had the investigation begun, one that had steadily grown darker and more dramatic, first with the coroner's inquiry, then with the pathologist's report, and after that—and with murder in mind—Detective Alabrandi's meticulous combing of phone and medical records, the seizing of computers, the questioning of friends, associates, neighbors, all of which had finally culminated in a grand jury indictment, which in turn had led, at last, to this first day of my trial, myself seated at the defense table with the best "Jew lawyer" in Coburn County beside me, both of us now watching silently as Mr. Singleton made his way to the lectern, glanced at his notes, then began.

"Your Honor, ladies and gentlemen of the jury," Mr. Singleton said, "from this first day onward, and step by step, we will prove to your complete satisfaction that Sandrine Allegra Madison did not take her own life."

He wore a dark blue suit that first day. It fit him poorly, so there was a slight rise, like a small snake, across the back of his neck. I could see this round bulge quite clearly because his back was to me when he faced the jury. He was short and very thin, with wire-rimmed glasses that added a sense of physical weakness, perhaps even ill health.

"Singleton always looks like he's going to sneeze on you," Morty whispered with a quick smile he was careful to conceal from the jury.

This was true, I thought, but the prosecutor's physical problems didn't end there. For one thing, he was nearly bald, and he often swabbed his pink head with a white handkerchief. Many months before, when he'd asked me to come to his office for a "preliminary discussion," I'd noticed that his teeth were badly crooked, like rows of tilted tombstones in a desecrated cemetery. At that time, I wondered if he'd perhaps been a poor boy whose parents had not been able to afford braces, or whether he was simply the sort of man whose priorities did not include close attention to his looks. At any rate, the jagged configuration of his teeth had given him the half-starved countenance of a primitive creature, its every aspect adapted for survival in a mean environment.

By then I'd come to realize that I was the target of his investigation, the one man in Sandrine's life who, according to his discoveries, had had a reason to kill her—perhaps more than one reason—along with the moral benightedness required to do it.

Watching him now, I recalled that first visit quite well, particularly how self-assured he'd seemed as he'd said, "Professor Madison, I'd like to acquaint you with a few facts."

He thinks I'm soft, I'd told myself at that moment. He thinks he can bully me because I'm a weak, ivory tower intellectual, a poodle to his bulldog. For that reason, I'd hidden my fear of these "facts," put on a mask of complete confidence in my innocence of any charge he might level against me, replied, "I'm eager to hear them," then casually leaned back in the chair, folded my arms over my chest, and waited for his next move as casually as a clubman anticipating his afternoon martini.

For the next few minutes, Singleton had laid out his case against me, always in a grave voice, like a Spanish inquisitor enumerating all my many sins and heresies. There was the matter of this (antihistamines in Sandrine's bloodstream) linked to that (a sinister research history on my computer). There'd also been correspondence that, as he'd discovered by then, I'd attempted to delete. Other grave issues had followed one after the other like the blows of a hammer, and as I'd listened to this recitation it had become clear to me that if I did not crack, perhaps hint at a plea bargain, Mr. Singleton would not rest until I dangled from a noose. That had scared me, and it was then, and far too late, that I'd finally gone to Morty and told him everything I'd heard in the prosecutor's office.

Morty had quickly assured me that the case against me was absurdly weak, Singleton's recitation a bluff, and so I'd been genuinely surprised when Detective Alabrandi subsequently showed up at my door, this time with a man I'd never seen, large, surly even when silent, with a thick neck, and looking very much like a sports bar bouncer.

"You're under arrest, Mr. Madison," Alabrandi said politely, but with his gaze fixed in an icy glare.

There are moments when you feel something shift and know—not just sense but know—that some great wheel has begun to crush you. One morning, somewhere within that netherworld of middle age, you look in the mirror and see that time is doing to you what it has done to everyone before you. Or you suddenly feel a squeezing sensation in your chest and realize that, although it is probably just heartburn, there is a chance, a genuine chance now, that it is something worse.

You are under arrest.

It was at that moment that I'd first begun to experience one of life's deepest lessons: you are the most alive when you feel the most vulnerable, not when the arrow is still in the quiver but when it has been released by the string and is flying toward you. The inexorable gears of modest little Coburn's justice system have begun to grind, I'd thought at that instant, and you, my dear fellow, so perfectly insulated before now, aloof and professorial, armored by advanced degrees and unknowable depths of arcane information, you, Dr. Samuel Joseph Madison, tenured professor of English and American literature, are the perfect grist for its mill.

"We will prove it was that man," Mr. Singleton said as he turned and pointed toward me, "that man, seated there, who took the life of Sandrine Allegra Madison and made her his victim."

Victim? Sandrine?

I'd known her in her youth. I'd known her as a lover, a wife, the mother of our now grown daughter. I'd known her as a student and as a teacher. At no point in my life had I ever imagined her as a victim of anything. And yet it was as a victim that a great many others had come to view her by the first day of my trial, and thus to view me as a man who had much to explain, much to confess, much to repent, and much—very, very much—for which he should be punished.

"Sandrine Allegra Madison was the victim of a cold and vicious plot," Mr. Singleton said. "She was the victim of a murder that was premeditated for weeks, as we will show, and carried out by a man with many motives to take her life."

He'd used her full name throughout his initial remarks to the jury, but Morty had earlier that morning alerted me to the fact that Mr. Singleton would probably begin calling her "Sandrine" as the trial proceeded, and perhaps even "Sandy" during his closing argument, a diminutive I knew she would have hated. For Sandrine was no Sandy. She'd been studying ancient history when I met her, and it was history she'd addressed in the opening words of her last written statement: *I often think of Cleopatra in desert exile at twenty-one, surrounded by those blistering sands, she whose feet had walked on onyx.*

Morty had also advised me that, at some point during the trial, Mr. Singleton would certainly read this last note or letter or essay or whatever it was to the jury, and that he would do this in order to support his contention that Sandrine hadn't killed herself. Although it had remained unsaid, I'd learned enough about courtroom strategies by then to know that Morty's hope was that the last words Sandrine had committed to paper would make her look pretentious, writing about Cleopatra in her final moments when she should have been penning a loving—or at least explanatory—letter to her husband or her daughter. Unfair though the idea might be—and this Morty had said to me directly—it would work to my advantage if the jury came to think of Sandrine as an egghead. From this I'd gathered that it is easier to find a man accused of murdering his wife not guilty if his victim, during her last moments, was thinking of Cleopatra.

Yet was Sandrine's last bit of writing pretentious? I hadn't thought so when I read it. It was simply how Sandrine wrote, always in a tone that was slightly old-fashioned, but which was also graceful and carefully measured. She had used such connectives as "into whose" and "by which" and "according to whom" in order to string thoughts together, and she had taught her students to do the same. For her, the task of writing was to relate insights to information, or vice versa. "Sentences must join like the fingers of a hand," she'd said to me one evening in New York, when we'd both still been young and the wine bottle two-thirds full, "otherwise, they can't hold water."

Water, by which she'd meant wisdom, the collected fruit of those hard-won truths, all of which inevitably led to what she called "the bottom line," and by which she meant the irreducible and unavoidable facts of life.

One thing was certain. Sandrine had loved language the way others love food, and so, understandably, no doubt it had been the loss of that command of language she'd most dreaded in the end, the terrible fact that eventually she would begin to slur, not to mention drool and blubber.

"We will prove that a miserable charade was concocted by that man," Mr. Singleton continued. "It was a veil he hoped to conceal a murder."

It was a veil *behind which he* hoped to conceal a murder, I corrected Mr. Singleton in exactly the way Sandrine would doubtless have corrected him.

"That man," Mr. Singleton all but shouted.

That man, of course, was me, Samuel Joseph Madison, husband to the late Sandrine and father to our daughter, Alexandria, who sat behind me that first day, dressed entirely in black, with close-cropped hair, a daughter nowhere near as physically beautiful or intellectually gifted as her mother. Because of that, I'd found myself wondering if Sandrine's death had removed a competitor from the field. After all, with her dazzling mother dead, Alexandria would never be unfavorably compared to her again, and surely that would bring her a certain, unmistakable relief. There is nothing quite so painful as invidious comparison, after all, and for that reason I'd sometimes wondered if Sandrine's death might not have been altogether unwelcomed by her only daughter.

Dark thoughts.

Such dark thoughts.

Murder's bedfellows.

"It was a crude and cruel act of selfishness that Samuel Madison attempted to disguise as suicide," Mr. Singleton declared.

I glanced behind me and noticed that Alexandria's expression had turned scornful at this latest of Mr. Singleton's pronouncements. Even so, it was impossible for me to know if she believed Coburn's lean and hungry prosecutor or whether she'd accepted my version of her mother's death: that it had been by her own hand and that I'd had nothing to do with it. A few weeks before, I'd dined with my daughter at Le Petit Court, Coburn's notion of a French bistro, and she'd bluntly asked, "You really had no idea, Dad?"

"There were hints," I admitted. "But nothing solid."

"It just seems so strange that she would do it, well, out of the blue, the way she did," Alexandria continued. "You go to your class and you come back and she's dead. I mean, that she would just suddenly decide that she had . . . that she'd just had enough."

I shrugged. "Your mother had a mind of her own."

"But that night, if you'd known what she was going to do, what would you have done, Dad?"

"I don't know," I answered. "If your mother wanted to die, didn't she have that right? The Greeks would have given it to her, after all."

It was then I'd suddenly glanced left and right, noticed my fellow diners at Le Petit Court, noticed those first stares, heard those first whispers, and sensed that the shock troops of Coburn were gathering against me.

Even so, I'd boldly proceeded on.

"This case is made for scandalmongers," I said.

Alexandria's gaze grew darkly still but she said nothing, so different from her mother, as I'd thought at that moment, less able to accuse me of every crime imaginable, save the one I'd actually committed.

"It's made to order for the type of people who read those tabloid newspapers," I added. "First of all, it's a case involving two college professors, and intellectuals are still the most hated people on earth. To have one accused of murdering the other? It's red meat for their fangs.

Especially a woman like your mother, so very . . . photogenic. My God, how much juicier can it get?"

But in his opening argument Mr. Singleton had made it even juicier than various media outlets—both local and national—had already made it. In the most perfervid language of which he was capable, he'd described a deadly intrigue hatched in the hothouse atmosphere of a small town liberal arts college, with emphasis, of course, on "liberal."

That wasn't all.

I don't read genre literature but I'd seen enough movies based upon those sorts of books to understand that into Coburn's pristine, even pastoral setting Mr. Singleton had introduced a generous helping of noir. He'd pointed out Sandrine's insurance policy, for example, a rather obvious nod to *Double Indemnity.* And, based on that first salvo, I'd guessed that as the trial moved forward he'd almost certainly describe me in such a way as to ensure that the jury would indeed hear the postman ring twice. He would build his case against me brick by brick. By the time of final arguments he would have painted the portrait of an arrogant and foolish man—by any standard an immoralist—who'd clumsily conceived and even more clumsily carried out a plot to kill his wife, his motivation being money, sex, or simple selfishness, take your pick. The jury would hear all this and, after they'd heard it, they would cheerfully send me to the Great State of Georgia's heart-stopping, muscle-relaxing equivalent of the gallows.

"Sandrine Allegra Madison did not die of natural causes," Mr. Singleton gravely intoned in the final line of his opening argument. "Sandrine Allegra Madison was murdered."

With that statement, delivered with a quite sincere show of quivering moral outrage, Mr. Singleton returned to the prosecutor's table. He did not smile but I knew he was quite satisfied with his performance. He glanced at Morty as if to say, *Top that, Jew boy!*

Opening Argument:
For the Defense

I glanced at Morty, who does indeed look like an anti-Semitic version of a typical yeshiva boy with his curly black hair, slightly crooked nose, and thick black glasses. He nodded softly, assumed his "What, me worry?" pose, and rose slowly from his chair. Once on his feet, he drew in a deep, theatrical breath then strolled with a deliberate lack of urgency toward the plain wooden lectern that rested a few feet in front of the judge's bench. A thoroughgoing actor, Morty gave every appearance of thinking it quite unnecessary to make any opening statement at all since nothing Mr. Singleton had said was actually worth addressing. His gait was unhurried, and to this leisurely pace he added an air of weariness by which he wished to convey to the jury that he shared their opinion that Mr. Singleton was a pathetic little wimp who had given them nothing but empty rhetoric by way of opening argument, and that he was absolutely certain they had found every single word of it a stupendous waste of time.

"Your Honor," he began once he reached the podium, "ladies and gentlemen of the jury."

He brought no notes with him, and so he looked only at the jury as he continued. Who needs notes, he was asking them with this ploy, when there is no evidence whatsoever against poor Sam Madison, a grieving widower now unaccountably charged with the murder of his beloved wife?

"You know, I'm sorry that you good people have to be seated in the jury box today," he began, "because I'm sure you'd rather be at your jobs or at home with your families. And frankly, ladies and gentlemen, you shouldn't be here, because before bringing a person to trial, the State is obligated not just to have evidence but to have evidence that is beyond a reasonable doubt. No. Let me correct myself. This is a murder case. A capital case, if you can believe that, and, frankly, ladies and gentlemen, I have trouble believing it. But here we are in a capital trial so, no, the prosecution is obligated to present evidence that will convince you not just beyond a reasonable doubt but beyond the shadow of a doubt. That's why each and every one of you should be at work today, ladies and gentlemen, or at home with your families, going through your usual routines. Because there is *no evidence* in this case. Not even enough to have brought Mr. Madison to trial, let alone try him for his life."

I faced the jury silently as Morty continued, faced these twelve women and men who, I felt certain, were quite prepared to kill me. It was obvious to me that they despised me, and I knew precisely the cause of their hostility. For wasn't it just such windy professors as myself who'd poisoned their children with atheism or socialism or worse, who'd infused their previously unsullied minds with dreamy fantasies of changing the world or writing a great novel, while at the same time teaching them not one skill by which they might later find employment and thus avoid returning to their parents' homes to sit sullenly in front of the television, boiling with unrealizable hopes?

How odd that I was to be judged by these people, I thought, as I allowed my gaze to drift over to the jury, all of them dressed neatly and with quite somber expressions on their faces. How many had I passed on the street or glimpsed in the park with no anticipation that they might ever have any power over me, much less the awesome one they now possessed?

To the extent that I'd thought of them at all, it had been as characters in some Coburnite version of the *Spoon River Anthology*. There'd even been times when I'd sat in the park or on the town square and made up gravestone poems about the people passing by, cynical little rhymes that Sandrine had rarely found amusing, and in the midst of which she'd sometimes risen and walked some distance away.

What had she been thinking at those moments, I wondered suddenly, and on that question I once again saw her lift her eyes from that study of Iago: *cynics make good murderers*. Could Sandrine have sensed something dangerous in my mocking quips, I wondered, and had her sudden rising and walking away from me been only the first small steps toward the final, isolating distance she'd imposed upon me during the last weeks of her life?

She'd changed so much during those last months, I recalled as I returned my gaze to the front of the courtroom. She'd become so quiet, so still, at least until that last smoldering night when her fury had boiled over and she'd actually thrown a cup at me. Prior to that night, and because she was still so young and because there is nothing more infuriating than bad luck, I'd expected her to rage against death, rather than against me, but she'd exploded like a roadside bomb, her fury so fierce it had finally driven me from the house.

Things had been very different before that night, however. In fact, during that last week, a gravity had settled over her, so that I'd often found her sitting in complete silence, no longer reading or listening to music but simply, darkly thinking. Had it been in the midst of one of those sessions of deep thought that she had come to some monstrous judgment on her life? Is this what I had seen in that little sunroom, Sandrine wrestling with her past as her future closed, coming to grips with the cruelest of her "bottom lines": that she could not add a single second to the clock, the one precious second that would have allowed time for her to . . . what?

In Sandrine's case, I had to confess that I simply didn't know.

On that thought, and quite suddenly, while Morty continued his opening argument, I recalled Sandrine's suggestion that we retrace our first trip together, make it our second honeymoon.

"Let's book a trip around the Mediterranean, Sam," she'd said excitedly several months before her death. "We could return to all the places we visited on that first trip." She smiled happily. "We could start in Athens and end in Albi, the way we did when we were young."

I'd been at a loss as to how I might respond to this, and so I'd said nothing as she'd raced on.

"We could go to Alexandria, where the great library was." She thought a moment. "Yes, Alexandria." She smiled. "The city we named our daughter for."

Alexandria, yes, a name I'd always been careful to pronounce clearly and distinctly. *Al-ex-an-dree-ah* . . . not Alexandra. And certainly never Alex or, God forbid, Ali.

Oh, how much can now be made of my daughter's name, I thought as Morty finished his initial remarks to the jury, a version of our family life that was meant to convince the jury of just how perfect things had been in that little house on bucolic Crescent Road, the house, surely, of a devoted couple, a house right out of *Good Housekeeping*, with its bright green lawn and red bird feeder and tinkling wind chimes.

"This home was a warm home," Morty told the jury. "It was not a cold, dark place." He paused and gave its expressionless members a penetrating look. "The house on Crescent Road was not a place of plots and schemes. The home that was made by Sam and Sandrine Madison was a place of love."

19

I cringed at this, but I kept my discomfort with the final words of Morty's opening argument to myself. Still, the sentimental language rankled because it turned our house into a Hallmark card. Sure, there'd been love at 237 Crescent Road. Years of love, as a matter of fact. But has anything in a marriage ever been that simple?

In my mind, I saw Sandrine's hand lift from the bed and stretch out into the gloomy air. For a moment I'd thought it a gesture intended to draw me back to her after having hurled that cup. But then that same hand had violently grabbed the white sheet and pulled it over her as if I were no longer entitled to see her body. Oh, of course there'd been love in our house on Crescent Road. But what else had been there?

Seeds of discontent?

Seeds of infidelity?

Seeds, at last, of murder?

As Morty headed back toward the defense table at the close of his argument, I thought of Sandrine when we'd first settled into the house in which, some twenty years later, she would die. It had been a bright spring day, and she'd worn a brilliantly colored sundress, and for a single, exquisite moment she'd seemed gloriously happy. "Oh, Sam," she said as she flung herself into my arms. "Let's be careful." She stepped back, looked at me quite seriously, then added, "Let's be careful not to change." Then she'd kissed me very sweetly and gently, a kiss that had been made one hundred percent of love, and which had probably bestowed upon me, as I realized quite suddenly, the single happiest moment of the life I'd shared with her.

Oh where are they, I asked myself, recalling what Sandrine had believed the saddest sentiment in all poetry, and which she had first read to me in French: *Mais, où sont les neiges d'antan?*

Oh where are the snows of yesteryear?

Strange, but as Morty resumed his seat beside me at the defense table and picked up some document or other, then rose again and headed toward the bench, it struck me as rather curious that, although Sandrine had quoted those lines many times over the past two decades, I had not felt their dreadful warning, time's ever imminent peril, until then.

As if returned to that bright day, I was on the lawn with her again, her body pressed against mine as we walked to the front porch and sat down in the swing, her voice soft but firm, as if talking back to time. "Nothing will go wrong, Sam, if we don't let it."

How quietly they can begin, as I would starkly realize on the last day of my trial, the journeys that return us to our crimes.

Motions

They came in flurries after the opening arguments, a host of motions that flew out of the current proceedings like butterflies emerging from the long incubation of pretrial activity. Motions to dismiss the charge. Motions to reduce it. Motions to exclude this or that. There'd been a good many motions before then, of course. So many I'd already lost track of all save the one that had actually had some merit, at least sociologically, a motion for change of venue that Morty had expected to be rejected, but the denial of which might serve to buttress my case in the event I needed to appeal. And besides, Sam, he once told me, it's pretty clear that the people here in Coburn don't like you very much.

I knew this was true, of course. In addition to the dreadful things I'd done to their children, the people of Coburn no doubt resented the fact that I'd done it while living a very privileged life, at least some of it paid for by the exorbitant tuition required to send their children to Coburn College. But this hostility had remained more or less mute before Sandrine's death. After it, the media had gone on a feeding frenzy, the result of which was that by the first day of my trial I'd become a person much despised in this little town. To them, I was a man who'd had a great job, if you could even call it work, what with summers off and sabbaticals at full pay and holidays for every religion known to man. I was a tenured professor, which to the people of Coburn was a free ticket to a carefree and semiluxurious retirement. I couldn't even be fired—so the locals assumed—no matter what I said in class, or even if I failed to show up in class at all. But this Samuel Joseph Madison character had wanted something more, they said to themselves and to each other. A cushy life had simply not been enough for the esteemed professor, expert on Melville, Hawthorne, and God knows how many other lesser-known literary figures. Here was a man who'd lived high on the hog despite the fact that he conceived nothing, built nothing, invented nothing, maintained nothing, sold nothing. Here was a man who lived high on the hog by . . . talking.

The townspeople had considered all the professors at Coburn College similarly pampered, of course, but Sandrine's death had put the spotlight squarely on me. She was beautiful, which is probably what had fueled the initial media interest. The local paper had published pictures of her in her twenties, most of them taken during our one great trip to Europe and the Mediterranean. In the most provocative of these photos she was in a bathing suit, her skin alabaster white against the black sands of Santorini, those long, perfectly shaped legs. In another, she posed seductively among the flowers of Giverney, and in their midst she seemed equally in exquisite bloom. How, these photos asked, could so gorgeous a woman have come to such a sad, despairing end? To die alone? To die in a dark room? Perhaps to have been murdered by her scheming husband? And if she'd been murdered, these photographs demanded, then what kind of man was I to have wanted such a woman, so bright and beautiful, dead? For God's sake, those pictures said, could this woman's husband not have known how lucky he was to have her?

But what could such people know of Sandrine's long hours, the endless private sessions she had with Coburn College's eternally mediocre students? Had they ever felt neglected? Had they ever felt abandoned? Had they ever felt secondary to an ever changing cast of hopeless, uninspired students? Yet Sandrine had seen these students differently. To her they'd been so in need of help that they'd come to take the place of the poorer ones it had been her earlier and quite idealistic dream to teach. Worst of all, by devoting herself to teaching, she'd completely lost interest in the great book I'd expected her to write.

I remembered a night when she'd come home particularly late and quite exhausted, so that I'd said, rather irritably, "Another night you've squandered when you could have been working on your book."

She swept past me, then stopped, whirled around, and said, "I'm never going to write a book, Sam. Not even a small book, much less that great one you think I should write." Then she'd pointed a finger at herself as if it were a pistol. "I am my book." Her gaze sharpened. "And just for the record, it's not my unwritten book you resent, Sam, it's yours."

How easy it had been to want such a woman dead, I thought suddenly, relieved, as I glanced at the jury, that such thoughts couldn't be read.

Why had this brutal exchange returned to me so suddenly, I wondered, as Morty and Mr. Singleton continued to argue their motions before the bench. Was it the sheer idleness imposed by endless courtroom procedures that had opened up that floodgate, or was I still responding to Morty's earlier admonition that I must, simply must remember everything because in a murder investigation, as he'd warned, it is almost as bad to misremember as it is to lie.

So had I recently fallen into the habit of obsessively reliving my life with Sandrine simply in order to cover my tracks? I couldn't tell. I knew only that I'd think of something she said, then rifle through my memory in a desperate search for the specific occasion, the exact circumstances, where and when it had been said, what my response had been. Wisdom, Sandrine once remarked, is the comprehension of context.

This quotation sent my mind off on yet another chase. Had Sandrine made this remark when we were young? Before or after we were married? Had we been in some foreign country when she said it or were we mired here in Coburn?

Mired? It surprised me that so unforgiving a word had surfaced in my mind. And yet it was true, I admitted. I had felt mired in Coburn, a man going through the motions, with no sense of anything bubbling underneath, no lurking secret needs until that afternoon in the park when I'd stared into those famished eyes. Not Sandrine's eyes. Not dark and searching as hers had been. But small, watery blue eyes that had given no hint of anything sinister, of a woman lurking in dark corners or hatching grim plots.

I suddenly realized that it is a slow process, the numbing of a life, and that at the end of that process the road not taken must come to seem no better than the one you took.

Perhaps it was this numbness I'd wanted to escape. I saw my fingers tapping out fanciful mentions of faraway places, of "escaping" Coburn, of "breaking chains," of the unspecified "desperate measures" that would be necessary in order to break them, all of which had at last met the eyes of Detective Alabrandi.

Another of Sandrine's comments hit me suddenly, this one said only a few days after she'd first revealed the forbidding nature of things in the no less forbidding darkness of our bedroom: *You only notice the little things you think you lost, not the great one you really did.*

What the hell had she meant by that? And who was *you*? Was it all mankind? Was it us? Or just me?

It was on the heels of that question that I suddenly saw Sandrine as clearly as I'd seen her on the night I'd found her alone in the backyard, moving slowly in the swing that hung from the great oak there.

"Are you okay?" I asked.

She was dressed in a white blouse and long dark-blue skirt that lifted slightly as she drifted forward.

"Sandrine?" I said, when she didn't answer.

For a time she remained silent, then, as if it were a hard-won truth, she said, "The problem with regret is that in the end it's always pathetic."

Had that been the moment, I wondered now, had that been the moment, as I'd lingered in the cold eddies of that hard-won truth, when I'd first reached for the rapier in my gown?

I looked at the judge's bench, the opposing lawyers in my case still debating the merits of the latest motion. From the judge's expression I got the feeling that he was denying one after another of Morty's attempts to make some legalistic end run. His arguments were no doubt characteristically Talmudic, but they wouldn't fly in down-to-earth Coburn. The charge against me would not be dismissed, as I well knew. Nor would it be lessened. Khayyám's moving hand has written, and that was that. I would be tried for Sandrine's murder by a jury of my peers in the presence of my daughter and anyone else who happened to find a seat in this crowded courtroom. No evidence would be excluded. My life would be dissected like a body in the morgue, my glistening innards spread across a steel table, everything displayed for all the world to see. That is the true horror of my current situation, I realized at that moment, the brute fact that nothing is too intimate to be exposed because, simply put, a trial is an evisceration.

Strange as it would later seem to me, I had never actually thought it possible that my life might be so mercilessly probed until the first day of my trial. With surreal insistence, this unreality had maintained its iron grip upon my otherwise discerning consciousness. For weeks I'd acted as if this were just a long nightmare, one from which I would eventually awaken. But the nightmare had not ended, of course, so that I'd come to feel like Kafka's baffled Joseph K, on trial, yes, but uncertain of the actual charge. Oh, sure, the charge was murder. But there was more to it than that. It had taken a long time for me to realize this but that morning, on the first day of my trial, I'd looked at the faces of the jury and, behind their expressionless stares, I'd seen quite clearly that I was charged, more than anything, with the crime of being me.

Realizing this I also realized that no motion in the world could save me from this rising tide.

And so the mystery that gripped me was how in the world, before now, I had failed to understand just how dire my situation was. Alabrandi had been right in what he'd said to me many weeks before. I was not going to get away with it, a fact that should have been clear the minute I'd seen the names on the prosecution's witness list. And yet somehow I'd made myself believe that at a certain point it would all go away. Mr. Singleton would realize the thinness of his evidence, and being sensible, as well as politically astute, he would finally concede that though he suspected me of murder he lacked the evidence necessary to charge me.

But just the opposite had occurred. With every rumor whispered in his ear, with every photograph of bright and beautiful Sandrine, with every report from the vigilant and highly competent Detective Alabrandi, Singleton had grown more certain of my crime and more determined to make sure that I would not get away with it. So you think you're so goddamn smart, Professor Madison, he must have said to himself at some point during the investigation, well, let's just wait and fucking see.

The circle broke and Morty and Mr. Singleton made their way back to their desks. The judge looked thoroughly put upon and aggravated, a man eager to go home, put all this legal business behind him, a man already looking forward to his beige little den and leather easy chair, and who, even as he prepared to hear the first witness in my case, was probably considering whether tonight's dinner would be surf or turf.

"It's just what we thought," Morty said when he returned to his seat at the defense table.

27

I had long ago noticed that with Morty everything was always "just as we thought."

"The motions were denied," Morty continued. "The state can proceed with its case."

I had also noticed that, in Morty's admirably neutral parlance, Mr. Singleton was no longer a man who was trying with all his skill and might to kill me. He was the state.

"There was no finding of incompetent, prejudicial, or wrongful conduct on the part of any party during the course of the investigation," Morty went on.

This was a mouthful but I got the gist of it. No cops erred in matters either large or which could be made to look large. No minor official had expressed his or her dislike for me within the hearing of anyone else who was willing to report it to the court. No court official or duly designated officer of the court had done anything beyond the scope of his or her authorized duties. Every document that had needed to be signed had been signed, and no document had been signed by any person other than the one in full possession of the authority to have done so. Legally speaking, every *t* had been crossed and every *i* had been dotted.

"In other words," Morty said, "all your constitutional rights have been protected."

"God bless America," I whispered.

Morty glared at me. "That's just the kind of smart-ass remark that can put a rope around your neck, Sam."

"Sorry," I said. But this sotto voce apology was not enough for Morty.

"How many times do I have to tell you this?" His eyes narrowed. "A trial isn't about what happened, it's about what a jury comes to believe happened. It's about appearances. And believe me, making some snide remark about America doesn't play."

"Sorry," I repeated, hoping that would end it. But Morty was on a roll.

"You're not at some Ivy League faculty tea," he continued. "This is Coburn, Georgia, for Christ's sake."

"Believe me," I said with a hint of resentment, "that much I know."

"Well, I sure hope you do," Morty shot back.

Surely this will end it, I thought, but I was wrong.

"You ever heard of a witch trial, Sam?" Morty asked. "Well, we're about to have one, if you're not careful."

"I'll be careful," I assured him since it was clearly this assurance that he sought.

He looked at me doubtfully.

"I will. I promise."

Morty nodded crisply, then sank into paperwork. I looked across the aisle and saw that "the state" was doing the same, his pencil flying across a page.

I waited.

At last Judge Rutledge said, "Mr. Singleton, is the state ready to proceed?"

"It is, Your Honor."

"Then please call your first witness."

"Yes, Your Honor," Mr. Singleton said, then he glanced into the crowd—or was it a mob?—that had gathered to follow my case and summoned his first witness to the stand.

Call Chanisa
Evangela Shipman

With those words it finally began, the actual substance of my trial, all else before it little more than practice before the game.

I watched as the first prosecution witness approached the witness box, the initial elements of Mr. Singleton's case against me to be offered by a short, compactly built black woman, one of the many telephone operators who worked the evening shift at the headquarters of the grandly named Coburn Office of Emergency Preparedness and Response, a name about which I'd once quipped that, after the World Trade Center tragedy, the town council had evidently concluded that Coburn would be next.

Once on the stand she took the oath, then, by way of answering Mr. Singleton's first routine question, she stated her name, and in one of those time shifts to which I'd recently fallen prey I went back to the evening when I'd made that 911 call and first heard the voice of Chanisa Evangela Shipman.

I'd come home from my last class of the day, gone directly to the "scriptorium," the august name I'd given to the cramped space into which Sandrine and I crowded our two small wooden desks, and in which we planned our lessons and wrote our lectures. Once there I'd graded a few of the generally incoherent and sometimes subliterate papers the students in my survey of world literature class had handed in that same day, frightfully mindless little jottings filled with every imaginable error of grammar and spelling, not to mention the utter absence of interesting ideas. I'd managed to get through a few of them by sunset but I'd stopped in a seizure of frustration at the opening line of the latest of them: *You've probably heard the old joke about Rome falling because of led in there plates and cups.*

It was then I'd gone looking for Sandrine, found her not in the little sunroom where she often read at the end of day but in our bedroom, in the dark, with even the table lamp turned off.

"I want it dark," she explained as I opened the door and came into the room.

"Why?" I answered.

"Just let me stay in the dark," she said sharply.

"Okay, but . . . are you all right, Sandrine?"

"Come back later."

"You don't want any dinner?"

"No. I want to rest for a little while, then I want to talk to you."

"Talk to me?" I asked cautiously.

"I have something I want to tell you."

"Sandrine, I—"

"Later."

"All right," I said as I eased back out of the room.

Her tone had been dark and hard, with an undertone of anger that had sent a shiver of foreboding down my spine. Even so, I hadn't suspected that things were as bad as they'd later turned out to be, that this latest exchange was but prelude to a full-scale assault.

None of this had anything to do with the current testimony, of course, since it had preceded Sandrine's death by several hours, and so

I tried to keep my mind from wandering, tried to stay focused on what was being said at present.

"Now, what is it that you prefer to be called, Ms. Shipman?" Mr. Singleton asked.

"I'm not a Ms.," the witness corrected. "I been married fourteen years and have three kids. Just call me Evie. That's what people do."

"All right, Evie," Mr. Singleton said agreeably. "All right. So, tell me, what is your job?"

She had been a 911 dispatcher for six years. She'd first worked the day shift, but because her husband worked nights she'd changed to the night shift as soon as a position had become available. Had she not done so, she would not have been on duty and thus she would not have answered the call that came into the 911 switchboard at 1:14 a.m. on the evening of November 14, nor heard what she now described as a man's voice.

"Did this man identify himself?" Mr. Singleton asked.

"Yes. He said he was Professor Madison and that he was calling to report the death of his wife."

"*Professor* Madison? He didn't introduce himself using his first name?"

"No, sir. He said 'Professor Madison,' and that his wife had died."

"Did *Professor* Madison say how his wife died?"

"No, he didn't. He just said she was dead, so there was no need to hurry."

"No need to hurry?"

"Because she was dead, I guess," Evie explained.

Dead, yes, and lying on her back in the bed, the white sheets hardly ruffled, as I instantly recalled. Earlier that same evening, when I'd left her, there'd been a notebook on the table beside her bed, along with a few pens, a book, all of it amid the bedside clutter I'd gotten used to by then, a box of tissues, a tube of ChapStick, her Nano with its white earbuds.

"Now there is a procedure with regard to calls of this kind, isn't there, Evie?" Mr. Singleton asked.

"Yes."

"What is that procedure?"

"Well, you have to find out if the dead person was expected to be dead."

"Expected?"

"I mean, if it's an old person, like a grandmother, or somebody like that. Or somebody who's been sick a long time. Or under hospice care. So you've been expecting them to die, is what I mean, so you can just call the person's doctor to get a cause of death certificate. After that, you can call the funeral parlor or wherever you want the deceased person to be taken. What I mean is, if I get a call like that, I don't have to call the police."

"I see," Mr. Singleton said. "But you did call the police, didn't you?"

"Yes, I did."

"Why?"

"Because we ask a few questions, and if it turns out, for example, that the dead person is young, then we send a police officer. That's what the rule says. In this case, the dead person was forty-six. That's young enough that a police officer is dispatched."

For the next few minutes, Mr. Singleton took Evie through the other questions I was asked that night, none of them particularly relevant, but all of them designed to show that Chanisa Evangela "Evie" Shipman was a fully competent public service dispatcher. I noticed that Mr. Singleton did not, at any point, inquire about my tone of voice that night, whether I'd sounded frightened, angry, aggrieved, or even whether or not I'd shown any emotion at all at the time I'd reported Sandrine's death. Even before my trial, I'd seen enough courtroom dramas to gather that such questions would be asking for a conclusion of the witness, thus subject to defense objections. Such objections would distract the jury and slow down the proceedings, something Mr. Singleton obviously wanted to avoid. Mrs.

Shipman's testimony was the opening chapter in the story of a murder, and he'd clearly decided that the flow of this sinister narrative was better left uninterrupted by show-stopping challenges from the defense.

And so, for a time, the witness continued her testimony, vaguely technical though it was, a well-trained woman simply doing what she had been trained to do.

Then, quite abruptly, and far more quickly than I'd expected, it was over.

"That will be all," Mr. Singleton said to the witness. "Thank you."

Morty rose, walked to the podium, and smiled sweetly at Chanisa Evangela "Evie" Shipman. Three members of the jury were black, and so he made sure to indicate that he had nothing but the highest regard for this dutiful civil servant.

"May I also call you Evie?" he asked.

"Sure."

"All right, now. How many questions would you say you asked Mr. Madison when he called to report the death of his wife?"

Evie's eyes grew thoughtful as she made her calculation. "Well, I'd say, maybe ten or so. You have to get addresses and phone numbers and things like that."

"Did Mr. Madison answer these questions without hesitation?"

"Yes."

"And, later, did you find that any of the answers Mr. Madison gave you that evening were incorrect?"

"No, sir."

"He told you that his wife was forty-six, isn't that right?"

"Yes."

"I have here the birth certificate of Sandrine Madison," Morty said. He handed the certificate to Evie. "Could you read the date of Mrs. Madison's birth?"

Evie did.

"How old was Sandrine Madison at her death?"

"Forty-six."

"In fact, in every particular of those ten or so questions you asked Mr. Madison that evening, he gave you a correct answer, didn't he?"

"As far as I know, he did, yes."

"And he gave these answers without hesitation, isn't that your prior testimony?"

"Yes, it is."

Again Morty smiled. "Thank you for the work you do for our community, Evie," he said, almost reverently. "No further questions."

Evie left the stand, and because the byways of the mind are unknowable, it struck me that I'd pictured her as a considerably larger woman than she was. She'd had a husky, no-nonsense voice, like one of those enormous women you see in the grocery store or the mall, a huge rear end covered so tightly by stretch pants the fabric seems to groan with the strain of holding back all that flesh. But Evie was small and wiry, a little bantamweight of a woman. Her step was springy, and I suspected that she could tear up the dance floor, a woman who knew how to have a good time, but also one who, once at work, did her job carefully and without much sense of play.

She didn't look at me as she passed. Witnesses rarely do, according to Morty. They keep things impersonal, at a distance. Sorry if what I said helps send you to Death Row, they seem to say, but, hey, I gotta tell it like it is.

Within seconds she was gone, and Morty and Mr. Singleton were at the judge's bench discussing some detail.

My mind wandered again, and I recalled leaving the bedroom that last night, leaving it while Sandrine was still alive, leaving it in a sputtering rage at what she'd said to me, how cold and cruel it had been, and how quietly she'd said it: "Sam, I'd rather be dead than live with you another second. Do you know why? Because you're a . . ."

On hearing the final word she'd added to that sentence, and dodging the cup she'd hurled at me as she'd said it, I had immediately slammed the door of the room, walked out into the night, looked up at the stars, that storied immensity, and for a moment hoped I might find some way to recover from this attack, go back to her, do what I could to salvage what was left of all we'd once had. I had immediately dismissed that same hope, however, and with that final dismissal accepted the grim fact that I didn't want to go on this way because she'd made it clear that whatever love she'd once had for me now lay as shattered and irreparable as the cup she'd tossed at me as I fled our bedroom.

A terrible numbness had settled into me after that, an emotional neuropathy that returned to me now as Morty and Mr. Singleton stepped away from the bench and headed back toward their respective tables, the little matter settled, evidently, so that Mr. Singleton was free to proceed to his next witness.

But I wasn't ready to proceed. I was still on Crescent Road, out in the yard, peering up at the night sky, though the hour had changed, and by then Sandrine was dead. And still I'd felt nothing. So had she been right in that last accusation, I'd asked myself, the one that had so wounded me? It was at that moment, while I was still gazing at the uncomprehending stars, that it had suddenly occurred to me I had a daughter, and that she had to be informed of her mother's death. Even so, I'd waited for a while, trying to find the right words. I never really found them, and so, when Alexandria answered, I'd simply repeated that most common of introductions to grim tidings.

"Alexandria, I have some bad news."

"It's Mom, isn't it?"

I found it strange that my daughter had leaped so immediately to this conclusion, especially given the fact that she'd been with Sandrine that same afternoon, the two of them sitting in the sunroom, Sandrine in that vaguely African-looking caftan, Alexandria quite prim and proper in her dark pantsuit. Even so, I said only, "Yes, it is." A breath then. "She's dead, Alexandria. There were pills beside the bed."

"So she committed suicide?"

"Yes."

After a silence, Alexandria said, "Why would she have done that, Dad?"

"I think you know why."

"But she seemed so alive," Alexandria said. "She was talking about a book."

"What book?"

"A book about Cleopatra. She said it was better than any book she could have written about her."

"I doubt that," I said with a hint of my long bitterness that Sandrine, my brilliant wife, had never gotten around to writing the great book I'd always felt certain was in her.

There was another silence, this one curiously edgy.

"It's just hard for me to imagine that Mom was thinking about killing herself," Alexandria said. "She just didn't seem suicidal."

"Maybe that was all just a ruse," I told her. "That business of seeming so excited or engaged or whatever it was. Maybe it was just your mother's way of covering her tracks, putting you off the scent."

"The scent?" Alexandria asked, as if she found the word inappropriate.

"That she was going to do it," I explained.

There was a third silence, during which it occurred to me that Alexandria hadn't gasped or burst into tears or given any of the responses expected of a daughter who'd just been informed of her mother's suicide.

"All right," she said finally. "I'll drive down now."

"You can wait until later this morning, if you like."

"If I like?" Alexandria asked sharply. "My mother . . . your wife just killed herself, shouldn't we be together?"

"Well, yes, I suppose."

"Dad, you sound like you're . . ."

She hadn't finished the sentence but Sandrine had finished it for her some hours before, the resounding accusation she'd so brutally hurled at me as she'd thrown that cup: a *sociopath*.

"I'm in shock, I guess," I explained quickly.

"You sound perfectly calm."

"Well, how else should I sound?" I asked. "What's done is done."

Alexandria said nothing in response to this, so that there was a long silence before I said, "Alexandria, are you all right?"

"Yes," she said, though she didn't seem so. "I'm on my way."

"All right," I said and started to hang up.

"And Dad?"

"Yes," I said, expecting to hear some tender expression of love for her mother, or sympathy for me, so that her words took me entirely by surprise.

"Don't touch anything," she said.

Even at that early moment I asked myself, as this memory faded, had my daughter suspected me of murder? Suspected me even before the officer whose name Mr. Singleton now called as his second witness in my trial?

Call Wendy Hill

Her name when spoken, rather than read, was somewhat amusing, but I showed no hint of this amusement in my face. Morty had been quite stern in his admonition that no matter what I saw or heard in the courtroom I was, on no account, to be amused. My eyes might glisten. I was even permitted to weep. In fact, such dramatic demonstrations of intense feeling might serve my case. But under no circumstances was I to smile.

And so I stared straight ahead, stone-faced, as Wendy Hill lifted her right hand and took the oath.

She was of medium height, slender, and she was dressed in her police uniform. Her hair was gathered up and pinned at the back on this day one of my trial, but early on the morning of November 15, when she'd arrived at 237 Crescent Road, she'd worn it in a short ponytail that swept back and forth quite jauntily as she made her way toward me. I recalled this jauntiness because it had seemed so playful and light spirited considering the gravity of the circumstances, and at that moment I'd remembered Sandrine when she'd been about the same age as I assumed Officer Hill to be at first glance.

She was older than I'd thought, however, a fact that came to light as she responded to Mr. Singleton's initial questions.

"I graduated from the state police academy three years ago," she answered. "When I was twenty-three."

"And how long have you been a member of the Coburn Municipal Police Force?" Mr. Singleton asked.

"Two years."

Before that, as her subsequent answers to Mr. Singleton's questions made clear, Wendy Hill had served in the United States Navy, two tours in Iraq, thus a war veteran, and for that reason—at least in the jury members' eyes—loyal, courageous, and truthful, thus quite pointedly my opposite number, even down to the fact that I'd never worn a uniform or served my country in any official capacity.

"Now, Officer Hill, at approximately 1:33 a.m. on the morning of November 15, did the police dispatcher inform you of a recent death at 237 Crescent Road in the town of Coburn?" Mr. Singleton asked.

Indeed, Chanisa Evangela "Evie" Shipman had so informed Officer Hill.

"What did you do in response to that information, Officer?"

"I went to the address she gave me."

I remembered that the air had been crisp and cool in those early morning hours, but in my memory's more dramatic reconstruction it is very dark and there is a thickness to it, so that I'd felt a strange sense of suffocation. The patrol car's flashers weren't pulsing as it pulled into the driveway at what I would have described—had I been asked—as a leisurely pace. Obviously, the dispatcher had told the officer behind the wheel that there was no need to hurry. A woman was dead and nothing could be done about it.

"What happened when you arrived, Officer Hill?" Mr. Singleton asked.

She met me, or should I say I met her, at the door. She was in uniform, of course, and I noticed that her holstered automatic pistol hung low, like a western gunslinger, and that her hand cradled its handle in the wary manner of one unsure of what to expect.

"I understand there's been a death," she said.

I nodded. "My wife."

"Where is she?"

"In the bedroom. I'll show you."

I led her down the corridor and into the room Officer Hill now began to describe to the court.

"The room was in a mess," Officer Hill informed the jury. "There were papers all around. And books. It was really sort of a cluttered place, because everything was covered with stuff. Mostly books and magazines, that sort of thing."

Our bedroom had always looked in disarray, so I'd made no apologies for it as I'd led Officer Hill into the room. Even so, I'd earlier thought of straightening it up a bit, then heard Alexandria's warning in my mind, and for that reason I touched nothing at all within the room save those scattered bits of porcelain cup, which I'd carefully swept into a dust pan and deposited in the large plastic garbage receptacle on the back deck, an act I'd hardly considered incriminating at the time.

"Where was Professor Madison at this point?" Mr. Singleton asked.

I'd been standing in the door of the bedroom, watching as Officer Hill glanced about the room. She'd seemed to find it strange, all the many books and papers, how untidy it all was, and which I now suspected to have generated her first suspicion that perhaps all was not well ordered at 237 Crescent Road. Could it be that this was the reason, I wondered, as she continued her testimony, she'd later reported the bedroom's disarray to Detective Alabrandi? Had a murder, or the idea that there might have been one, first begun to take shape in this former navy recruit's sense that some sort of domestic dispute had taken place in this room?

Had we thrown these books at each other, Sandrine and I? Had things gotten tossed about during the course of a struggle?

"Did you notice any of these books?" Mr. Singleton asked.

"I noticed the one that was open."

"Where was this book?"

"On the floor beside the bed. I guess Mrs. Madison had been reading it. But it looked like she'd put it on the floor before she died."

"Do you remember the subject of that book?"

"It was about Cleopatra. It showed a picture of her, and the title was in big letters."

"What else did you notice?"

"A piece of yellow paper. Legal size."

"Where was this paper?"

"It was also on the floor beside the bed."

"Next to the book?"

"Right beside it."

"It was lying flat?"

"No. It was folded in the middle and sort of made to stand up. Like a tent."

"Was anything written on the outside of the paper?"

"No."

"Did you read the paper, Officer Hill?"

"Not at that time."

Not at that time, because it was then that two EMS workers had arrived, dispatched no doubt by Chanisa Evangela "Evie" Shipman, presumably as a matter of established practice in such cases. They'd come in an ambulance, Orville Todd and Leno Kaneda, and, according to their report, they had found Sandrine "apparently deceased," a surmise later confirmed by a stethoscope (Leno's).

While Officer Hill recounted these activities, I was left to recall them, the flashing light of the ambulance, the way it had rhythmically swept the room, the puzzled look on Orville Todd's face when he first saw Sandrine, how beautiful she was, perhaps as beautiful in the serenity of death as she had ever been in life, a beauty both EMS workers had obviously noticed. I'd seen the way they looked at her, then glanced knowingly at each other as if to say—guy to guy—Jesus, what a waste.

"All right," Mr. Singleton said. He was obviously impatient with the methodical but somewhat lethargic way Officer Hill had just chronicled the arrival, actions, and departure of the EMS workers. As testimony it had been matter-of-fact but to the jury, as he clearly feared, way too slow, a lag in the action that threw off his presentation's carefully calculated pace.

"All right," he repeated. "Now, Officer Hill, did you have occasion at this point, after the EMS workers had left the room, did you have at that point occasion to look at that yellow paper you'd noticed earlier?" He glanced at the jury as if to remind them to be attentive. "The one that was folded and placed upright beside the bed, as I believe you have earlier testified, like a tent."

She'd had such occasion, but she hadn't picked up the paper until she asked me a question.

"I asked Mr. Madison what that was, that paper," Officer Hill informed the court.

"What was his answer?"

"He said it was probably a suicide note."

"Was this Professor Madison's first statement to you with regard to the cause of Sandrine Madison's death?"

"Yes, it was."

Mr. Singleton nodded. "Could you tell us if Professor Madison said anything else regarding the paper he referred to as a suicide note?"

"He said I could take it."

Because I'd assumed she would anyway.

"Did he indicate that he'd read it?"

"He said that he hadn't."

Which was true. I hadn't read it. Why? Because in order to read it I would have had to pick it up, and so once again my caution had betrayed me. Who would have thought, I asked myself as Officer Hill continued her testimony, that being careful might have such perilous results?

"Professor Madison had made no attempt to read what he assumed to be his wife's suicide note?" Mr. Singleton asked to emphasize the point.

"That's what he said, yes."

"And he just told you to take it?"

"Yes," Officer Hill answered. "Those were his exact words. He just said, 'Take it' and waved his hand."

I looked at the jury and sensed just how odd they found all this. Had this man no feelings at all? Or even any curiosity, for that matter. Had this Professor Madison become so estranged from his wife, or so indifferent to her or so repulsed by her, that he'd not the slightest impulse to read her last note?

They would be responding to a mood, of course, rather than to any particular piece of evidence. Officer Hill had not actually described this mood, but I feared that some element of it had wafted up from her testimony and drifted over to the jury box. It was like an odor, and this odor disturbed them. They'd felt something strange and sinister in the way I'd told Officer Hill that she could take Sandrine's note, something even stranger and more sinister in the fact that I hadn't read it.

I was certain that Mr. Singleton saw this, too, though he gave no indication of it to the jury. It was way too soon for him to give the impression that they were already in his pocket. He was posing as a man who was nothing if not humble, a modestly paid civil servant who could be making much more money defending the indefensible scum who were daily sowing their malicious chaos amid our otherwise purple mountain majesties and amber waves of grain. It was important that they think of him as one of them, a man who shops where they shop and buys what they buy and takes his family to the movies and stares with childlike wonder at blue creatures in 3-D. I was to be the alien in the midst of these ordinary, hardworking folk, a reader of books whose wife had a French name and probably even read books written in that snooty language.

Careful now, I told myself, don't let your face show the contempt you feel for Mr. Singleton's crude strategy, his quite obvious manipulation of this no doubt highly manipulateable (is that a word?) jury.

"Officer Hill, did you take that note?" Mr. Singleton asked.

"No," Officer Hill answered. "I was just responding to a call. I had not been assigned any duties with regard to an investigation."

Perhaps so, but that very night, it had been clear to me that she'd begun investigating almost immediately after entering the bedroom. I'd seen it in her eyes, that dark sparkle of suspicion, her sense that something wasn't right. She'd moved about the room slowly, guardedly, as if she were already playing her cards close to the vest, a behavior I'd found rather melodramatic. For that reason, I'd dismissed Officer Hill as a typical small town cop, one who'd watched plenty of episodes of *Law & Order* but who'd never confronted anything in sleepy little Coburn that could possibly resemble the high drama of a television police opera.

Now, as I listened to Officer Hill's testimony, I had to concede that she might legitimately have begun to question what she saw in the shadowy light of Sandrine's death room, the way there'd been a plate of uneaten food on the floor beside her bed, a pair of pajamas balled up and thrown into the corner, that oddly folded tent of yellow paper. Was it possible that this woman had not died of natural causes? Was it possible

that her death had been brought about by a hand other than her own?
It had been Officer Hill's duty to ask these questions, and she had done
her duty, of course, and as she continued her testimony it struck me
that, had she been a professor rather than a cop, she might have been
a far more devoted one than I.

"And did you have occasion, Officer Hill, to observe the bed?" Mr.
Singleton asked.

She had had such occasion, of course, and what she'd seen could
not but have added an element of the macabre.

"And Mrs. Madison in that bed?" Mr. Singleton asked.

"Yes. I saw Mrs. Madison."

I knew what was coming, because for days after Sandrine's death
it was this image that would not leave me, the curious tableau that had
greeted me when I'd gone into the bedroom, expecting to find one scene
but astonished to find a quite different one.

"Can you describe what you saw to the jury, Officer Hill?" Mr.
Singleton asked.

This: Sandrine, lying on her back, her dark, wavy hair swept up
and over to her left so that it seemed to float above her, as if she were
immersed in water. Sandrine with the white sheet pulled down to expose
one perfect breast, its small pink nipple, the round white orb, even in
death, oddly erotic. Sandrine with her right arm in repose upon the
sheet, her fingers delicately holding the dried rose that had once rested
in a small vase in the scriptorium. Sandrine with her lips painted and
her cheeks lightly blushed, her eyes open slightly, drowsily, as if on the
verge of sleep.

It was a scene that had been reflected in the glass bottles and single
crystal decanter that rested on the small wooden table beside the bed,
a sinister tableau that surely must have given pause to Officer Hill.
Had it looked to her, I wondered now, as if Sandrine's body had been

purposely arranged in this way, a peaceful death in appearance but, in reality, something else?

The answer to this question was not long in coming.

"Now Officer Hill, confronted by this . . . scene . . . did you ask Professor Madison if this was exactly the way he'd found Sandrine Madison?" Mr. Singleton asked.

"Yes."

"Why did you ask him that question, Officer Hill?"

"Because it just seemed strange to me that a woman who was going to kill herself would put on makeup," Officer Hill answered. "And the way everything looked, the bottles, for example. It just seemed like things had been set up. There was something that didn't look natural about it. It was more something you'd see like maybe in a movie."

Arranged "like maybe" in a movie indeed, I thought, and so it had certainly been Officer Hill's duty to explore the possibility that Sandrine's death might have something of ritual about it. Had she tentatively entertained the possibility that we'd been members of a satanic cult, Sandrine a human sacrifice?

"Would it be fair to say that it was because of these things that you began to view the bedroom as a possible crime scene?" Mr. Singleton asked.

It would indeed be fair to say this, for as her continuing testimony made clear, Officer Hill had done just that.

"When you returned to the Coburn police station, did you make these observations known?" Mr. Singleton asked.

"Yes, sir."

"To whom did you speak?"

"I spoke to the duty officer, and he called Detective Ray Alabrandi," Officer Hill said. "Detective Alabrandi subsequently came to police headquarters and I told him what I'd seen in Mrs. Madison's bedroom."

"And what was Detective Alabrandi's conclusion?"

"Same as mine, that the coroner should be called right away," Officer Hill responded. "That's what he told me he was going to do."

"You felt the coroner should be called in right away?"

"Yes, I did."

"But the coroner would have been called for in any event, wouldn't he, Officer Hill?" Mr. Singleton asked. "Because Professor Madison had already mentioned that the yellow piece of paper beside her bed might have been a suicide note."

"Yes," Officer Hill answered. "If there's any reason to suspect a suicide, then there has to be an autopsy."

"But you wanted to make sure that this official inquiry began right away, didn't you, Officer?" Singleton asked.

"Yes."

"Why is that?"

"I don't know," Officer Hill answered. "It was just an . . . itch."

Singleton smiled. "Thank you, Officer Hill, for your work on behalf of the citizens of Coburn," he said softly. "No further questions."

Morty walked to the podium.

"Officer Hill, isn't it true that even before Mr. Madison had mentioned this about a possible suicide note, you'd begun to feel that something was criminally amiss?" he asked.

Officer Hill stiffened slightly. "Criminally amiss?"

"An itch," Morty said dryly.

"I guess so," Officer Hill admitted.

"You guess so? Well, upon returning to Coburn police headquarters, you spoke immediately to the duty officer, isn't that your testimony?"

"Yes."

"And later you spoke with Detective Ray Alabrandi?"

"Yes."

"Now, Detective Alabrandi is a homicide detective, isn't he?"

"He's a detective," Officer Hill answered. "I guess he investigates homicides."

"In any event, you reported your observations regarding the scene of Mrs. Madison's death to a duty officer at police headquarters, then to a full-fledged detective, even though you must have known that the coroner would certainly be called into the case, isn't that true?"

"Yes."

"All right, so something gave you that little itch, right?" Morty asked. "It would be fair to say that, wouldn't it?"

"I suppose so."

"All right, what did you tell Detective Alabrandi when you had occasion to speak to him regarding the death of Sandrine Madison?"

"Well, for one thing, I described the room."

"How did you describe it?"

"It was a mess, like I said. Stuff was scattered all over the place. It was hard for me to imagine that a woman would let a bedroom get like that, and so, well, I sort of wondered if she'd . . ."

"She'd what?"

"If maybe she'd been kept there."

"Against her will?"

"Yes."

"So it was the general disarray of the place that brought about that little itch, is that right?"

"Yes."

"Because women, being natural-born cleaners of rooms, and Mrs. Madison being a woman, you concluded that she might have been . . . imprisoned . . . by her husband?"

"I didn't know by who."

"And that perhaps Mrs. Madison's death might not have been a natural one?"

49

"I knew it wasn't natural. Mr. Madison had already said it was a suicide."

"But you didn't believe Mr. Madison, did you, Officer Hill?"

"I wasn't sure," Officer Hill admitted.

"Well, if Mrs. Madison had not committed suicide, how had she died?" Morty asked.

"I didn't know."

"But you had a suspicion, didn't you? And this suspicion was that Mrs. Madison had been murdered. That was your true suspicion, wasn't it, Officer Hill, your itch?"

Officer Hill stiffened slightly, and I saw that here was a woman who was not afraid to state exactly what she thought, and that to some degree she was doing it out of deference for Sandrine, in an effort, honest and determined, to render justice in her case.

"Yes, it was," she said.

"So we have clutter, a woman, and from this the idea of a murder?" Morty asked, then quickly lifted his hand before Officer Hill could answer, or Mr. Singleton object, and immediately fired off his next question.

"Officer Hill, do you remember being called to 439 Dancers Street on the night of October 10, 2009? The house of Janice LePlane?"

"Yes."

Morty took a photograph from the stack of them he'd placed on the lectern and showed it to Officer Hill.

"Is this the room in which Mrs. LePlane was found?" he asked.

"Yes."

"How would you describe it?"

"Well, it's . . . cluttered. Magazines on the floor. Some white food containers. You know, Chinese food."

"It's not dissimilar to the state of the bedroom in which you found the body of Mrs. Madison, is it?"

"No, sir."

"How did Janice LePlane die, Officer Hill?"

"She killed herself. That was the coroner's verdict."

"How did she kill herself?"

"She took pills."

Morty retrieved the photograph from Officer Hill, gave it to the foreman of the jury, then walked back and handed the witness a second photograph.

"Do you recall this room, Officer Hill?" he asked

"Yes," the witness answered. "I don't remember the woman's name, though."

"Her name was Martha Gillespie."

"Okay."

"How would you describe Mrs. Gillespie's room, Officer Hill? Would you say that it's cluttered?"

"Yes."

"And there are dirty plates and papers all over the room, isn't that true?"

"Yes, there are."

"How did Martha Gillespie die, Office Hill?"

"I don't recall."

"Was it suicide?"

"I don't think so, but I'm not sure."

"Was it murder?"

"No."

"In fact, Martha Gillespie died of natural causes, didn't she?"

"Yes, she did."

Morty took the photographs Officer Hill had just identified and gave them to the jury foreman, who stared at them briefly, then passed them to the juror to his left.

Morty was now back at the podium. "Officer Hill, did you return from either of these rooms, the dead bodies you observed in cluttered rooms, and speak to anyone at police headquarters with regard to any suspicions you had regarding the manner of those deaths?"

"No, I did not."

"Then why did you have any doubts as to the nature of Mrs. Madison's death?"

Officer Hill shifted uneasily in her seat. "It was just a feeling, I guess."

"Just a feeling," Morty repeated with a pointed glance toward the jury.

"Yes, sir," Officer Hill admitted a little hesitantly.

Morty paused, pretended to study his notes. Then he produced another photograph and handed it to the witness.

"Have you seen this picture, Officer Hill?" he asked.

"Yes."

"It's Mrs. Madison, isn't it?"

"Yes, it is."

"Taken by the coroner," Morty added.

"I don't know who took it."

"Okay, but you made mention that Mrs. Madison had put on makeup, isn't that right?"

"Yes."

Morty smiled. "I notice that you're wearing lipstick, Officer Hill. And today, right now, you're wearing other makeup, as well?"

"A little," Officer Hill responded warily.

"Blush?"

"A little, yes."

"And like a great many women you apply a little makeup to enhance your looks, isn't that correct?"

"Yes."

"Are you married, Officer Hill?"

"Yes."

"Do you sometimes put on makeup in order to please your husband?"

"I guess I do."

"Because you want to look beautiful to him, correct?"

"Yes."

"Because you love him?"

"Yes."

"Would you say that Sandrine Madison might have felt the same about her husband?"

Mr. Singleton rose immediately. "Asking for a conclusion, Your Honor."

His objection was sustained, but Morty had made his point and he knew it.

He nodded softly. "Thank you, Officer Hill. No further questions."

He was back in his chair at the defense table seconds later, looking quite satisfied with his cross-examination of Officer Hill.

"She despised me from the beginning," I said after Morty returned to his seat beside me.

Morty's eyes shot over to me. "From the beginning?"

"When she first laid eyes on me."

"When you met her at the door, you mean?"

"Yes."

Suddenly I realized that Officer Hill had seen nothing of Sandrine's death room at that point, not her body in the bed, nor the books scattered around it, and certainly not that yellow tent of paper. So what had she seen, I wondered, what had she seen in my eyes?

"Demonstrating prejudice is like shooting whales in a barrel," Morty whispered cheerfully. He offered me a broadly reassuring look.

"You're the victim in this case, Sam. Don't forget that. You're a victim of unwarranted suspicions that put you on the police radar, and that's what we're going to show."

I had learned by then that this was to be Morty's set-in-stone strategy. I will be portrayed as a victim of small town prejudices, and by this means my lawyer will turn the tables on the jury. He will show that these prejudices were vile and that they contorted the facts. If he is successful, the jurors will see that this is true and guard themselves against exhibiting these same prejudices. In effect, Morty will immunize them from themselves.

It is all very clever, but suddenly it also seemed very sad, so that I felt an odd spark of buried feeling, a surprising ache of pity for something other than myself.

"People are lost," I whispered.

Morty shrugged and returned to his notes, but the sadness and pity that had just swept over me lingered, and as it lingered it reminded me of the first feeling I'd gotten from books, particularly from Melville, tales I'd read long before I'd either taught or been taught them. I thought of the resigned way in which Starbuck had tossed his pipe into the sea, then the bleak sigh of "Oh humanity" that ends "Bartleby, the Scrivener." At that moment, my mind turned unaccountably to Yeats, and I recalled the sorrows he'd glimpsed in Maud Gonne, the pilgrim soul he'd seen in her, sorrows that even her beauty could not sweep from her "changing face."

And somehow all of this returned me to Sandrine in her bed, with that one red rose, her hair arranged just so, a candle set at just the right position to cause that many-faceted reflection. By the time it was all over she'd been made to look for all the world like a woman with no expectation of death. Either that, or something still less incriminating, like a woman in a state of serene but blissful eroticism, one who'd welcomed death as if it were her demon lover.

"So let's see now," Judge Rutledge said. He was looking at the clock. "It's getting rather late, I think." He glanced at the jury, then at Mr. Singleton, and finally at Morty. "It seems to me that in light of the hour, it may be best to adjourn for the day," he said. "Does either the defense or the prosecution have any objection to an adjournment?"

Neither did.

"All right, then, we will resume tomorrow morning at nine a.m.," Judge Rutledge said.

We rose as the jury left the room. I stood silently, watching them file out, each of them careful not to glance in my direction, as if the way I looked was, itself, in some way prejudicial.

"Okay," Morty told me once the last of them had departed. "Get some sleep."

I turned to Alexandria, her face in that fixed look of strain and worry.

"I'll take you straight home," she said, as if I were a deadly microbe, a creature, primitive and deadly, that shouldn't be released into the air.

I stepped away from the table, turned to leave the courtroom, then stopped cold at the sight of Jane Forbes, a fellow professor at Coburn College, a woman Sandrine had sometimes met for early morning trots around the reservoir. She was standing rigidly in a shadowy corner of the courtroom, wearing a burgundy overcoat, her hands sunk deep in its pockets, a woman whose eyes unaccountably returned me to the now thoroughly incriminating ones that had once gazed at me in the green shade of the park. I had no idea why Jane had chosen to attend my trial, and yet, at that moment, her presence suddenly suggested an as yet unrevealed aspect of my case, the key to a room I had not entered yet.

"Dad?" Alexandria called.

"Coming," I said, then fell in behind her, moving quickly now, past the benches where reporters and spectators alike were gathering up their things, pulling on their coats and jackets, then more quickly still as I surged past them.

Once outside the courtroom we headed toward the parking lot, the corridor filled with the flotsam that inevitably swirls about any small town courthouse, people under restraining orders or seeking them, people answering summonses of various kinds, people in debt, people in trouble, the twisted knots in which so much of life seems perpetually entangled.

Ah, humanity, I heard in the low, sorrowful voice I had long imagined as Melville's.

"What is it?" Alexandria asked. "You look . . ." She stopped, then shrugged. "I don't know . . . strange."

We were outside the courthouse now, the parking lot only a few yards away, and unaccountably I'd stopped dead at the top of the stairs.

"Dad?" Alexandria asked worriedly.

I shook my head. "It's nothing," I assured her as I returned to myself.

"Are you sure?"

I nodded, then found my legs and headed down the stairs. "Nothing," I repeated.

But that was a lie. For it had indeed been something, a feeling I'd hardly recognized because it seemed so curious, a sense not of life's sorrow but of its wrathfulness, the conviction that it was a coiled serpent forever striking here then there, a slithering, poisonous thing whose malice no one could at last escape.

I glanced behind me, up the courthouse stairs, still shaken by this thought, fully expecting to see some B-movie river of blood cascade down those same stairs, red and thick, bent, consciously bent, upon engulfing everything.

A panic seized me, one so fierce I thought I might surely break into a run.

I knew better than to do anything like that however, and so I simply straightened my shoulders and headed down the stairs.

"Let's go home" was all I said.

Home Bound

"I'll drive," Alexandria said as we approached the car. She was reaching into her purse, searching for the keys, a gesture that told me she did not intend to argue the point. I'd just appeared mysteriously shaken, and so I was to be driven home, and that was that.

"Okay," I said.

I'd learned by then that an accusation, any accusation, leaves the accused decidedly weakened. An accused person is a straggler in the herd. This is a recognition I'd come to slowly, and had fully understood only after the various local news media had labeled me a "person of interest" in regard to the investigation into Sandrine's death. No charges had been made against me at that point, and certainly I'd not been arrested. But the accusation had been enough for Charles Higgins, the young, go-getter president of Coburn College, to summon me to his office and, while I sat silently and a little dazed by what I was hearing, request— unofficially, of course—my resignation. The college was in the middle of a fund-raising campaign to build a new sports center, he'd explained, and my "situation," as he'd called it, might threaten its success.

"As you must know, Sam," the president said gravely, "attendance at sporting events brings in a great deal of money." As if this weren't enough to sink the spear, he added, "And, of course, there's always the question of alumni donations, which can easily drop off in the face of poor publicity."

Given all the damage I was doing the right course was clear. I should do my duty to dear old Coburn College and resign.

Charley ran his fingers down his lapels and waited for my response, his gaze neutral, save for the supplication, as if Coburn were a homeless shelter whose residents my staying on would cast into the cruel cold.

It was impossible for me to guess whether he thought I'd killed Sandrine. It wouldn't have mattered anyway. Being a distraction is, itself, a sort of crime, the minimum penalty for which is the loss of your job. I suppose that, had I considered my circumstances more clearly, I would have expected this to happen. Even so, I made a little show of being treated unfairly. After all, as I might have reminded him, my trial had not yet even begun. But it had by then become obvious to me that the presumption of innocence was a legal nicety the athletic program at Coburn College simply could not afford.

"But what am I supposed to do, Charley?" I asked helplessly. "I mean, if I resign."

"Well, perhaps you could work on your novel," he answered.

"I haven't worked on my novel in twenty years," I informed him coolly. "My novel is a dead baby."

He looked at me expressionlessly though I could tell that he regretted he'd been unable to use the book myth most of my colleagues entertained, their way of convincing themselves they still had something to say along with the will and the talent to say it.

"I see," Charley said. "Well, at any rate, I'm sure you'll find something to do."

He had no moral ground to stand on and he knew it but that couldn't matter either. He had other responsibilities. Coburn was the bottom rung for him, a springboard to some later, more distinguished college presidency. He was young, with miles to go before he slept, and he would not let my current predicament get in his way.

59

I knew all this, but losing my job would be so ruinous I was compelled to state the simple, if humiliating, truth. "I have bills to pay, Charley," I told him. "Big bills. Legal bills."

Higgins shook his head. "I sorry, Sam. I truly am. And I hope this whole unfortunate matter will clear up in time." His gaze turned stony. "But for now I'm afraid the board has left me no choice. We could be sued, you know. I don't know for what, but some lawyer could figure something out, I'm sure. We are responsible for our faculty, for exposing our students to our teachers."

So no alleged murderers on board, I thought.

"If I don't resign, you'll fire me?" I asked.

"It would be suspension without pay," Charley answered.

"You've already thought this through," I said. "Laid out the steps if I refuse to resign."

"I'm afraid so." He shrugged. "I hope things eventually clear up and I can reconsider your appointment," he added. "After you've resigned, I mean." He shrugged again. "Until then," he said, and shrugged a third time.

Until then I would be out of work.

No, not "until then." Forever.

No matter what the outcome of my trial I would be radioactive at Coburn College. And beyond Coburn, what college would hire a professor who'd brought such a cataract of bad publicity to his school?

And so I'd left the president's office knowing full well that I would never teach again, but the loss of my job had paled compared to this other loss, the one made painfully obvious by Alexandria now sitting at the wheel of my car, the loss of the traditional powers of fatherhood, the fact that I had become a kind of invalid to my own daughter.

This was not a subject I wanted to discuss with her, however, and so I said, "How do you think it went in court today?"

She turned on to Crescent Road. "Okay."

Her voice was flat, inexpressive, a nod to the fact that she simply had no way of knowing how it had gone, what the silent members of the jury might now be thinking. With that recognition, the inexplicable nature of my situation settled over me again. How had so clever a fellow ended up like this?

This was a question I'd asked myself at each stage in the process that had begun with Sandrine's death. Even late in that legal process I'd kept expecting it to halt. But it hadn't, and so as Alexandria turned the wheel and we glided smoothly into the driveway of the house on Crescent Road, I could no longer be certain that it ever would.

"Edith's out sweeping the driveway," I said drily with a nod to the woman who lived next door, Edith Whittier, long divorced, head-over-the-hedge friend of Sandrine, but nonetheless one of the last people to see her alive, a name recently added to Mr. Singleton's list of prosecution witnesses. She nodded back, but coolly, and with a hint of repugnance, as if she'd just recently discovered my name on the state's sex offender registry.

"She hates me, too," I said mordantly.

Alexandria wheeled the car into the driveway. "Ignore her," she said.

Once in the house, I went to the scriptorium and read while Alexandria made dinner. I'd been perfectly capable of making dinner but she felt that I needed time to relax after a day in court. She'd been right, and yet even as I tried to lose myself in a book I incessantly replayed Morty's earlier remark to me, how prejudice could be easily unearthed in a witness. But what would Officer Hill have had against me?

I mentioned this to Alexandria over dinner.

"Don't be naive, Dad," she said.

"What do you mean?" I asked.

"She probably thought you were pretty weird," Alexandria said bluntly.

"How could she have thought that?" I asked. "I hardly said a word to her."

Alexandria's eyes whipped over to me. "Well, that's weird in itself, don't you think?"

"What was I supposed to say to her?" I asked. "Nice night, isn't it, Officer Hill. Think it'll rain by the weekend?"

Alexandria shook her head. "It wouldn't have mattered anyway. She would have gotten a bad impression, what with the way things look around here, like you and Mom are old hippies."

"We were never hippies," I said. "To begin with, the hippies were way before our time."

"I'm talking about the way the house has always looked, Dad," Alexandria said. "Like you and Mom just moved in. Everything scattered around."

"The house was untidy so I'm a murderer?"

Alexandria lowered her eyes to her plate.

"Well?" I demanded.

She looked at me. "Dad, did you and Mom never notice that when we went to other houses, professors and people like that, they didn't live like this?" She indicated the adjoining living room, where papers and books and CDs were scattered all about. "The house was always a big mess, just the way it is now. At those other houses everything was neat. Books were put away. You and Mom never noticed that?"

"Oh, we noticed those houses, believe me," I told her. "And you know what, Alexandria? We didn't want anything to do with the way those houses looked. Everything in its place. Everything scrubbed and polished. We didn't want that kind of house because we didn't want that kind of life."

"Yeah, okay, Dad," Alexandria said somewhat glumly. She returned to her food, toying with the green beans she'd cooked to a mush.

"What do you mean, 'Yeah, okay, Dad'?" I demanded.

Alexandria faced me. "What else can I say? You don't ever take anything back. It's like a point of honor for you to win every argument. Even Mom said that."

"Really?" I asked sharply. "When did she say this?"

"About a month before . . . she died," Alexandria answered. A vision of Sandrine in her last days appeared to surface in her mind. "She seemed really sad. I remember one time she said that most people died wanting an apology, but that she would die wanting to apologize."

"To whom?"

"You," Alexandria answered.

"Me?" I asked. "Why?"

"I don't know," Alexandria answered, her gaze suddenly so disturbingly penetrating I found it hard to look her in the eye.

"Let's talk about something else," I said.

She pointed to my untouched food. "Eat something. You have to keep up your strength."

She had become like this since Sandrine's death, a little brusque and authoritarian. I'd allowed this new way of dealing with me because I'd come to believe she wanted to feel more competent. She'd graduated from college only three years before, and although she'd hoped to land a job at a New York publishing house, she'd ended up in a small Atlanta literary agency that was little more than a mail-forwarding service for people who couldn't get reputable agents. "A vanity press is pathetic enough," she'd once told me, "but a vanity literary agency, that's really sad."

There was little conversation after that. I mentioned this book or that movie, something on *Frontline* or a *Masterpiece Theater* episode. I avoided any further reference to my first day in court.

More than anything I avoided any talk of Sandrine. Even so she was everywhere. I thought of that line from one of Sondheim's songs: *Every day a little death . . . in the buttons, in the bread.* Sandrine had listened to that song over and over during her last weeks. She'd downloaded every version she could find. Then she'd sat for hours in the scriptorium, with those white earbuds and her pale green Nano. She'd hardly ever read. She was tired of words and pages, she said. I want to stream, Sam, she told me one evening when I'd mentioned a book she might admire. Please, just let me stream.

After dinner, I went back to the scriptorium, then to the bedroom I'd shared with Sandrine and in which she'd died. I'd gotten rid of the bed a few days after her death. It was just too much, sleeping on the same mattress where she'd lain, half covered in the light of that flickering candle. I'd had the mattress hauled away, along with all our bedding. We'd never actually had a bed, just the metal frame that held the mattresses, with no headboard or bedposts. That, too, must have looked weird to Officer Hill. It must have looked cold and unloving, that stark metal frame pushed up against a bare wall, the whole thing surrounded by the accumulated droppings of our various intellectual interests.

The bed I'd chosen to replace that steel frame hadn't been made up in several days, and for a moment I simply stared at it. I'd chosen it hastily because I didn't like to shop. It was made of oak but stained to look like mahogany. It was very plain, with a low headboard. A Shaker would have approved of everything but the somewhat glossy stain.

I looked for an alternative to climbing into the bed but this was Coburn, and after nine o'clock bed was all there was. There were no nightclubs in the town, no theater save for the Coburn County Thespians who did a lot of Neil Simon, and the last showing at the movie house was already halfway through. But I wouldn't have gone to the movies anyway. Morty had long ago advised against my going anywhere in the town. His fear was that some not yet selected member of the jury might spot me enjoying myself. Nothing could be more prejudicial than that, he said. A widower—especially one whose wife killed herself or, worse, one accused of her murder—should never smile, and certainly never laugh. The lightness of being had to be weighted down until the trial was over. Widower's weeds were all that I could wear.

But surely widowers could go walking in the neighborhood, I reasoned, and so I headed for the door.

"Where are you going, Dad?"

Alexandria's voice was like a hook in my mouth.

"For a walk."

"You want company?"

"Not really," I told her, "but thanks for asking."

Seconds later I was strolling down Crescent Road, breathing in the crisp night air.

Early on, during our first weeks in Coburn, Sandrine and I had often walked together in the evening. She would look up at the stars, and a curious happiness would settle over her. "I never really wanted to be an expat, Sam," she'd said on one of those occasions, "that Hemingway type, drinking too much, hanging around in cafés. It was never what I wanted."

"What did you want?"

She laughed. "To be one of those much-maligned do-gooders," she answered. "What we talked about before we came here . . . building a school."

Was it in the wake of that lost ideal that things had begun to go awry, I asked myself as I continued my solitary stroll down Crescent Road. Had there been within the welter of Sandrine's youthful dreams one of such singular force that in failing to achieve it she'd come to think of herself as having failed in everything? Had she thought of it as I had thought of my unwritten novel, and had it worked upon her heart as corrosively as that novel had worked on mine?

Some truths hit harder than others, but none drops you to the mat like the sudden awareness not that it had ended badly but that it had begun badly. In Sandrine's case, with an idealistic dream of building a school in some forsaken corner of the world.

I walked around the block one time, then returned to the house. Alexandria was sitting in the living room. She had obviously been waiting for my return.

"I'm not eight years old," I told her. "Or eighty."

She looked at me sourly, like a little girl scolded.

"I'm fine," I assured her, now trying to show genuine appreciation for her concern. "Really."

She rose, then walked down the short corridor. "Good night," she called as she stepped inside what she still called her "old room."

She had been sleeping there since her mother's death, and I had no doubt that she would sleep there until the verdict was announced. Then, one way or another, she would go on with her life. But how, I wondered, thinking of that last day, of Sandrine in the dark of that last night, the unspeakable things we'd said to each other, could I go on with mine? Some things crack, and some things shatter, and after that final exchange I'd known that our marriage was like the little white cup Sandrine had hurled at me, beyond repair . . . so why go on?

There are times when a darkness falls over you, thick and impenetrable, and later, as I lay alone in my bed, I experienced one of those moments. I didn't want to read or watch television, but more than anything I didn't want to sleep. Sleep had become the time when I felt vulnerable, a police interrogation room where my mind threw up issues I'd rather not confront.

And so I lay in the darkness, fighting that moment when my self-control would lose its grip and I would drift helplessly into whatever thought assailed me. But to my surprise it was simply a memory that came to mind, and a pleasant one at that.

I am in Washington Square, sitting on one of the park's many benches, reading. It is an autumn day, and despite being quite engrossed in my book I become aware of someone standing motionlessly just a few feet in front of me. At first, I don't even know if it is male or female, but the minute I glance up the question is resolved because what stands before me is as lovely a young woman as I have ever seen.

"You're not very handsome," she says. "But you look very intense."

I nod shyly, still for all my graduate studies a small-town boy, dressed in frayed jeans and a checkered shirt.

"What do you do?" she asks. "When you're not reading?"

"I'm finishing up my doctorate here at NYU."

"Is that all?" she asks.

"Well, I'm working on a novel," I confess.

Clearly she has heard this before. "Anything else?"

"At the moment, I'm teaching retarded kids. Not far from here. On the Bowery."

"What do you teach them?"

"Basic skills," I answer. "Keeping clean, making change. Things that will help them get through life."

She smiles and something in her eyes touches me as physically as the tips of her fingers might have. "Well, that's the bottom line," she says.

"I guess you could call it that," I say.

"We would be an odd couple," she says, then smiles as she sits down beside me, takes the book from my hands, reads a little of it, then looks up at me, her gaze at once penetrating and tender. "Perhaps that's our destiny." She offers her hand. "Sandrine."

Still adrift in the ebbing tide of that moment, I felt something give way, and with its loosening came a flurry of those disturbing questions I'd come to dread each night when I went to bed: What had Sandrine been thinking as she died? Had she gone to her death still confident that I would never hurt her, having never glimpsed the nature of my crime?

PART II

The trial of Samuel Madison for the murder of his wife enters its fourth day at the County Courthouse in Coburn, following three days of testimony from various EMS workers, along with that of the county pathologist. Mr. Madison is accused in the death of his wife, Sandrine, on November 14 of last year. Mr. Madison was a professor of literature at Coburn College, a post from which he has resigned. It is not yet known whether he will testify in his own behalf.

Coburn Sentinel

January 14, 2011

DAYS TWO AND THREE

Time

The next two days of testimony had been excruciatingly boring. The good news was that they'd passed in a haze of technical issues I'd had no need to recall and Morty had had no need to dispute. The EMS workers had testified that Sandrine was dead when they arrived, and that they had retrieved the body and taken it to the Coburn County mortuary. Officials at the mortuary attested to the fact that her body had never been moved after its arrival. The pathologist, one Dr. Earl Mortimer, had testified next, surprisingly uninteresting testimony, given that I'd long ago been apprised of his findings, details Mr. Singleton had surely not forgotten, as Morty assured me, and which no doubt would arise in some other, later testimony. Others came and went, all of them witnesses whose task it was to establish the fact that nothing having to do with the care and treatment of Sandrine's remains in the time following her death could possibly be used by the defense to argue that the chain of evidence had at any point been broken or that any part of said evidence had been tampered with.

Thus had the hours dragged by.

Of course, as a reader, I knew that a great many things had been written about time. It was a river. It was a thief. It was money to Benjamin Franklin and a dream to Conrad Aiken. Tolstoy had thought of it as a warrior, but as my trial continued I found myself recalling that it had been the peculiar power Shakespeare had ascribed to time that Sandrine had most often quoted, the notion that it voided cunning, that nothing could outfox it. In other words, that murder, in the end, would out.

As for myself, I knew only one thing for sure about time, that during the second and third days of my trial it had moved at a snail's pace as one witness after another took the stand, droned on for a while about nothing of any true relevance to my actual guilt or innocence, then stepped down from the witness box.

Only memories had made the clock's turgid movement bearable, and during those many hours of tedious testimony I'd spent a great deal of time remembering my years with Sandrine.

I remembered that she and I had gone for a long walk after that first meeting on Washington Square, all the way north, in fact, and into Central Park. I was tall, but not dark, and hardly what anyone would call handsome. In fact, if truth be told, I'd looked like the lanky farm boy I was, a kid from Minnesota who'd miraculously been admitted to NYU and who, over the following years, had gone further and further up the academic ladder, getting increasingly better scholarships, garnering a few English Department awards. The PhD had come pretty much as a matter of course, but I'd found it insufficient to guarantee a high academic post. That had mattered very little to me, however, because my heart had been set upon writing a great novel, something I'd felt quite certain of doing at some point. College teaching, with its long vacations and occasional sabbaticals, would provide the time.

And so it had been a man in the grip of a grand artistic hope that Sandrine had come upon that fall afternoon when I'd appeared "intense" to her, and she'd appeared beautiful to me, a vision sweeping over to sit beside me, joking about what an odd couple we would be, then sweetly adding that such might be our destiny.

I had never known a woman like Sandrine, a woman as gifted in so many different ways, and yet who seemed absurdly unaware of those very gifts. She hardly noticed the heads she turned, the eyes that drank her in. She hardly noticed when she uttered some elegant turn of phrase or came up with some piercing insight. She offered everything save any awareness of all the many things she offered, and in that way she was, and always remained, so it had seemed to me, spectacularly down to earth. A few weeks after we'd met, when I'd asked her flatly what she wanted, her answer had so astonished me that I actually laughed: Someday, a baby.

We'd been in my closet-sized apartment, together on my thin mattress, wrapped in my cheap sheets, and she'd suddenly sat up, the upper half of her body immaculately white as the sheet fell from her.

"Why does that make you laugh, Sam?" she asked.

I laughed again. "Anyone can have a baby. I'm talking about what you want out of life."

She looked at me very seriously. "Someday, a baby," she repeated firmly. "Maybe with you."

I took her at her word this time. "Why me?"

I'd considered this an entirely legitimate question at the time. I'd had little to offer her, after all. Sure, I was smart, but so were God knows how many other young men in New York City. I spoke only English, and had traveled very little, while Sandrine spoke fluent French and had lived abroad for extensive periods. My stock was humble, to say the least, my parents simple working people. Sandrine was the favored daughter of two university professors.

So, yes, I thought now, as yet another witness trudged toward the stand, yes, it had been a quite honest and heartfelt question I'd asked Sandrine that afternoon, and repeated now, Why me?

She'd watched me for a moment, clearly sifting through all the information she had by then gathered about me until she'd found the one thing that, for her, answered my question. Then she drifted back down to me and rested her head on my shoulder in that classically tender, trustful pose.

"Because you're kind," she said.

There are moments when our accumulated errors and missteps invade us like a hostile army, and by the end of the third day of my trial, when this memory assailed me, it was an invasion whose unexpected force threatened to break the calm demeanor I'd so far presented to the court. Before that moment I'd sat in utter silence, completely still. I'd faced the witnesses squarely and offered no visible response to anything they'd said. But in the surprising insistence of that particular recollection I felt the emergence of a second, far darker tribunal, the grand inquisitor in his black robe, demanding to know what really happened, how with so starry a beginning I'd reached this starless night.

To regain control of myself, I battened down the hatches of my own memory, concentrated on the happy moments, the simple, justice-of-the-peace marriage upon which Sandrine had insisted, our brief Mediterranean idyll, the job offers Sandrine had found waiting for her upon our return.

There had been quite a few of them, all of them from prestigious universities, a great career opening before her, the chance to teach in Boston, Stanford, or Chicago, the promise of fine libraries, brilliant students, time to write the great book I knew was in her. But only Coburn had made a double offer, jobs for both of us.

"Let's take this one," she said as she handed me a letter on light blue stationery.

She was sitting on the floor of our tiny apartment, her legs stretched across the hooped rug we found in a flea market.

I drew it from her fingers. "Coburn College?" I asked.

"We're married, Sam," Sandrine said. "Married people stay together."

76

She'd seemed entirely satisfied with the house we later bought here, and which she'd never expressed the slightest desire to leave or expand or renovate. She'd thrown herself into her teaching and in her spare time set up an easel in the backyard and painted, though with no interest in exhibiting her work. "No, I'm an amateur, Sam," she'd answered when I'd quite honestly suggested that her work was worth exhibiting. "I do things for the love of them."

The "someday, a baby" moment had arrived the following year, and the painting gave way to motherhood. During those early months, while I'd slaved at my intransigently stubborn novel, she'd often carried Alexandria into town and strolled about the square, going into this shop or that one, showing off our new daughter to the surprisingly large number of townspeople she'd come to know by then.

Once, when Alexandria was five, I'd found them gathering a few brilliantly colored fall leaves in the town park.

"We're going to make a crown," Sandrine told me happily. "Caesar's laurel, only from oak leaves."

I was tired and disheartened at the progress of my novel. Hope deferred does make the heart sick, and it was in the grip of that sickness that I'd spoken. "So I guess it's to be a laurel of Coburn leaves rather than a book on Cleopatra or Hypatia or any of—"

"Stop it," Sandrine interrupted. She looked at me sternly. "So what if I never write a book," she said, her head proudly erect. "It's not a crime."

She didn't wait for a response.

"You're the one who wants to write a book, Sam," she said defiantly, "not I." Then she reached down and took Alexandria's hand and led her away from me, across the broad lawn, a glowing sea of red and yellow leaves, Coburn arrayed in all its autumn splendor.

I'd always expected that if Sandrine betrayed me it would be for love of another man. But that afternoon, growing angrier as she and

Alexandria drifted farther and farther away, I felt I'd been cuckolded by a town.

The sound of Judge Rutledge's gavel returned me to the present, a hard banging that seemed not unlike the one I suddenly and quite disturbingly felt thudding in my chest.

"Court will resume tomorrow morning at nine o'clock," he said.

And thus was heralded, as some nineteenth-century novelist might put it, the fourth day of my trial.

DAY FOUR

Call Milton Douglas Forsythe

The man who answered to his name on the fourth day of my trial was rather short, and a little round, with such an abundance of snow-white hair I'd at first mistaken it for an Andy Warhol wig. It was no such thing, of course, yet even then, as he made his way to the witness stand, I had to think that some of the jurors were briefly of the same opinion. Two of them were bald and one had prematurely thinning hair. How could they not have suspected that Milton Douglas Forsythe was wearing a fright wig?

He was dressed in a beige suit, with a pale green shirt and brown tie, a mix Sandrine called "dirty salad."

Where had she said that? I couldn't remember, though it sounded like something from her youth, something said on a bus or a subway, whispered into my ear and followed by a nod in the direction of the poor soul who'd drawn her fire, but also, and as a matter of course, her sympathy.

By the time I'd emerged from this surmise Mr. Forsythe had already been sworn in and identified himself as the Coburn County coroner, an alliterative job if ever there was one.

"How long have you served in this post?" Mr. Singleton inquired.

"I have been the coroner of Coburn County for the past thirty-two years," Forsythe answered.

We were then treated to the usual list of professional societies to which the coroner belonged and the various training programs he'd attended and from which he had received certificates. This recitation moved us forward in time so that the jury at last found itself in Forsythe's office on the morning of November 15, when the phone rang.

"It was Detective Ray Alabrandi of the Coburn Police Department," he informed the court. "He told me that earlier that morning he'd spoken to a uniformed officer about a death that had occurred here in town the night before."

"Do you recall the name of that officer?" Mr. Singleton asked.

"Officer Wendy Hill."

"And what had Officer Hill told Detective Alabrandi?"

"She'd given him information concerning the death of Sandrine Allegra Madison at 237 Crescent Road. And based on that information Detective Alabrandi thought I should look into it. The death had the appearance of a suicide, he told me."

Appearance, I thought, yes.

"Detective Alabrandi wanted me to go to the house before the body was removed," Mr. Forsythe continued.

"Why so quickly?"

"He said there were odd circumstances," Mr. Forsythe answered. "So he wanted me to launch a formal investigation right away."

"A formal investigation," Mr. Singleton repeated. "And what would that entail?"

"Well, first of all, it would halt any effort to dispose of the body," Mr. Forsythe answered. "Then there'd be an autopsy, of course. Any suspicion of a suicide would immediately trigger an autopsy. But in this case, as I said, Detective Alabrandi asked me to go to the address of the deceased."

"All right, and did you subsequently go to the crime scene?"

Morty rose. "Objection, Your Honor, 237 Crescent Road is a house, not a 'crime scene.'"

"Sustained," the judge said. "Careful with prejudicial language, Mr. Singleton."

"Sorry, Your Honor." He returned his attention to Mr. Forsythe. "All right, did you subsequently go to 237 Crescent Road?"

"I did."

And indeed he had gone to 237 Crescent Road, looking a bit tired, as I now recalled, a man edging toward retirement and with something in his eyes that suggested he'd seen too many dead bodies over the years.

"I'm Doug Forsythe," he said when I opened the door. "I'm the Coburn County coroner. I'm very sorry for your loss."

I couldn't tell if his small sad smile was genuine or official.

"I'm sure you understand that in a case like this," he said, "a relatively young woman, the issue of a suicide, that the county requires that I make an investigation."

I'd known no such thing but I said, "Of course," and waved him into the house.

He glanced about but appeared to register very little, his face expressionless, eyes that told me nothing.

"My wife is down there," I said with a nod to the corridor.

It was eight in the morning but Forsythe looked like a man who'd already worked a full shift, his movements slow, his gaze betraying none of the considerable powers of observation he actually possessed and about which I'd learned only after he'd completed his report.

"My daughter came home at around four this morning," I told him. "To be with me, I mean, after I told her what happened. She's sleeping down the hallway."

"No need to disturb her," Forsythe said amiably. "I won't be here long." He smiled. "And I'll try to be quiet." And with that he'd softly, and quite thoughtfully, padded down the corridor to where Sandrine still lay.

As Mr. Forsythe continued his testimony, I unaccountably thought of my long-deceased mother, the easy way she'd dealt with people, the softness of her voice, how slow to anger she had been. She'd held down a job of killing monotony, and yet, from those small wages, and even after she'd finally divorced my utterly indifferent father, she'd sometimes sent the checks I'd find in the mail from time to time, ten dollars here, twenty dollars there, always with the notation: for my son. It was a memory that returned me to that younger man, so grateful for those small contributions, without bitterness, harboring no resentments, working on a novel I'd titled "The Pull of the Earth" and which I'd described to Sandrine as being about "the tenderness of things," a man who now seemed far, far different from the one who'd escorted Mr. Forsythe into the bedroom of his dead wife.

"And what did you observe at 237 Crescent Road, Mr. Forsythe?" Mr. Singleton asked.

"Mr. Madison met me at the door, where I identified myself. Then he escorted me to a back bedroom. That's where I found the victim."

Morty was on his feet again. "I don't mean to hold things up, Your Honor, but for the record I'd like it noted that Sandrine Madison was a deceased person, not a 'victim.'"

"Duly noted," the judge said with a nod to the stenographer. He then turned to the jury. "Ladies and gentlemen, please strike the word 'victim' from any thought you might have concerning Mrs. Madison. It has not been established that she was a victim of any act, criminal or otherwise, committed by the defendant or anyone else."

With a feeling of genuine surprise, I found myself rather admiring the exquisite fairness of this, the pains that were being taken to protect me, and to honor during this otherwise inconsequential and decidedly small-town judicial proceeding the august requirements of the Constitution of the United States.

Judge Rutledge turned to Mr. Singleton. "Continue."

"Now, Mr. Forsythe," Mr. Singleton began again. "Can you tell us what you observed in the bedroom Professor Madison escorted you to?"

"I found a deceased female," the coroner answered. "She was in the bed, lying on her back. She was naked from the waist. Whether she was completely naked wasn't something I could tell because there was a sheet over the lower part of her body."

For the next few minutes, the coroner recited observations not unlike those of Officer Hill. The room is cluttered. There is a yellow piece of paper beside the bed. He also sees an empty glass "about the size you'd have with iced tea," a pill container with the cap on, various books scattered about. "And there was a candle burning."

"A candle?" Mr. Singleton inquired.

"Yes," Mr. Forsythe answered.

"Where was this candle?"

It was on a small shelf near Sandrine's bed, I recalled, and I'd put it there because she'd asked me to do it. We'd bought it many years before in Albi, the little French town that had been the last stop on what she had always called our "honeymoon trip," though we'd been married for almost a year before my spinster aunt died unexpectedly, leaving me with a small behest. We'd thought of starting a little nest egg with this money but had decided on a trip instead. There'd be plenty of time to save money, Sandrine had pointed out, but the chance to travel around the Mediterranean, visit all those fabled places, might never come again.

"A large red candle," Mr. Forsythe added.

Sandrine had wanted me to retrieve it from a box in the basement. There were quite a few such boxes, and it had taken me some time to find this particular candle. She'd smiled when I finally came into the room with it, taken it from my hand, and rather lovingly turned it beneath the lamp. Then she'd uttered one of her enigmatic remarks: I wish you could retrieve everything so easily.

Retrieve, I thought now, a word Sandrine had no doubt chosen carefully, and which, at least for her, had surely been fraught with significance. But what had she meant? And did I now have to parse every sentence she'd uttered in order to retrieve its meaning?

Rather than enter into this discussion with myself, I returned my attention to the courtroom.

"Was this candle lit?" Mr. Singleton asked.

"Yes," Mr. Forsythe answered.

It was lit because Sandrine had wanted it lit. She'd also wanted it placed in a particular spot on the shelf to the left of her bed. She'd asked me to light it when I came into the bedroom that last night, and, as if ignited by its flame, she'd then launched into her attack, her voice very cold and hard when she said, "That candle, Sam, that little candle, is all that's left of Albi."

Singleton knew none of this, of course, so I couldn't imagine why he bothered to ask Mr. Forsythe about a candle that had no relevance whatsoever to my trial.

I glanced toward Morty and gave him a quizzical look. In response, he merely shrugged, as if to say, Sometimes testimony just goes off track. Don't worry, Sam, the state will pull the train back onto the rails soon enough.

And Singleton did, dropping the whole business of the candle and returning to the subject of the general condition of the bedroom. He'd anticipated Morty's rebuttal and established that although a bit in disarray our bedroom gave no sign of a struggle. Nothing was overturned, nothing broken. Under Mr. Singleton's questioning, Mr. Forsythe told the jury that he saw no bruises on Sandrine's body, nor any sign that she had ever been physically abused. He used the word "angelic" to describe the features of Sandrine's face, and it struck me that they'd been exactly so. He then told the jury she'd looked "at rest," which she surely had, words that immediately returned me to the final moments of that last night's fury, with what wicked depths I'd wanted never to hear her voice again or defend myself against her accusations, the thrashing wounded bull I'd been.

"Now, Mr. Forsythe," Mr. Singleton said, "at some point during your visit to 237 Crescent Road that morning, did you have occasion to speak to Professor Madison concerning the death of his wife?"

He had had such occasion, of course.

"Would you tell the court the gist of that conversation?"

"He said that his wife had killed herself," Mr. Forsythe answered.

"Did he say how?"

"He said his wife must have been stockpiling a painkiller for some weeks."

"Did he give you the name of this painkiller?"

"Demerol."

"And did he suggest to you how Sandrine Madison had administered this drug on the night in question?"

"He said that he'd picked up the glass beside the bed and it had smelled of vodka," Mr. Forsythe informed the jury. "He said that his wife had probably taken the pills with this vodka."

"Did he say that he was with his wife when she took her own life?"

"He said that he was not."

Mr. Forsythe went on to reveal additional facts regarding our conversation that morning, none of which seemed particularly notable until he reached the point where, standing at the door, as he was about to leave the house, he'd turned back to me and said, "I noticed a guidebook."

"A guidebook?" I asked.

"It was tucked just beneath the sheet," Mr. Forsythe said. "I noticed it when I examined the body more closely."

I had not examined Sandrine's body more closely, and so I hadn't noticed the book at all and told him so.

"What kind of guidebook?" I asked.

"A travel guide," Forsythe said. "The title was something like *Around the Mediterranean.*"

"The Mediterranean," I said softly. "She was probably thinking of the trip we took to the Mediterranean when we were young. It was the travel guide we used on that trip. It was twenty years old, but she never threw it away, I guess."

"So it was nostalgia, you think?" Mr. Forsythe asked. "The reason she was reading it?"

"I suppose so, yes," I said. "It was a good time for us. When we took that trip." I paused, then before I could stop myself, added, "We were happier then."

Something in Forsythe's eyes darkened. "I see," he said. "So she hadn't been planning a trip?"

"No."

I was trying to recall the exact words of this exchange when Mr. Singleton suddenly turned, walked over to his desk, picked up our old travel guide, the one Alabrandi had later seized, and handed it to Mr. Forsythe.

"Is this the book you saw in the bedroom at 237 Crescent Road?" he asked.

"Yes."

"And the title is what?"

Mr. Forsythe shifted the book to get a better light. "*Around the Countries of the Mediterranean, a Travel Guide*," he read.

"All right, did you later have occasion to take a look at this travel guide?"

He had.

"And did you notice if any page had been marked."

"The corner of one page had been turned down, yes."

"And what did this turned-down page mark?"

"A town in France," the coroner answered.

"Which town?"

"The town was named Albi."

"Thank you," Mr. Singleton said. "I have no further questions."

Morty gave my shoulder a reassuring squeeze as he rose from his chair. His hand was big, beefy, and I felt somewhat like a little boy whose father has just confidently signaled him that, despite the unexpected and steadily building odds against it, he will win the game.

"Forgive me, Mr. Forsythe, but would you state again how long you have been the Coburn County coroner?" Morty asked.

"Thirty-two years."

"And if you don't mind, would you tell the court how old you are?"

"I'm seventy-one."

"And just for the record, you did order that Mrs. Madison's body be autopsied, correct?"

"Yes, I did."

"And that would be entirely routine, wouldn't it? It was enough that Mr. Madison had mentioned suicide as a possible cause of death?"

"Yes, that would have been enough."

"In fact, Mrs. Madison's age alone might also have been enough for you to order an autopsy, yes?"

"Yes," Forsythe answered. "Unless her death had been expected."

89

I knew exactly what Morty was up to with this line of questioning, of course. He was going to show that had not Officer Hill gotten her "itch," and subsequently reported it to Detective Alabrandi, then there would have been no reason for the wheels of justice to begin turning as rapidly as they had in my case. This speed had been the result of nothing but a few initial and very prejudicial observations, Morty was saying, and they were but the first of many that had, at last, made Samuel Joseph Madison, loving husband of Sandrine and loving father of Alexandria, the true victim in my case.

"But this mention of a suicide alone wouldn't have been enough to make you call upon Mr. Madison the very next morning, would it, Mr. Forsythe?"

"Probably not."

"It was Detective Alabrandi's phone call that gave you this sense of urgency, isn't that correct?"

"Yes."

"And, as you've stated, you went to 237 Crescent Road, and after returning from there you ordered Dr. Benjamin Mortimer to conduct an autopsy on the body of Sandrine Madison, isn't that true?"

"Yes, it is."

This time, Morty had brought his notes to the lectern. He glanced at them, then looked up. "Now, Mr. Forsythe, would you say that you've seen several suicides during your career?"

"Unfortunately, yes."

"All right, and from your experience, you've learned a few things about what a suicide looks like. It would be fair to say that, wouldn't it?"

"It would."

"Mr. Forsythe, did you see anything in Mrs. Madison's bedroom that indicated to you that her death had been caused by anyone other than herself? By this I mean, did you see anything physical that might have given you that impression?"

Mr. Forsythe hesitated slightly. He was obviously an old hand at giving testimony, and so he knew that this was a heavily loaded question. For a moment, I watched him closely, suspecting that he might find a way to slither out of answering with a flat no, perhaps give an evasive answer, or one more damaging to me. He was, after all, a prosecution witness.

"No," he said.

"Nothing at all that indicated a murder?"

"No, nothing," Mr. Forsythe answered firmly.

It was an answer so completely honest and professional that I was quite surprised by it.

And so I offered him a tiny smile, almost invisible, but one I hoped sufficient to express my appreciation for his simple honesty. Subtle though it was, the coroner appeared to see this smile, though he made no response to it that could be read by anyone but me.

"Thank you," Morty said. "No more questions."

Mr. Forsythe didn't look at me as he left the stand but stared straight ahead, and within seconds his "dirty salad" suit was just a swath of beige in my peripheral vision.

I turned my attention toward the judge's bench. Morty and Mr. Singleton were talking to Judge Rutledge. Then both turned and headed back to their respective tables.

"There's going to be a short delay," Morty said. "Singleton's next witness is just now parking." He smiled. "Well, the coroner didn't hurt us."

I nodded in agreement though I had little doubt that Morty would have said the same even if the coroner had produced whatever in my case would be the smoking gun.

He sat back casually. "So what's the deal with that candle?"

I shrugged. "We bought it in Albi, a little French town. It was when we were young, that first trip we took."

"The page your wife turned down in that guide, right?"

"Yes."

"What's so important about this town?"

"I don't know." I thought a moment, then added, "Well, it's what started the argument. Sandrine mentioned Albi, and somehow from there we got into that fight."

"What fight?"

"The last one," I answered. "The one I told you about, the one we had that night."

I recalled again the fury of our final exchange, how raw and hurtful it had been, with what ferocity Sandrine had attacked me and with what terrible final statement I had struck back.

"I can't imagine why Singleton would ask anything about that candle," I added. "It was just a cheap souvenir. Like everything else on that trip, I bought it with a little money I got after my aunt died."

I saw something catch in Morty's brain. "How did your aunt die, by the way?" he asked.

"After a long illness."

"Were you there when she died?"

"You mean, in the room?"

"In the vicinity."

I gazed at him bleakly. "For Christ's sake, Morty, do you think I killed my aunt too?"

Morty stared at me silently.

"No, not in the vicinity," I said flatly. "My aunt was in Minneapolis. I was in New York." I glared at him. "If you need any further proof that I didn't murder my aunt, I'll try to provide it."

"I don't think that will be necessary," Morty said. He smiled but it was a cold dead smile. "I was just checking, Sam. There is nothing more damning than innuendo, or worse than a surprise."

"There won't be any surprises," I told him. "You know everything there is to know."

And it was already far too much, as I'd learned by then, far, far more than I would have thought possible before my trial, though I also suspected that Mr. Singleton's little paws were still at work.

When I looked back at Morty, he had a curious and uncharacteristically troubled look on his face.

"The time line, Sam. When did you leave your wife? The day she died, I mean."

"I left her twice that day. Once for my afternoon class and, later, for my evening class."

"The second time you left, that was after you had that fight, correct? When she threw that cup at you?"

"Yes."

"Where was Alexandria at that point?" Morty asked.

"Why does it matter?"

"It matters because if Singleton got desperate he could call her as a witness." He saw how surprised I was by this. "You have no constitutional protection against your daughter, Sam," he reminded me.

"Alexandria would never testify against me," I said. "Besides, there's nothing she could testify about."

Morty's gaze remained steady. "What about that last fight you and your wife had?"

For some reason, the image that returned to me was of Alexandria making lunch that day, standing in the kitchen, cutting bread. She hadn't turned when I called to tell her that I was headed for my noon class but only given a short jerk of the knife.

"She wasn't in the house when that happened," I told Morty. "She'd gone into town."

"But she came back after that fight, didn't she?" Morty asked pointedly. "After you'd already left, I mean."

"Yes."

"And so she no doubt said goodbye to your wife," Morty said.

"Of course," I said. "But Sandrine would never have told her about that terrible last argument."

"She might not have had to tell her."

"What do you mean?"

"Well, there's that cup."

I felt a cold dread. "Yes, the cup."

"Your wife didn't clean that up," Morty reminded me. "You did, remember? You did it after your wife's death."

I nodded.

"So Alexandria might have seen it."

"If Sandrine was still in the bedroom, yes."

"Did you ever ask Alexandria what she and your wife talked about that last evening?"

"No."

Morty started to add something else but suddenly glanced back toward the entrance to the courtroom. "Ah," he said softly.

I turned to see a woman in a dark pantsuit.

"You spoke to her only a few times, right?" Morty asked.

We'd gone over all this previously, but it was clear that even my lawyer doubted either my memory or my intentions, both of which could prove damaging to my case.

"Yes," I told him. "But the only conversation we had was when Sandrine and I went to her office. And even then she did most of the talking. It wasn't a conversation, really."

"And you never met her outside her office?"

"No."

Morty watched as the woman moved down the aisle, toward the front of the courtroom. Her gait was brisk, like someone used to being on time and quite aware that she wasn't.

"Well, we're about to hear what she has to say," he whispered.

I steeled myself.

"Indeed."

Call Dr. Ana Ortins

Dr. Ortins was of medium height, with straight, no-nonsense brown hair, and though she was a tad plump for a physician who so often counseled against being overweight, she looked quite healthy on the day she took the stand. I'd seen her trotting around Coburn's neat little reservoir on occasion, and the local news had often reported that she was running in this or that marathon. For the past few years she'd been our local television station's favorite medical talking head. In the summer she regularly appeared to remind us to use sunblock, and in the late fall she advised seniors to get their flu shots. On television, she dressed only in solid colors, probably for their slimming effect. Her eyes were large, and I'd known from personal experience that she could make them quite soulful when she chose, a trick she'd pulled off very well indeed on the one occasion I'd actually spoken to her face to face.

I'd never met Dr. Ortins before Sandrine chose her, and during the one office visit I'd made with Sandrine she sat in her snug consulting room, always behind her desk, as she indicated this or prescribed that. At the end of that visit, she tried to look on the bright side of an admittedly dark situation: *You have many years ahead of you, Sandrine.*

Even weeks later I found I remembered that office quite well. Like other physicians, Dr. Ortins had festooned its walls with the usual array of diplomas and certifications, but to these she'd added a large and very colorful poster of the human body, all its interior parts vibrantly displayed. I'd found something rather macabre in the look of it, a body skinned in this way, and in less solemn circumstances I might have made a quip about them, called her "Dr. Dexter," or "the serial curer," or something of that sort. But on the day of our visit there'd been no place for humor, and I'd simply sat with my hands in my lap and waited, Sandrine silent in the chair next to mine, looking, for the first time in her life, oddly broken.

When Dr. Ortins reached the stand she glanced at me briefly, then away as the bailiff approached.

As usual, the preliminaries were soporific recitations of colleges attended, degrees held, length of practice in charming Colburn. Dr. Ortins answered Mr. Singleton's tedious questions with an amiable, unthreatened air, as if she were applying for a job she knew she would get but already had no intention of taking. She went through her education and training, the fact that she'd specialized in neurology, which was no doubt why Sandrine had chosen her.

A quarter hour of testimony went by before Sandrine at last appeared in Dr. Ortins's office. She had been alone on that first visit, the doctor told the court. As her office records showed, Sandrine had come in at precisely 11 a.m. on the morning of April 7. Spurred by my subsequent recounting of that morning in Morty's office, I'd recalled that although the drive to Dr. Ortins's office would have taken only five minutes, Sandrine had left our house an hour before her appointment and not come home until almost two hours after it, a curious stretch of time I'd thought nothing of before Detective Alabrandi appeared at my door some days after her death, notebook in hand, his gaze a tad distant when he'd made his telling comment: "A few unusual items have turned up," and to which I'd replied, "About me?" His reply had sent an icy finger down my spine. "No, about your wife."

Sandrine had been in relatively good spirits the morning she left for Dr. Ortins's office, though she'd still been unsure she had made the right call in Dr. Ortins herself. Because of privacy issues, I'd warned her to stay clear of any physicians associated with Coburn College.

"You can bet they chatter like magpies about what professor has herpes or AIDS or who takes Viagra," I told her over breakfast one morning. "They're like old ladies at a quilting party. They couldn't keep a secret in a jar."

For her part, Sandrine had already decided to avoid any doctor whose practice smacked of a "holistic" approach.

"I don't want some vegan doctor telling me about the benevolence of nature," she said, "or that a tumor is okay as long as it's growing."

I'd laughed out loud at that one but Sandrine had only smiled.

Only smiled, yes, but tensely, because by then she must have been quite frightened of the possibility that something was seriously wrong with her.

The first signs were not much different from the usual changes that occur as one gets older, and since Sandrine was forty-six she'd dismissed them at first. It was several weeks before she'd even mentioned them to me, though I later learned she must have been asking herself why she should have such mysterious weakness in her muscles.

Then, out of nowhere, her speech began to slur occasionally, and for Sandrine this must surely have sent a cold dread through her soul.

She was born of parents already rather old, and who'd died in their late seventies, a few years before, and so she had little reason to fear an early death. And yet, for all that, I'd seen that fear in her eyes the morning she was to see Dr. Ortins, and which I'd tried unsuccessfully to quell.

"You're fine, I'm sure," I told her.

She nodded crisply. "Probably," she said cheerily, then rose from the table and gathered up her things. "Back soon," she said.

I'd assumed that she was headed immediately for Dr. Ortins's office, but that had turned out not to be the case, a fact I learned only later from the tightly drawn lips of Detective Alabrandi.

She'd returned at just after six. I'd noticed very little change in her demeanor, a fact that now struck me as rather odd in light of what was presently being said on the witness stand.

"Mrs. Madison was quite alarmed," Dr. Ortins told the court. "She had been experiencing certain disturbing physical changes for a long time."

"How long?"

"Over a year."

Over a year, and yet, as I thought at that moment, she'd mentioned nothing of these changes to me, not one hint of what must have been a steadily growing dread.

"What kind of problems?" Mr. Singleton asked.

Serious problems, as I finally learned, and of whose dire nature the jury was now to hear.

"Mrs. Madison had noticed what she called a 'constellation of effects,'" Dr. Ortins answered. "I know she used that term because I wrote it down in my notes."

"Why did you write it down, Dr. Ortins?"

"Because it suggested to me that Mrs. Madison had been doing her own medical research," Dr. Ortins answered. "And frankly, when I know a patient is doing that, I'm a little more careful in how I approach things with them because they may have gathered some quite incorrect information, usually from the Internet."

"But that was not the case with Mrs. Madison, was it?" Mr. Singleton asked.

"No," Dr. Ortins answered. "Mrs. Madison had done quite good research."

"And had she come to any determination with regard to her research?"

"If you mean by way of self-diagnosis, then yes, as it turned out, she had," Dr. Ortins answered. "Of course, I didn't know that her research had generated a correct diagnosis. You need several tests to determine that."

"And did you order those tests?"

"Yes. I did an electrodiagnostic, which included electromyography and a nerve conduction velocity test. Also the usual blood and urine tests, including high-resolution serum protein electrophoresis, thyroid and parathyroid hormone levels . . ."

She seemed suddenly to realize that her answer had overshot the question by half and she quickly brought her answer to a halt. "Along with other tests, of course," she added.

"All right, so what was the diagnosis that resulted from those tests, doctor?"

"Amyotrophic lateral sclerosis."

"That disease has a more common name, doesn't it, Dr. Ortins?"

"Yes," Dr. Ortins answered. "It's more commonly referred to as ALS or Lou Gehrig's disease."

Hearing those words again, I couldn't imagine that for weeks before seeing Dr. Ortins Sandrine must have had them fluttering like bats in her mind. Even so, she'd certainly given no indication of so dark a suspicion. Not even the afternoon she'd returned from her first visit to Dr. Ortins. Of course, there'd been a reason for that, as the doctor made clear.

"But on her first visit to my office, I assured Mrs. Madison that it was quite unlikely that she had ALS," Dr. Ortins told the jury. "There are many reasons why a person can feel muscle weakness, and as for the occasional slurring she'd noticed, that is sometimes the result of fatigue. Although Mrs. Madison didn't appear tired in that way, she did seem . . ."

Here Dr. Ortins stopped, a pause that focused my attention because she was clearly searching for the right word.

"Sad," she said, when she found it.

And so my wife, so lovely, so brilliant, still quite young and probably healthy, with a marriage that was by all outside appearances quite happy, had seemed "sad" to Dr. Ortins. How in all the months and weeks and days before she appeared in the good doctor's office, I asked myself suddenly, had I not seen that?

And what, I further asked myself at that moment, would have made Sandrine sad?

Mr. Singleton did not ask Dr. Ortins this question, because he knew that it would be leading the witness or calling for a conclusion, and Morty would no doubt object, and his objection would certainly be sustained.

For the next few minutes, Dr. Ortins reviewed the results of the tests she'd ordered, along with her analysis of the test results, and finally the awesome certainty to which she'd come and of which she'd informed Sandrine on the afternoon of April 12.

"I told her that her initial self-diagnosis was unfortunately the correct one," Dr. Ortins said. "She, of course, already knew the prognosis. Even so, as I would with any patient, I detailed the likely progress of the disease and how Mrs. Madison might prepare for it."

"Did Mrs. Madison appear to be interested in how she might prepare?"

"Yes," Dr. Ortins answered. "She asked quite a few questions. And, of course, she was interested in just how long she had to live. I told her that she might well live another ten years, and that during that time there might be some breakthrough in medical research. She asked about this research, and I went into some of the work that was being done."

"Did Mrs. Madison say anything else to you at that point, Doctor?" Mr. Singleton asked.

"Only one thing," Dr. Ortins answered.

101

"And what was that?"

"She said she didn't want to die," Dr. Ortins told the jury. "And that she intended to live as fully as she could to the last breath."

Mr. Singleton was still watching the jury when he very pointedly asked Dr. Ortins his next question.

"To the last breath. Those were Mrs. Madison's exact words?"

Nor did he turn from them when she gave her answer.

"Her exact words, yes."

Only two hours or so after Sandrine had said this to Dr. Ortins, I'd returned from my classes to find her in the bedroom in the darkness: *Come back later, Sam.*

Which I had done, though by then she'd left the bedroom, so that I'd found her in the scriptorium, sipping a glass of red wine, reading a biography of Cleopatra.

"What would make a woman a true queen of the Nile, Sam?" she asked as she closed the book.

"Courage, I suppose," I said. "Daring. What do you think would make a woman a true queen of the Nile?"

"The ability to face the truth," Sandrine answered. "To try to change what there's still time to change and accept what you can't."

I laughed. "That's from the serenity prayer, isn't it?" I asked. "Have you been going to AA meetings?"

She watched me silently, and her expression told me everything.

"It was something bad, wasn't it?" I asked. "From the doctor."

She nodded.

"What is it?"

"I have Lou Gehrig's disease," she said flatly.

With this news, I'd experienced that famous cliché, the sense of being hit very hard in the stomach. But was it at that very moment, I asked myself now, as Dr. Ortins continued her matter-of-fact testimony,

102

that I'd begun to run the awful scenario of what was to come, the profound changes that lay ahead, all of them quite dreadful?

"Are you sure?" I asked her. "Is the doctor certain about the diagnosis?"

"Yes."

I offered no response to this, and during the following silence I saw something in Sandrine's eyes change, and with that change a terrible sadness settled over her, one so profound she seemed physically to deflate, as if all the light and air had suddenly left her soul.

"I have to think things through," she said in a voice that struck me as suddenly very distant, something said to herself and whose meaning she alone understood, so that she looked as if she'd just received a blow somehow deeper and more wounding than her diagnosis, something that smelled even more of death.

"Think what through?" I asked.

Rather than answer, she glanced down at the book she'd been reading, let her gaze linger there for a moment, then looked up at me and said, "I wish I had something to leave you, Sam." She watched me closely, as if she were looking for some small light in a steadily darkening room. When that light failed to appear, she said, "I was thinking of *Who's Afraid of Virginia Woolf?* The way George stares off into infinity and says, 'Sunday. Tomorrow. All day.'"

"Why that of all things?" I asked.

"Because when he says that, he's really lost hope that anything can change," Sandrine answered. "That's the hope I don't want to lose."

When I reached over to touch her hand, she drew it back quickly and reflexively, as she might have drawn it back from a wasp or a spider.

"You won't lose hope," I assured her.

Something very strange had come into her eyes at that moment, I recalled now, a look I'd never seen before, half fear, half care. Then, just as suddenly, her gaze had hardened into determination. "No," she'd said firmly, "I won't lose hope."

Dr. Ortins was closing in upon the last of her testimony by the time this memory played out, but what lingered in my mind was the fact that I'd been certain Sandrine had been speaking about her illness at that point, the fact that she hadn't wanted to lose hope that Dr. Ortins might be right in telling her about the research going on, the possibility that there might, indeed, be a breakthrough.

My question now was simple. Was that what she'd meant or had she been speaking of some different hope she'd feared to lose? Hope for herself? For Alexandria? Or had it been some unspoken hope she'd had for me?

I thought suddenly of the candle from Albi, how Sandrine had asked me to place it exactly on the spot where its light would play directly on the glass jars and bottles she'd later put on the table beside her bed. Why had she done that?

So many odd questions were emerging now, a debris washed up by my trial, questions that were subtle and unfathomable and which in some way were beyond my guilt or innocence of the crime for which I was charged.

Mr. Singleton, however, had a very different question on his mind.

"When did you next see Mrs. Madison?" he asked Dr. Ortins.

"She came to my office with her husband," Dr. Ortins said. "I went over what would be expected in the coming years, the work of the caregiver in a case like this."

"And that's a lot of work, isn't it?"

"Yes."

"Why is it a lot of work, doctor?"

"Because a person suffering from ALS becomes increasingly unable to care for herself."

"And so Mrs. Madison would become more and more difficult to manage, isn't that true, Doctor? On a day-to-day basis, I mean."

"Yes," Dr. Ortins answered. "I explained to Mr. Madison that his wife would begin to lose her ability to use her muscles."

"In the end her muscles would entirely desert her, correct?" Mr. Singleton asked.

"With a few exceptions like blinking her eyes, that's true."

For the benefit of the jury and to emphasize this dreadful point, Mr. Singleton now took Dr. Ortins through the grim steps of Sandrine's horrifying decline.

"So, in the end, Mr. Madison would have to feed his wife?" he asked.

"Yes."

"Bathe her?"

"Yes?"

"Even take her to the toilet?"

With this question, I noticed several members of the jury turn to look at me, a grim surmise already in their minds, I felt certain, the grave possibility that I'd plotted then carried out the selfish opposite of euthanasia, a murder motivated by my simple desire to rid myself of the loathsome tasks that would soon be mine.

"Yes," Dr. Ortins answered.

"So what it comes down to is that during this office visit you informed Mr. Madison that his wife would eventually become completely unable to carry out any of the physical functions of life, did you not, Dr. Ortins?"

"That's what I told him, yes," Dr. Ortins answered. "And I warned him that he might become depressed. That almost certainly he would, in fact, become depressed."

Mr. Singleton glanced at his notes, studied them a moment, then looked up. "When did you next see Mrs. Madison?"

"I never saw her again."

Mr. Singleton gave every appearance of being surprised by this.

"She never returned for any sort of treatment or consultation?" he asked with a show of almost childlike wonder.

"No."

Mr. Singleton walked to his desk, retrieved a small square of paper, and handed it to Dr. Ortins.

"Do you recognize this, Doctor?"

"Yes. It's a prescription. I wrote it for Mrs. Madison."

"But I thought you said you had no further contact with Mrs. Madison."

"I didn't," Dr. Ortins said.

I knew what was coming because Mr. Singleton now turned toward the jury so that he could see its reaction to Dr. Ortins's answer.

"Then how did you happen to write this prescription?" he asked.

"I was contacted by Mrs. Madison's husband," Dr. Ortins answered. "He called and said that his wife was having quite a lot of back pain. Very severe, he said. Debilitating. She had fallen, he said, and he thought perhaps she'd compressed a vertebrae or something of that sort. He said she needed something strong."

"But this 'fall' was never confirmed by Mrs. Madison?" Mr. Singleton asked.

"I never spoke to Mrs. Madison," Dr. Ortins told the court. "Only to her husband, when he called to tell me about her fall, her pain, that she needed something strong."

"Now, Dr. Ortins, have you had occasion to read the pathologist's report on Mrs. Madison?"

"Yes, I have."

"So you are aware that Dr. Mortimer could find no sign of a back injury in his examination of Mrs. Madison."

"I have read his report, and, yes, he found no back injury."

"Is it fair to say that when Mr. Madison told you of this back injury, he was not telling the truth?"

Morty got to his feet. "Objection, Your Honor."

"Sustained," Judge Rutledge said. "Please rephrase the question, Mr. Singleton."

Mr. Singleton nodded. "Dr. Ortins, did Professor Madison give you any instruction as to what sort of pain medication his wife's back injury would require?"

"Only that it should be something strong."

Mr. Singleton was still watching the jury when he repeated, "Something strong?"

"Yes."

"And did you prescribe a strong painkiller for Mrs. Madison?"

"Yes," Dr. Ortins answered. "I prescribed Demerol."

Mr. Singleton paused for a dramatic moment, then said, "I have no further questions for this witness."

During cross-examination Morty did his best to minimize the effect of Mr. Singleton's final few questions to Dr. Ortins. I knew that nothing prior to those questions could possibly have cast suspicion upon me, but at the very end of her testimony a dark curtain had parted and Morty clearly feared that the jury might have glimpsed something sinister behind it, the first, shadowy suggestion of a crime.

For that reason, Morty led the good doctor through a series of questions, all of which were designed to make her answer in the simple affirmative.

Is it common practice for you to write prescriptions without seeing the patient?

Is it common practice for you to do this at the request of a patient's spouse?

Is it common practice for you to prescribe Demerol for severe back pain?

Yes.

Yes.

Yes.

Then Morty switched to a series of questions designed to make Dr. Ortins answer in the negative.

It wouldn't be unusual for a patient in the first stages of ALS to fall, would it?

In such cases, it also wouldn't be unusual for such falls to result in an injury, possibly a serious one to the back, would it?

For that reason you weren't at all surprised to hear that Mrs. Madison had fallen, were you Dr. Ortins?

Or that she had injured her back?

Or that her husband was the person who conveyed this information?

No.

No.

No.

No.

No.

"So you didn't find anything at all unusual with regard to your writing a prescription for Mrs. Madison for Demerol at her husband's request, did you, Dr. Ortins?"

"No."

Then, a few, final questions.

"Dr. Ortins, have you had other patients with back pain?" Morty asked.

Dr. Ortins sensed trouble. Cautiously she said, "Every doctor does."

"That's true," Morty said. "And have you had patients who've complained of back pain and, despite your best efforts, you've not been able to find the cause of that pain?"

"That's sometimes the case, yes."

"Have you ever prescribed Demerol for such a patient?"

"Yes."

At that point, Morty faced the members of the jury in exactly the same way Mr. Singleton had faced them minutes before.

"It is possible for a patient to need medication for a back ailment or injury that medical science cannot find, isn't that true?"

"Yes, that's true."

Now Morty, in a tone designed to replicate in every vocal nuance Mr. Singleton's earlier statement, concluded with "I have nothing further for this witness."

It was all quite masterful, as well as wonderfully theatrical, and it seemed to me that Shakespeare would probably have made a lot more money as a lawyer. As Dr. Ortins left the stand, I couldn't help but imagine what stunning addresses to the jury the Bard would have made.

The stern look in Morty's eyes warned me that a slight smile had slithered onto my lips.

"Stone face," he whispered like a father disciplining a child. "Keep a stone face."

I looked down quickly, duly scolded, then lifted my head slowly.

"Sorry," I whispered back to him, though there was something in this little episode that had pierced me, the fact that Sandrine would have understood my smile and returned it to me. There'd been a time when I'd had no further questions for that smile. But now I wondered if it would have been one of shared amusement or the fingerprint of some old regret. "You see through everything, Sam," she'd once said to me. I'd taken this as affirmation of my disdain for all that I considered saccharine or sentimental, my peals of laughter, so to speak, at the death of Little Nell. Sandrine had meant it differently, however. For her it had

109

signaled a core change she'd perceived in me "But whatever happened," she asked softly, "to the tenderness of things?"

It was a question that once again returned me to those long lost days immediately after we'd met in Washington Square, the slow walks, the inexpensive dinners, the evenings of cheap wine and quiet talk, how in that distant time the goal of her education had been contained in her dream of passing it along, founding a little school somewhere, a vision of her life Sandrine had perhaps never entirely abandoned.

On that thought, I recalled the dingy loft I'd had on Avenue A in those days, how Sandrine had often spent the night with me there. Toward dawn on one of those nights, she'd quoted a line from *Love's Labour's Lost*, how, when asked the purpose of study, Ferdinand had replied that its purpose was simply to bequeath those treasures of heart and mind which, without it, would be lost.

Heart and mind, I thought, and with those words felt the gallows floor creak beneath me.

"Sam?"

I looked at Morty, who was staring at me approvingly, clearly pleased by the grim expression on my face.

"Much better," he said.

Lunch Break

I watched as the members of the jury left the courtroom to take their lunches. By then I'd noticed that, when court was in session, they behaved like ideal students, listening even to the dullest testimony with the attentiveness and seriousness I'd once given to my long dead novel, and considerably deeper than any I'd later offered to the rudimentary needs of my struggling students. According to the results of their judgment I would either live or die, and I could see that this burden did, in fact, weigh upon them. Sandrine had often referred to Pascal's observation that the lion's share of mankind's many evils derive from the simple fact of not being able to sit quietly in a room, and as the last of the jurors disappeared into the adjoining chamber I sensed that collectively they would achieve this stationary thoughtfulness.

Once they were gone, I made my way to the little room where I'd decided to have my lunch while my case went forward.

Some weeks before, Judge Rutledge had set my bail at a scant $50,000. I was a forty-six-year-old tenured professor of English literature with no criminal record, thus not at all, according to the judge, a flight risk. For that reason, I might have had lunch anywhere in Coburn, but I'd not availed myself of that freedom save for the day of my arraignment, when I'd casually strolled to a local sandwich shop. On that occasion, there had been a sufficient number of stares from the townspeople to cut through my usual obliviousness, and since then I'd taken my lunch in the small conference room down the corridor from the courtroom. Morty often joined me there, so that it was in this room some days before that we'd gone over the jurors' responses during the voir dire phase of my trial and at last selected the five men and seven women who had moments before filed out of the courtroom, not one of them casting a glance in my direction.

Morty came through the door a few minutes later, looking quite pleased with the morning's proceedings. He smiled, sat down, and opened his briefcase.

"Let's go over something one more time," he said. "Just to make sure there are no surprises."

A surprise could come from only one quarter, so I steeled myself for yet more painful questions.

"April Blankenship," Morty said.

Imagine a strip of parched wood, dried by a hundred desert suns, a stick of kindling that had never felt a match, and you would have April Blankenship when I met her.

"We've been over all this many times, Morty," I reminded him wearily because it was a ground seeded with land mines and I didn't want to cross it yet again.

"True," Morty agreed. "But I want to be certain, because without doubt at some point Singleton is going to call this woman to the stand and I need to know about anything and everything she might say to the jury." He looked at me pointedly. "Or read that story you sent her, the one you wrote." He drew in a somewhat labored breath. "My guess is that it was getting his hands on that story that was Singleton's tipping point as far as making a case against you." He shook his head. "Too bad April didn't burn that fucking thing. I mean, hell, it was just a story, for Christ's sake."

I instantly recalled the drizzly afternoon when April and I had been in bed together, her mention of how I was always reading, a remark that had somehow wound me back to my own past literary efforts, and to which she'd replied with a harmlessly sweet plea that I write something, as she'd put it, "for me to read."

"It was a novella," I corrected grimly.

Now I recalled those late nights in my college office, tapping out my tale of escape in serial e-mails to April, she the one who'd provided an eagerly appreciatiative audience for my work at last, my grand vision for "The Pull of the Earth" now reduced to a mocking pot-boiler imitation. It was an idea I'd once spoken of to Sandrine, to write a parody of noir fiction. She'd dismissed it out of hand, then put her finger on the deeper problem I'd failed to recognize. "Disillusionment is a shabby gift, Sam," she'd told me bluntly. "Isn't that what Fitzgerald said?"

April had thought it a fantastic idea, however, and so I'd tried my hand at it, the result of that effort now no doubt resting snugly inside one of Harold Singleton's desk drawers.

"The problem, of course, is that it's about a man who kills his wife so he can run away with his girlfriend," Morty reminded me. "And so you have to admit that in the context of what happened it could be a tad incriminating." He shrugged in a way that was clearly designed to calm my obvious agitation. "But look, Sam, I know you never intended to run away with April Blankenship," he added.

This was certainly true, but at that instant I found myself once again beneath the sheets with April, talking about the novel I'd struggled to write for years but never finished. How sweetly she indulged my maudlin tale of artistic woe, then quite softly asked me to conjure up a tale just for her, the writing of which she seemed to take as a great honor, thus a request my vanity had found it impossible to deny.

And so I had penned a novella I'd felt certain she would have destroyed at the end of our affair, but which, quite unaccountably and to my complete surprise, she hadn't.

"Now once again, Sam," Morty said, "you were past this affair before you even heard about your wife's diagnosis, right?"

"I hadn't seen April for three months by that time," I answered. "And I was never alone with April again except for that one time."

Except for that one time.

With those words, I saw her again at my door, thin as air, with her lips tightly pursed, glancing over her shoulder as if she feared she'd been followed, whispering despite the fact that there was no one around: *You're not going to tell them, are you, Sam?*

"The one time she came over after Sandrine's death, right?" Morty asked. "That's the time we're talking about?"

"Yes."

"And other than that last encounter, you'd had nothing to do with her for almost a year before your wife's death?"

"Nothing."

Morty had now fully taken on the role of Mr. Singleton, who would soon be my relentless cross-examiner.

"Now, Sam, by 'nothing,' I am to conclude that you have not seen this woman, nor written to her, nor called her, correct?"

"Correct," I answered.

"You understand that the state can present a case for dual motives," Morty said. "Or should I say interlocking motives, one reason egging on another, that sort of thing, until . . . I'm sure you get the picture."

We'd been over this many times, and so with confidence I answered, "Yes, I get the picture."

"One of them he can never prove, of course," Morty assured me. "By that I mean you wanted to get rid of your wife because she was going to get more and more dependent upon you, and you wanted to escape that burden and get on with your life." He paused, then added, "The other motive is April."

It struck me that April had always been "the other," the one passed over or discarded, whose feelings were not considered and whose loss of dignity had never mattered to anyone save to her husband, poor cuckolded Clayton.

"April is the 'other woman,' after all," Morty added.

The "other woman" is a label that could not possibly have seemed less fitting to this gossamer ghost of a woman, but the web of life entangles us all, and it had now ensnared April, who, by the time of Sandrine's death, had certainly felt herself well beyond the reach of so catastrophic a scandal.

Even I had expected that she would escape notice, no matter what inquiry might be made into the manner of Sandrine's death. It had been a tepid, short-lived affair, with little excitement and no love at all, cheap and tawdry, as bland as the rooms in which we'd met on those listless afternoons. April's last words to me had perfectly summed up the lackluster nature of our trysts. "I can never let myself go, Sam," she'd said with a shrug as she got into her car. "What can you do, if you just can never let yourself go?"

Other than the time she'd showed up at my door, I'd last seen April about a month or so after learning of Sandrine's illness. She'd been standing outside Waylon's drugstore as I'd driven by. She'd been wearing the same blue dress and digging into the same black purse from which, on our first rendezvous, she'd shyly withdrawn a pack of condoms.

I'd pressed down on the accelerator and the car bolted ahead. I'd been terrified she might glance up as I sped away, but in my rearview mirror I'd seen that she was still rifling through her purse. I made it to the corner and was rounding it when she finally lifted her head, but she was still close enough for me to see that it was her car keys she'd been looking for, a blue Toyota that was already three years old when I met her, a car a lot like April, made for routine chores. That she'd ended up in a cheap romance with one of her husband's colleagues could not have surprised her more, though I think she might have taken some fleeting plain Jane pride in bedding the man who was bedding the far—from every point of view—more desirable Sandrine. You could be with her, she'd asked with every awkward, self-demeaning glance, so why are you with me?

I had not once, either before or after this ridiculous affair, been able to answer that question in any way different from the way Sandrine had answered it with regard to her own father's serial philandering with a series of increasingly unattractive coeds: *it doesn't take much to fill a hollow man.*

"It was nothing, Morty," I blurted. "That thing with April. It was never love. It was never anything."

"It doesn't matter," Morty interrupted by way of dismissing any further discussion of April's complete innocence in regard to my current situation. "The point will be for the jury to think you're a shit."

An opinion Mr. Singleton will no doubt harden into utter ire, I thought.

"Ruth made us a couple of tuna sandwiches," Morty said casually as he took a paper bag from his briefcase. "No mayo on mine." He laughed. "For obvious reasons. But I think she put a little on yours." He handed me one of the sandwiches. It was wrapped very neatly in tinfoil.

"Singleton still hasn't exploded those bombs from the pathologist's report," he added. "I thought he might take Dr. Ortins through some of those troubling details, but other than the business of that back injury the state has decided to hold fire."

116

"Singleton's like some hack mystery writer, isn't he?" I asked. "He can choose whomever he wants to narrate his story."

Morty took a bite from his sandwich.

"He'll probably pick Alabrandi to do the heavy lifting," he said. "He was the lead detective on the case, after all, and besides a cop is always a good choice."

"Why?"

"Because the jury is likely to have heard cop narratives before," Morty answered. "They read those books you just mentioned. Cop books. Mysteries. Whatever you call them. And in those books, cops are often the ones telling the story, right?"

"I wouldn't know," I told him.

Morty laughed but it was an edgy laugh. "Just don't let the jury know you turn up your nose at their reading material, okay, Sam?" He went back to his sandwich, took a large bit, and chewed slowly. "Anyway, my guess is that Alabrandi will be on the stand for a very long time. He'll probably tell us everything the pathologist didn't with regard to your wife."

After that, we ate more or less silently, then I walked over to one of the long benches and lay down. There were still a few minutes before my trial resumed, and for the past two days I'd been plagued by a lingering weariness, along with a curious indifference to the books and music that had once formed the pillars of my inner life. I hadn't been able to think as quickly as I once had, either, and yet I'd come to feel that my thinking was growing deeper and more curiously seeded with poignant memories. One thing was certain, things that once mattered no longer did and in their vanishing they'd created more space in my mind. It was strange that by radically confining my life, Sandrine's death, along with its dire consequences, had in some way expanded my consideration of it.

"Yeah, good, take a nap," Morty advised. "You need to look rested."

I closed my eyes and, as always, I thought of Sandrine.

It had been a few weeks after her fateful consultation with Dr. Ortins. She had continued to teach, but the terrible news had been steadily sinking into her, the dreadful facts of her disease. We were sitting in the scriptorium. The first chill of autumn was in the air, and there was a small fire crackling. Sandrine was in the big, overstuffed chair, a checkered blanket over her legs, reading. I was on the sofa, doing the same.

Suddenly the book slipped from her hand, but rather than reach for it she simply stared at it a moment, then looked at me. "I've been thinking of my first published article."

It had been written not long after she'd graduated from the Sorbonne, and she hadn't spoken of it since.

"The one on Blanche Monnier," she added softly. "You remember?"

"Yes."

On the morning of May 22, 1901, an anonymous letter had arrived at the police station in Poitiers, a small town in west central France. The letter advised the authorities that a woman was being kept against her will at 21 rue de la Visitation. According to the letter, she had been locked in a room, half starved and living in her own filth, for the past thirty-five years.

The following afternoon, police arrived at this address and demanded admittance. After some resistance, they entered the house, searched it, and on the top floor found Blanche Monnier. She was fifty-two, and she had been imprisoned in this room, sleeping on a putrid mattress, since the age of eighteen.

In her article on the case, Sandrine had written with particular reference to Blanche's mother, the aristocratic Madame Monnier, her determination to prevent her wayward daughter from marrying the penniless suitor with whom Blanche had fallen in love. Sandrine had seen it all from a feminist perspective, of course, Madame Monnier almost as much a victim of patriarchy as the daughter she had imprisoned, an approach that made her article seem terribly dated now, a piece of work that would be remembered, if at all, only by way of a time capsule.

I didn't say any of this to Sandrine, of course.

"Why would you be thinking of Blanche Monnier?" I asked.

"Actually, I wasn't thinking of her," Sandrine answered. "I just happened to remember that André Gide wrote about her case, and that got me to thinking about how he once told someone that the tragedies of life amused him." Her gaze was quite penetrating. "Not that they moved or tormented him. Not that they broke his heart but simply that they amused him."

"What interests you about that?" I asked.

A smile struggled onto her lips, then withered. "His heartlessness."

"What about it?"

"I was wondering if there would have been any way back for him," she answered.

"Back to what?"

"Back to feeling something for people," Sandrine said. "Particularly people who are in trouble or who aren't very smart."

With that, she'd risen, drawn the robe more tightly around her body, then walked out of the scriptorium and into the kitchen, where I'd found her later sitting alone at the little table that looked out onto the backyard.

"What's wrong?" I asked.

"I'm afraid, Sam."

"Of course, you are," I said.

As she continued to look at me, her gaze took on an aspect of terror, and though she'd never said it I realized that it was me she feared, something in me.

119

What could she possibly have glimpsed in my eyes that had fright-ened her so, I wondered now. Was it something that had alerted her to my own dark thoughts so that she'd known at that horrible instant that the first of the state's perceived motives had been by far the most powerful one, that even then, weeks before her death, I'd been thinking grimly of what was to come, how the house would eventually be converted into a hospital room, everything shoved over to make way for a metal bed, for aluminum stands hung with transparent plastic bags, this house become a place of tubes and drips, the toilet fitted with a raised seat, every available surface covered with medicines, rubber gloves, tissues, cotton balls, plastic drinking bottles sprouting plastic straws, the whole horrid sprawl of invalidism. And not just invalidism, but a horribly protracted death that would stretch into the indefinite future, a death not in one month or two or even three but one that might go on and on, with the whole process of dying getting worse every single day for years and years and years.

Sunday.

Tomorrow.

All day.

A voice finally broke the silence that had descended upon me in the wake of this chilling recollection. It was Morty's.

"Wake up, buddy."

I opened my eyes.

"Yeah, okay," I muttered.

Morty's expression alerted me to the fact that he had glimpsed something he didn't like. "You all right?"

"I'm fine," I said crisply.

But I was not, because my mind had returned to an earlier vision, Sandrine seated in the scriptorium, looking oddly like the invalid she was doomed to become, her legs wrapped in a woolen blanket, her eyes fearfully in contemplation of her own frightful future, one I knew I was destined to share. Was that the first time I'd asked myself in dreadful, scheming earnest: Is there a way out of this?

I looked at Morty and was relieved that he'd seen little or nothing on my face of what was in my mind. Luckily, he'd been too busy lifting his own enormous frame from the chair.

"Show time," he said once on his feet, then added, "Jesus, I have got to lose some weight."

Call Gerald Wayland

I had known Gerry Wayland for almost twenty years, though only as the pharmacist who filled our prescriptions. In his friendly manner, he'd dispensed the usual warnings and advisories. Take this before meals; take that after them. This pill is sleep inducing, that one may cause agitation. Either entirely dutiful or absurdly literal, Gerry had even occasionally warned against our operating heavy equipment. But other than this comic observation what did I know of Gerry Wayland, despite the many years I'd "known" him?

Not much, really.

I knew that he was married and had two children, both of whom had graduated college and now lived in distant cities. I knew that his wife was bowling ball round and cherubic, wore big hats, had enormous, pendulous breasts, and had once owned a children's clothing store. In one of the few conversations I'd had with Gerry, he lamented that his wife's business had been "murdered" by Walmart. This was the only killing I had ever heard him mention, so it struck me as ironic that the wheel of circumstance had brought him here to give testimony concerning a crime he could not possibly have imagined before I was accused of it.

As Gerry lifted his right hand and swore to tell the whole truth and nothing but, I noticed how nervous he was. Clearly he hadn't wanted to be here. He'd always seemed a somewhat shy man, and so I suspected that he found the all too public role he had to play in my case faintly distasteful. For that reason, he would no doubt go about it like the guy who straightens the sheet after the actors have left the set of a pornographic movie, that is to say, at arm's length. Without question he had every reason to consider his testimony of little relevance, though Mr. Singleton had surely given him a clear idea of the piece he had been called to add to the puzzle of my crime. I was sure he would give this evidence quickly and matter of factly, then return to the clean, well-lit pharmacy where substances are less volatile and their side effects both better known and better controlled.

For the next few minutes Gerry, as had all the witnesses before him, established his professional credentials. He had been a pharmacist for thirty-three years. His degree was from the Mercer University College of Pharmacy. He was certified by the state board and was, of course, duly licensed to dispense drugs within the boundaries of the sovereign state of Georgia.

"This is a prescription from Dr. Ana Ortins," Gerry told the court.

He kept his eyes on a small, square sheet of paper, one of several Mr. Singleton held in his right hand.

"Now, Mr. Wayland," Singleton said, "can you tell us the date of that prescription?"

Gerry did so.

"And what is it a prescription for?"

"Demerol."

"And for whom is this prescription written?"

Sandrine, of course.

"Do you recall who gave you this prescription?"

Here Gerry's eyes flashed over to me, then away.

"Sam Madison," he said. "Her husband."

Mr. Singleton let this sink in before asking his next question.

123

"Have you had occasion, Mr. Wayland, to go back over your files and see exactly how many prescriptions for Demerol you filled with the name of Sandrine Madison written as the patient?"

Gerry had done this, of course.

"How many did you find?" Singleton asked.

"Three. Each with two refills."

"Now it's customary for anyone picking up a prescription to sign for it, isn't that correct?"

"Yes, that's correct."

"And have you had occasion to review your records as to who picked up the prescriptions for Demerol that you filled for this patient?"

Yes, he had done this.

"Who signed for them, Mr. Wayland?"

This time, Gerry's gaze remained on Mr. Singleton.

"Sam Madison."

"Was there any occasion when Mrs. Madison picked up her own prescriptions?"

"No."

Mr. Singleton smiled mirthlessly, then turned to Morty. "Your witness."

Morty rose but did not approach the witness stand. This gesture was meant to show that he didn't consider Gerry's testimony of sufficient weight to require him to press his mountainous bearing in upon the witness. His questions carried this purposeful trivialization a few steps further. They were quite similar to the ones he'd earlier asked Dr. Ortins, and in answer after answer Gerry affirmed that there was nothing unusual, or even of note, with regard to the fact that I was always the one who'd picked up and signed for Sandrine's prescriptions.

"In fact, isn't it true, Mr. Wayland, that had you detected anything of a suspicious nature with regard to the filling of these prescriptions you would have been required—by law—to notify authorities of that suspicion?"

"Yes, that's true," Gerry answered.

"Well, did you notify any authority with regard to any matter having to do with Mrs. Madison?"

"No."

"So, in fact, Mr. Wayland, you can say categorically that you had no reason whatsoever to suspect any unlawful activity on the part of Mr. Madison or anyone else with regard to the death of Mrs. Madison, isn't that true?"

"Yes, that is true," Gerry answered.

It was the answer he had to give because he was an honest man who'd previously sworn to tell the truth, the whole truth, and nothing but the truth. For this reason he must tell the jury that nothing I did had raised the slightest suspicion in his mind. He declared this in a clear, strong voice, but as he did so his gaze returned to me, and I saw just how great the distance is between what a man must say as a matter of law and what he harbors in his heart.

It wasn't until the end of the day, however, long after Gerry had finished his testimony, then been followed by a few other "pointless fact witnesses," that at last I'd gotten the chance to raise exactly that point with Morty.

By then court had adjourned for the day, and both Morty and I were standing in the nearly empty courtroom.

"Gerry Wayland thinks I killed Sandrine," I told him. "But, of course, so does the whole town."

"It's only what the twelve people on the jury will come to believe that matters now, Sam," Morty said. He added nothing to this as he gathered up his things, then headed out of the courtroom, I at his side, keeping pace with him until we exited the building, at which time he stopped and said, "Well, good night, Sam."

We were standing on the steps of the courthouse, the streets of neat little Coburn busy below us. I could see its shops, the park with its bandstand, the slides and swings and whirligig. Postcard America.

"I guess I thought I was trapped," I said softly, a remark that had seeped from me like heating oil from a tiny crack.

Morty's eyes whipped over to me. "Trapped?"

"My life," I explained. "The way it had turned out. Teaching at Coburn College, living here. It all felt like a vise. It was tightening every day. That's why I did it, Morty."

My lawyer's eyes narrowed and everything in him, from the largest muscles in his body to the smallest capillary, tensed. "Did what, Sam?"

"That thing with April Blankenship," I answered. "It was that I felt trapped in this little town and so—"

"Just don't show any of that to the jury," Morty interrupted, his voice not at all stern this time but filled with a relief that the "what" I'd just confessed was not the murder of Sandrine. "They live in this town, and most of them, Sam, don't feel your contempt for it."

Contempt seemed a harsh word, but I realized that contempt really was what I'd felt for this little town with its modest liberal arts college.

As if whispered by the air around me, I heard Sandrine's voice, repeating one of the many dreadful things she'd said to me on that last night: *Failure is a cold bedfellow, isn't it, Sam?*

Trapped, I repeated in my mind as Morty lingered beside me on the courthouse steps, rifling through his briefcase. But this time, as if on the wings of that word, I suddenly flew back in time to find myself in the bedroom of 237 Crescent Road. Sandrine was reading in bed, the room very much as Officer Hill would later see it, scattered with learned detritus, piles of books and papers beside the bed, peeping out from under desks and chairs, rising in jagged towers from every available surface. We'd lived so much like a couple of scholarly vagabonds that Alexandria had kept her room sparkling clean and well ordered as a gesture of teenage rebellion. It was an erudite chaos I'd worn as a badge of distinction, a proud disorder that had let me feel that I was different from the rest of the faculty. I'd even referred to our colleagues as "the Republicans," though few had ever voted for anything but the Democratic slate.

Sandrine had looked up from this literary dustbin, her head cocked slightly, so that I thought some phrase from the Pavarotti aria playing in the background had suddenly struck her. But the thought that had occurred to her had had to do with Pavarotti's person, rather than his song.

"It's said that Pavarotti once asked his teacher what it took to be a great singer," Sandrine said. "The teacher answered that it was ninety percent great singing. But that the final ten percent, the part that lifted great competence to grandeur, was something else."

"Really?" I said. "And what was this something else?"

"I don't know," she said. "But I think it would still be there, even if he didn't sing."

The topic of this conversation was way too abstract or magical or just plain *woo-woo* for my thinking, and more or less to bring it to its conclusion I said, "So it could never go missing, I suppose."

"No, it could go missing," Sandrine said. She leaned forward and snapped off the music. "The question is whether it could be gotten back."

I quickly ran back the calendar, and it was clear that Sandrine and I had had this exchange only a few days after she'd gotten Dr. Ortins's diagnosis, obviously a time during which she'd been going through a very difficult time, the "thinking things through" she'd earlier spoken of.

The snap of Morty's briefcase brought me back to the present.

"Alexandria's waiting," he said.

Dinner

I headed down the stairs and got into the car, but this time I made no effort to engage Alexandria in conversation and so we'd gone all the way home in near silence.

"Go in and relax," she told me as she pulled into the driveway. "I'll bring in the groceries."

I did as I was told, and to aid in the relaxation I opened a bottle of wine and walked into the kitchen, where for some minutes I was lost in undefined and inchoate thoughts, shards of memory whirling about like bits of paper in a mental storm.

"Drinking already?" Alexandria asked after she'd gotten a whiff of my breath. "You haven't even had dinner yet, Dad."

"It was a stressful day," I answered by way of explanation.

"There are going to be days a lot more stressful than today," Alexandria responded.

She looked at me as if I were a shark fin she'd glimpsed in the distance, something scary moving slowly but inexorably toward her. I couldn't help but wonder if she were thinking that now might perhaps be a good time to get out of the water.

Rather than face so final an abandonment, I began to unpack one of the grocery bags she'd lugged in from the car. She'd bought fruit and vegetables and several salmon fillets, all very sensible. She'd obviously noticed that I had begun to go to seed, everything sagging as if invisible weights hung from my cheeks and jaw and eyebrows.

She made no comment about this, however, but simply and quite methodically began to put away the groceries.

"You can cut the zucchini," she said.

I drew a kitchen knife from one of the drawers and went to work. For an instant she looked at the blade warily, as if it were the pistol introduced in Act I and thus must inevitably reappear before the curtain falls.

"Not too thick," she instructed.

She is very methodical, my now half-orphaned daughter. The vegetables go into the vegetable bin. The bread goes into the breadbox. Our domestic chaos taught her to value design, it would seem. She has seen the whirlwind that disorder sows, and she will have none of it in her life, not even in the buttons and the bread.

She is right, save in one thing, I decided, the fact that moderation is possible, even in disarray. One can know, as Jean Cocteau once noted—this yet another learned reference stolen from Sandrine—how far to go too far. But where along time's famed continuum, I asked myself, should I have reined in the tiny nipping angers and frustrations that were ceaselessly tearing at me? And had Sandrine seen that, although outwardly calm, on the inside I was a thrashing pool of piranha?

Time now hurtled backward, as it had when I'd stood on the courthouse steps with Morty, and I found myself in the NYU library reading, of all things, Paul Verlaine, no doubt to impress Sandrine.

She glanced at the book as she came toward me. "Paul Verlaine threw his three-year-son against a wall," she said, "during an argument with his wife."

I closed the book. "I didn't know that."

Sandrine's dark eyes were motionless. "You would never get that angry with me, would you, Sam?"

"No," I said. "There would have to be something missing in a man to do something as cruel as that."

"Something missing, yes," Sandrine said.

Had she sensed that missing thing in me, I wondered, sensed it or something worse, actually saw it with devastating clarity as I faced her in the scriptorium all those years later, casually brushing off an anecdote from the life of Pavarotti while the sword of Damocles swung closer to her by the day?

"Dad?"

Alexandria was looking at me oddly because the knife in my hand had suddenly gone deathly still.

"You've stopped cutting," Alexandria said.

"Oh, sorry," I explained. "Just thinking."

"About what?"

"Your mother's mind," I said with an infinitely fragile smile. "How knowing she was."

She looked at me sourly. Such talk only irritated her now and in her eyes made me seem hopelessly oblivious to how things had turned out.

"Finish cutting the zucchini," she told me.

I remembered the earlier conversation I'd had with Morty, his questions about Alexandria's whereabouts on the day Sandrine died, and particularly the nature of any conversation they might have had. For a moment, I thought of asking her outright about that conversation, but I stopped myself because I feared that Sandrine had, in fact, told her all the hateful things she'd said to me, and I was in no mood to hear them repeated.

A few minutes later we ate dinner in the same nearly unspeaking way in which we'd earlier driven home from the courthouse, and after that I retreated to the scriptorium with a glass of wine.

At around ten I returned to the kitchen and put the glass in the copper sink. It was an old sink, hand hammered, and it had the rough, uneven texture of things made by hand. I'd barely noticed it until the afternoon—this now two weeks after the consultation with Dr. Ortins— I'd come upon Sandrine standing before it, peering into its battered basin. She'd looked quite lovely, framed by the window, her dark hair flowing down her back. But I'd long ago gotten used to her beauty so that was not what stopped me. Rather, it was the way she'd reached down and run her fingertips over the pits and gouges as if she were seeking something precious within them, a tiny jewel of some sort, minuscule as gold dust.

I'd assumed that she was thinking about her illness, the horrid way it would progress, all the powers that were at that very moment diminishing and would continue to diminish until they disappeared entirely. There really is a sorrow beyond words, and I suspected that in reaching into that copper basin Sandrine was touching that deep place.

When she sensed my presence, she turned and faced me. "I've made my decision," she said.

I'd felt quite certain I knew exactly what that decision was, and had felt, God forgive me, a surge of relief that she had made it, that she would not put herself—or me—through years and years of grim decline.

But now, rethinking this scene, feeling the ghost of Sandrine's hands on my face, recalling the dark glint in her eyes as she made this announcement, I no longer felt so sure that I knew what her fateful decision had been, or even if it had been about herself at all.

How long the nights have become without her, I thought suddenly, or with her only in my memory, only as a ghost. If she were here, I realized with a truly tragic irony, I would discuss my case with her, go over all that led up to it, all that has been discovered as a result of it, and where it all might end. During the slowly moving hours I would describe the little quakes that have shaken me during these few days of my trial, along with what they have revealed about the woman for whose

131

murder I stand accused, how this grave accounting has returned me to those first years with her.

On that thought, I abruptly remembered a morning in Antibes. The day before we'd been at Neapolis, in Siracusa, where we'd tested the famed acoustics of the Ear of Dionysius. Sandrine had thought the story of Dionysius having been able to hear his slaves hatching plots against him by means of their voices bouncing off the exposed stone quite unlikely, and she'd been right. I'd stood at the point said to be perfect for transferring sound to that tyrant's hearing and whispered, "I'm going to kill you," and Sandrine, stationed at the king's listening post, had heard no word of murder.

Remembered joy is a heartbreaker, especially when the long view holds future tragedy, but at that moment I found myself quite rejoicing in this memory of Sandrine, the sweet life we'd led in those early days.

Thinking of that distant time returned me to music, and for a moment I considered putting on a CD and playing Sandrine's favorite piece, "Air on a G String," a musical title that, given its inherent double entendre, she'd always found rather funny. But simple as it is, Bach's little air is decidedly classical, and so I recalled Morty's caution, and I wondered what might be the effect should some errant member of the jury pass within hearing distance of my house. Would those gentle, meditative tones be detrimental to my case, further proof of my elitism, my snobbery, the ethical morass into which my life was sunk, and which, taken collectively, had created a man so lacking in moral boundaries that he could easily slide into murder? I could almost hear the cautionary didacticism that would emerge from any of my so-called peers' consideration of all this, the fact that life is not a mountain or a valley but the slippery slope that leads from the heights of one to the depths of the other. I knew they'd put it just that way, use me as an example of how badly a life can go wrong.

The doorbell rang.

When I opened the door, he smiled.

"How'd it go?" he asked.

I looked at my neighbor Carl Santori and saw the product of his many ailments. He has lost one kidney and has had bypass surgery, and for these reasons I had certainly expected to outlive him. This is an expectation I can no longer entertain, however. In the words of Mr. Singleton: "The plot was too cruelly premeditated and carried out over too long a time not to warrant death."

"Honestly, Carl, I never know," I answered.

Carl nodded softly. He has dropped by once a week since Sandrine's death, always, as now, with a hot meal from his restaurant: spaghetti, manicotti, eggplant rollatini. We have been neighbors for eleven years. His life has been seasoned by misfortune. Along with his own poor health he has known widowhood, and his son, now fourteen, has never been well. We've borrowed tools from each other and from time to time had short conversations about nothing I could later recall, but it was the night I'd quite by accident saved his son's life that had turned acquaintance into friendship, at least in Carl's mind.

On that particular night, he had suddenly gotten the idea that he'd left one of the restaurant ovens on and had rushed to his car. He was barreling toward the street when I noticed his son, Anthony, facedown in the driveway. He'd had one of his seizures, and at that instant it was clear to me that he lay directly in the path of Carl's car. As anyone else would have done, I bolted for Anthony, swooped him up, and dove, with the boy in my arms, into the safety of the adjoining yard just in time to miss the right rear bumper of Carl's Saturn. We were still on the ground when Carl rushed over to us. He leaped from the car without first putting it in gear so that it had continued on down the driveway and rammed into the brick mailbox at the end of it. Carl had seen none of this, however.

He was focused on Anthony. We both immediately dashed over to my car and rushed him to the local hospital, where he'd quickly recovered.

Anyone would have done what I did but Carl thought it heroic, and from that moment on he pledged to be my friend eternally. Since Sandrine's death, with his visits and his gifts of steaming Italian food, he has proven to be just that.

"I put in some garlic bread," he said.

"Thank you, Carl."

"Enjoy," he said as he pressed the bag toward me.

He had always been deeply inarticulate, and the trouble I was in had only made him more so. Even under normal circumstances he would have had little to say. Now every word seemed the product of a long travail.

Carl eased away from me as if to the sound of a ticking bomb.

"Well, good night, Sam."

"Good night, Carl."

He seemed to dissolve almost instantly, leaving me alone and staring at the bag of food he'd brought me.

Normally I'd at least have a taste of that garlic bread, but at that moment I had no appetite for anything. In fact, encased within the bleakness of this occasion, I wondered if I'd ever have a taste for anything again. Whatever the food, it would remind me of Sandrine. If it were Middle Eastern I'd think of our few days in Istanbul. If it were French I'd think of her in Paris. If it were Italian I'd think of strolling the streets of Rome with her or swimming with her in Capri. Or would I think of Venice, drifting beneath the Bridge of Sighs, that storied kiss. Some years later, I'd asked her quite seriously if she thought that moment would perhaps be that the one she would most remember about our Mediterranean trip. Her answer had been swift and sure. No, she'd said, her gaze very soft and loving, that will be Albi.

Albi, I thought now, where that candle had come from. Albi, the page she dogeared in the travel book she'd taken to her bed on that last night.

"You really should try to get some sleep, Dad."

I turned to find Alexandria standing a few feet away, backlit and motionless, a figure that struck me quite suddenly as rather sinister, a woman in the house who was not Sandrine. My daughter, yes, as I realized quite achingly, but even so a woman I did not actually know.

"A long day tomorrow, remember?" she added.

"I remember," I said quietly. "Okay, I'll go to bed very soon. You should get some sleep yourself."

She nodded, turned, then disappeared in the same ghostly way as Carl had vanished moments before.

I put the food Carl had brought me in the refrigerator, then washed, brushed my teeth, went to the toilet, and finally, with no alternative, crawled into bed.

It was late but I couldn't get to sleep. Alexandria was right. Tomorrow would be a long day. I had seen the witness list and so I knew that as of tomorrow the case against me would build steadily and grow more sinister.

I grabbed the remote and turned on the television.

On the screen, a beautiful young actress was talking to a middle-aged late-night host about her new movie. In the film she played a comic book character rather than a person.

"Is it easier to be a comic book character than a human being?" the host asked her in the slightly mischievous bad-boy way of late night hosts.

Surprisingly, the young actress appeared somewhat troubled by the question. A hint of gravity appeared in her eyes, as if she'd glimpsed the looming approach of a force bent on killing her.

"Safer," she said.

Well, that much is true, I thought, then glanced over to the bureau where Sandrine had kept her scarves and blouses along with the faded jeans and floppy sweatshirts she'd often worn around the house. Beautiful women are even more beautiful, as Willa Cather once observed, in a state of dishabille. This had certainly been true of Sandrine, a fact made entirely evident by the photo that rested in a little chrome frame on top of this same bureau, and which showed her sitting on the steps of the Coburn College library.

I was still drifting in the remembered beauty of those early days when Alexandria tapped at my door.

"It's one-thirty, Dad," she informed me. "You really should go to bed."

"Sleep is for the dull," I said, knowing quite well that there would be little sleep for me that night.

"Whatever," Alexandria muttered.

The bedroom door was closed but I could hear her step away and move on down the corridor to her room. I couldn't see the expression on her face, of course, but I knew it was sour. She had previously made it clear that I was one of those people who always had an answer, and I had to admit that for most of my life I had, in fact, always had one. But since my trial it seems that I'd had only questions for which I can find no answers, though I continued to feel that they were there waiting for me, these answers, and that I would eventually find them. In one of Sandrine's unpublished essays, she wrote that there should be no distinction between questions for the head and questions for the heart because no compelling answer could be offered to either without giving voice to both.

Sociopath.

Her voice sounded so clearly in my mind at that moment that I actually spun around, as if expecting to see her standing before me as she had that night, her eyes aflame as she'd reached for that white cup.

Sociopath.

Perhaps she'd been right, I told myself, as I twisted around and turned off the light. Perhaps I am even now strangely disconnected to the very events that are most critical to my life, and thus increasingly hard-pressed to defend myself against the many charges made against me. The only thing about Catholicism that ever made sense to Sandrine was the confessional, and in this she was right. More, perhaps even more than someone to love and love us back, we need someone to whom we can tell the unvarnished truth about ourselves. That is what I found myself missing most at that moment as I stared into the darkness. What I missed more than ever, and would forever miss, was simply and irreducibly Sandrine, her heartbreaking truths, the way she'd released the last of them like an arrow into darkness.

You are nothing, Sam. Nothing, nothing, nothing.

Her last words to me.

Part III

County District Attorney Harold Singleton has said that he is now preparing the most crucial aspects of the state's case against Professor Samuel Madison for the murder of his wife, Professor Sandrine Madison, both of Coburn College, a trial that has captured the attention of both national and regional media and is thought to be the most famous ever held in Coburn County.

Coburn Sentinel
January 15, 2011

DAY FIVE

Morning

I was surprised when, on the fifth day of my trial, I came into the kitchen and found Jenna sitting with Alexandria. But there they were, Sandrine's sister and Sandrine's daughter, poised around a butcher-block table. In a vague paranoia no doubt induced by a sleepless night they looked to me like two witches from *Macbeth,* keeping the pot astir, summoning toil and trouble.

"Good morning, Sam," Jenna said.

"Hi," I replied, somewhat drily, since I knew Jenna has always felt that in choosing me Sandrine had made the wrong choice.

"I happened to be in Atlanta," Jenna said, "so I drove over to see how Alexandria is holding up."

Meaning that for me she had not the slightest care, an attitude she'd exhibited quite thoroughly since Sandrine's death, distancing herself more or less completely. She'd stayed in touch with Alexandria but I'd dropped off her radar like a crashed plane. Still, I wasn't sure she'd gone so far as to think I'd murdered Sandrine. On that particular subject she had yet to weigh in.

"Alexandria's doing fine," I assured her. "We Madisons are made of stern stuff."

Jenna's smile could have cut a diamond. "I wanted to see that for myself." The smile widened but kept its hardness. "I have only a few minutes, I'm afraid."

"And then where are you off to?" I asked.

"I have a meeting in Chicago at noon tomorrow."

"Then you're not spending the night here?" Alexandria asked.

Jenna shook her head. "I'd like to but I have to get back to Atlanta."

Was that true, I wondered. Or was there something about this house that frightened Jenna, the notion perhaps of sharing it with a murderer?

"Well, I'm sorry you can't stay," I said, though I doubted Jenna would believe this.

She was Sandrine's older sister, and she had always played the role of her protector. In that role, she'd doubtless hated the fact that her brilliant, beautiful sister had gotten involved with a scraggly graduate student, lived with him in grimy apartments, then unaccountably married him and had a baby with this same undistinguished soul.

Yet I had little doubt that her heart went out to Alexandria for my daughter's bad luck in being my only surviving relative, heir to the host of disreputable behaviors that had now culminated in, of all things, a murder trial.

"Alexandria tells me that today may be pretty tough," Jenna said.

"It could be, yes." I looked at Alexandria. "But we're getting used to it being rough, aren't we?"

Alexandria took a sip of coffee. "We have no idea how long it may last," she said to Jenna. "The trial, I mean."

I offered a dry laugh. "Or the appeals or the appeals of the appeals."

"So it's going badly?" Jenna asked.

I suspected that the prospect of my case going badly was Jenna's devout hope. She would, it seemed to me, like nothing more than that I spend the rest of my life on my knees in a grimy cell giving head to a Mexican drug lord. After all, I'd betrayed her sister, and she may even believe I'd killed her. And yet she had to be cordial with me, if only for the sake of Alexandria. Such is the burden, along with the sorrow and the pity, of extended family.

I shrugged. "I have no idea how it's going, Jenna," I told her.

"For one whole day it was the pathologist," Alexandria said. "A Dr. Mortimer."

"Aptly named," I quipped. "For *mort,* which means death in French."

A chilly smile trembled on Jenna's lips. "I would, of course, know that, Sam," she informed me icily, "having grown up in Montreal."

I walked to the refrigerator, took out the milk, sniffed it because this is a compulsion of mine, then poured a small amount into a cup. I added coffee, but I had no appetite for anything more. Even if I had wanted an actual breakfast, I would have refrained from having it in front of Jenna. It would look unseemly, a big hearty southern breakfast of eggs, bacon, toast, butter, jam, the works, in a man on trial for the murder of her beautiful, brilliant, deserving of much better sister. That is one of the oddities of my case—or of any case like mine—that the ordinary pleasures, or at least the public enjoyment of them, quite convincingly argues not only that you are guilty of the crime of which you are accused but that, in addition, you feel not a speck of remorse. Smile or, God forbid, laugh when your child is missing and no one will doubt that you know where its body is.

I strategically stuck to coffee, a little milk, but absolutely no sugar.

"It's amazing how dull it is, a trial," Alexandria went on in a tone that seemed quite disconcertingly matter-of-fact, as if, as my ordeal ground on, she'd begun to rate it as entertainment, a system that in my case would garner no more than two stars.

"So this Dr. Mortimer had nothing to say that would—" Jenna stopped, quite obviously at a loss as to how she should continue.

"Convict me?" I asked with a dry laugh. "No, not really. He confirmed that Sandrine died from an overdose of Demerol, along with a tumbler of vodka 'seeded,' as he put it, with antihistamines."

145

He'd gone on to testify that there'd been no bruises, cuts, or lacerations on her body, which indicated, of course, that there'd been no sign of a struggle. Either Sandrine had poisoned herself of her own volition, as Dr. Mortimer concluded, or someone had poisoned her.

"It's the antihistamines that are the problem," Alexandria said.

"And the fact that they were crushed," I added. "Which would evidently have made them undetectable. So that Sandrine wouldn't have known she was taking them. I mean, she wouldn't have tasted anything, and so, theoretically, I might have used them to . . ."

"I see," Jenna interrupted. "But why would she have taken antihistamines at all?" she asked.

"To stop her from vomiting up the Demerol," Alexandria answered. "That's what the prosecutor says. And so they were added to the vodka because Dad wanted Mom to keep down the Demerol."

"I see," Jenna repeated softly.

For a moment, she stared at her hands, then she looked up and her eyes whipped over to me. "Is it true someone was looking for antiemetics on your computer?" she said. "I read that in the Atlanta paper."

"Yes," I said. "It's true."

I could now assume that Jenna had also learned that in addition to an effort to find "strong" antiemetic drugs, my computer had recorded several sinister searches having to do with "painless suicide," as well as with various drugs that could bring it about, among which was Demerol, facts long made public, along with my less than adequate explanation that Sandrine's computer had been having problems so she'd used mine.

"Obviously, Sandrine wanted to die," I said. "And naturally she wanted it to be painless."

When Jenna looked at me doubtfully, I continued, "As for those antihistamines, I'm not positive Sandrine took them in order to make sure the Demerol did the job."

146

"What other reason would she have had?" Jenna asked.

I gave the only answer that I thought made sense. "Sandrine was . . . kind. She wouldn't have wanted to make a mess."

"A mess she knew you'd have to clean up, right?" Jenna asked.

"Yes."

"How thoughtful she was, Sam," Jenna said. Her gaze hardened. "And how loyal."

"Loyal, yes," I said, then fled back to the safer subject of incriminating evidence.

"Anyway, as far as the painless suicide research, I didn't know she'd done any of that," I said.

A question clearly came into Jenna's mind, one she briefly hesitated to ask before at last giving in to her insurmountable urge to ask it.

"And if you had known?"

"Well, as I told Alexandria, maybe Sandrine had a right to do it. I mean, the Greeks—"

"The Greeks, right," Jenna interrupted sharply, then immediately began to gather up her things. "I can do without pedantic references."

There'd always been something hard about Jenna, something dead-eyed and unforgiving, perhaps even a tad mercenary, her character almost the direct opposite of Sandrine's, thus a woman, as I thought now, who would never have had the slightest impulse to teach in some little college or, God forbid, open a school in some remote corner of the globe.

Because of all this, it struck me as quite odd that during the last months of her life Sandrine had invited Jenna for several visits, offers she'd always accepted, stays of two or three days during which I would often find them in conversation in the afternoon, the two of them sitting in the little gazebo Sandrine had wanted for the backyard, one of those cheap prefabricated affairs, assembled in a single day, and which was already beginning to fall apart.

It had served her for a season, though, and she had often retreated there, either to read or listen to music on her Nano, and on occasion to talk with Jenna over glasses of white wine, both of them glancing over when they caught sight of me, their conversation instantly falling off.

"Tell me this, Jenna," I blurted suddenly. Jenna was taken aback by how abruptly I'd called to her. "What did you talk about?" I asked her.

"Talk about?" Jenna asked tentatively.

"When you were with Sandrine," I said. "In the gazebo."

Jenna looked as if I'd posed this question with hostility.

"Nothing much," she answered coolly.

"Nothing much?" I asked. "But you came here often during those last weeks, when Sandrine had drawn completely away from me. I mean, she hardly ever talked to me during that time, but she talked to you quite a lot, so I'm just wondering what you talked about, whether it was . . . intimate?"

"Intimate?" Jenna said a little sharply. "Why shouldn't she have talked intimately to me?"

After all, Jenna was saying, weren't you "intimate" with that little whore?

I felt myself wither under the hard edge of her gaze.

"I'm sorry," I said softly. "Of course, she did. It's just that Sandrine wasn't talking to me much during those last weeks. She'd cut me off so I couldn't imagine—"

"Maybe she was tired of talking to you, Sam," Jenna shot back.

"She told you that?"

"Well, wasn't it obvious?" Jenna demanded. "You just said that she'd practically stopped talking to you."

"But why?"

"I don't know," Jenna answered. "She never said."

We both remained silent for a moment, then very quietly Jenna added, "We talked about life, Sam." Her eyes glistened suddenly. "Sandrine was my sister." She drew in a long breath and I could tell she was using it to regain her composure. "She was my only sister."

"And sisters talk, Dad," Alexandria added firmly, like a referee stepping between two boxers.

"Of course," I muttered softly, then pasted on a gentle smile that was all for Jenna's benefit, and which I offered at that moment because I was evidently learning to be . . . kind. "Of course they do."

Jenna resumed gathering up her things. "Stay safe," she said to Alexandria in a way that struck me as somewhat conspiratorial, those two Shakespearean witches in dark conclave again.

"You don't have to go," I said. "I'm not . . . evil, Jenna. I'm not . . . I . . ."

The fact was, I no longer knew what I was.

"Anyway," I muttered. "Thanks for checking in . . . on Alexandria."

Jenna had by then gotten on her coat, her eyes on me during the whole oddly frantic process. She seemed about to leave, but suddenly she stopped and faced me squarely. "Sandrine loved you, Sam." Her gaze was very steady, like a middle school teacher making a point. "If that's in doubt somehow."

And with that she left.

"What was that all about?" Alexandria demanded once Jenna was safely out of earshot.

"What was what all about?" I asked.

"Asking what Mom and Jenna talked about." She was clearly irritated by the question. She looked at me sternly. "Jenna's not the one on trial, Dad."

This was beyond the pale.

"And I am, right?" I snapped.

Alexandria both gave a little and held her ground. "You know what I mean," she said.

"Not really, Alexandria," I told her. "I know I have brought difficult times down on you, but I don't know what I can do about it. If you can think of something, please let me know."

She gave me one of her puzzled yet penetrating looks, then asked a question I knew must surely have been dogging her for a long time.

"Did Mom know about that woman?"

So at last we had arrived at April.

"Not that I know of."

"You never told her?"

"Confession is not my strong point, I'm afraid."

She paused and, during that interval, I felt a terrible heat wafting from her.

"And what about Malcolm?" she asked. "Did you know about him?"

I shook my head. "Not the whole story, no."

I saw that my daughter was reluctant to go any further into her parents' unfathomable marriage. I didn't want to go any further into it either, but at that moment I saw Malcolm Esterman quite vividly in my mind, an image of him strolling through the gold and yellow leaves of an autumnal Coburn College, balding and bespectacled, with his books under his arm, his jacket forever coated with a thin film of chalk dust. Central casting: Mr. Chips.

Malcolm Esterman.

Of all people.

His name had once conjured up quite a different emotion than it did now. Actually, his name had called up no emotion at all before Sandrine's death and Detective Alabrandi's subsequent investigation. Now there were images I simply couldn't get out of my mind, all of them more or less pornographic, sheets and naked bodies equally twisted, both sweaty. For a sound track I heard heavy breathing, Sandrine's growing more rapid and shallow until she releases the last one, which is, of course, long, exhausted, and fantastically satisfied.

"I didn't really know him," I told Alexandria. "I mean, I knew him. He's been teaching at Coburn for thirty years. Of course, I saw him around. At faculty meetings, graduations, that sort of thing. But the fact that he was—"

"Of course," Alexandria interrupted.

She let the subject drop, and so did I. It would all be detailed at the trial today or tomorrow or the day following. Malcolm's name was on the witness list, after all.

Alexandria looked at the clock on the microwave. "We'd better get dressed. We're running late."

With that, we parted, she to her room and I to mine. We did not see each other again until I strolled into the living room, where she was already waiting for me.

"Jesus, Dad," she said as I came into the room. "Your tie's a mess."

"I guess my fingers are a little unsteady," I told her.

Reflexively, I started to fuss with the knot, but she stepped forward and began to work with it herself.

She has had a few relationships, but none had ever lasted long enough or proved deep enough for her to bring the fellow home to meet Sandrine and me. Perhaps she feared that I would have disapproved of whomever she brought to us, and I probably would have, though I would have kept quiet about it and been pleasant to the chap. But once Alexandria had left with him I'd have no doubt shaken my head and wondered what in the world she must be thinking to take this guy seriously. And throughout all this I would have thought myself quite tolerant, that I was judging this young man not by some high, intellectual standard but by some simpler aspect of his character, as Sandrine had once judged me: because you're kind.

But lately I have come to think that it is Alexandria who is actually tolerant. After all, she has borne the shocking revelations of the investigation without once questioning the many secrets I kept from Sandrine and that she kept from me and that we both kept from our daughter. "You and Mom gave me the illusion that I lived in a happy home," she said to me after the first scandalous details emerged, "and I guess I have to thank both of you for that."

"This can't be fixed without undoing the whole thing," Alexandria said as she unwound the mess I'd made of my tie.

I bowed to the hard-won truth that there were many things like that.

"Hold your head up, Dad," Alexandria said as she pulled out the final knot and started over.

As she did this, her face was very near mine. I could feel her breath, and the simple fact that she was breathing, that my daughter lived, suddenly gave me a stroke of happiness, though not without an anguished sense of how easily we forget or take for granted these greatest and deepest of our good fortunes.

"There," she said and stepped back. "Okay. So are you ready to face the day?"

"Ready," I replied with a great show of self-assurance, a great show of being confident that nothing I would hear today or at any subsequent day during my trial could further shake the foundations of my life. "Absolutely ready," I added.

But I was not.

"Good, let's go then," Alexandria said. "Because judges don't like it when the defendant is late."

Defendant, yes. For more than ever, and even to myself, I felt myself to be precisely that.

Call Detective
Raymond Alabrandi

There's no story like a murder story. Mr. Singleton knows this quite well, and so I'd been expecting, though hardly anticipating, the moment when he would at last begin to present my case's events in the way of a cheap detective yarn.

With the calling of Detective Alabrandi, I knew that the moment had arrived.

Detective Ray Alabrandi was perfect for the part he played, tall, lean, appropriately graying at the temples. He marched to the witness stand like a soldier in the field, took the oath, and then, following Mr. Singleton's questions and in a clear, strong voice, he told the jury that he had been a policeman for seventeen years. Before that he'd been a soldier, but in a policeman's role, assigned to army CID. This was impressive, as was Detective Alabrandi, a cool professional, not completely cynical, but used to being lied to, just like the homicide cops the jury saw nightly on television or read about—or so I assumed—in detective novels.

He told the court that he'd arrived at 237 Crescent Road at 3:57 p.m. on the afternoon of Friday, November 21. He didn't add that it was raining that afternoon, but it was, and as he carefully responded to Mr.

Singleton's questions I recalled how a line of raindrops had settled upon his dark blue overcoat by the time I opened the door.

"Samuel Madison?" he asked.

I nodded.

He showed me his badge. "Would you mind if I came in? There are a few things we'd like to clear up."

I opened the door and escorted him into our book-lined living room. The shelves were packed with the great works but Alabrandi seemed to gather only one impression from them: the fact that I probably thought myself a great deal smarter than he was, an opinion with which I have no doubt he has since come quite confidently to disagree.

This recollection was interrupted by the sound of Mr. Singleton's commanding voice.

"So troubling questions had been raised with regard to Sandrine Madison's death, isn't that correct, Detective Alabrandi?"

"During the course of our initial investigation, yes," Detective Alabrandi answered. "And the autopsy, of course."

"What questions?"

They were questions that had not occurred to me until Detective Alabrandi had first confronted me with them on that rainy afternoon as we sat in the living room of a house whose clutter had earlier bothered Officer Hill, and which, by then, I'd somewhat cleaned up. But before the detective had launched into his substantive and disturbing questions, there'd been certain polite formalities of which Mr. Singleton wished the jury to be informed.

"Now, when you met Professor Madison that morning, did he have any questions regarding his wife?"

"Yes, he did," Alabrandi answered. "He asked me about the disposition of Mrs. Madison's body." He took out a small brown notebook and flipped to the appropriate page. "He asked me, 'Where's Sandrine?'"

"When did Mr. Madison inquire as to the whereabouts of his wife's body?"

"The minute he saw me," Alabrandi told the jury. "I was still standing on that little porch at the front door of the house."

I'd asked immediately because I'd had a bizarre and very disturbing nightmare while taking a nap that same afternoon, Sandrine on a metal table fitted with drains, her pale but still beautiful body further whitened by the glare of fluorescent lights, a man poised over her with a scalpel in his hand. But that had not been the worst of it. In this horrible dream the masked pathologist had demanded to know who'd taken her life, and she'd opened her eyes and with a terrible virulence had hissed through her clinched teeth: Sam!

"What did Mr. Madison say exactly?" Mr. Singleton asked.

"He asked me if the autopsy had been done," Alabrandi answered. "I told him no, but that it was scheduled for tomorrow morning."

At which point I could have responded only with a look of dread because some strange part of my disordered thinking at that moment argued that I would continue to be subject to this chilling nightmare until Sandrine had been cremated. And suppose I became disoriented by this nightmare, and while in the grip of some frantic need to escape it, an unguarded moment I could not anticipate, I blurted some incriminating remark? I was being watched now, and I knew it. Did it not make sense to rid myself of anything that might later damage my case?

"How did Professor Madison respond to this?" Mr. Singleton asked.

Because of this nightmare and the idiotic notion that I would keep having it until Sandrine's body was no more, I'd responded by way of the bizarre literary reference Detective Alabrandi now revealed to the jury.

"He said that her body was working on him like a telltale heart."

"A telltale heart?" Mr. Singleton asked.

Detective Alabrandi nodded. "It's a reference to a story by Edgar Allan Poe. That's what Professor Madison told me."

"Did you consequently look up that story and read it?"

He had indeed done just that, Alabrandi told the court, then went on to relate the story's details. As he did so I noticed two jury members lean forward. So that's what a good story does, I thought, at least minimally: it turns ordinary people into more sensitive observers.

Should I have kept that simple fact in mind as I'd struggled through draft after draft of "The Pull of the Earth," I asked myself now, each rendering more academic than the other, more clever and more learned, but also more snide, so that by the time Sandrine had read the last one she'd declared it "cold and unloving." I had, she said, "stripped it of every tenderness."

Had that been the first occasion when I'd actually found myself hating her, I asked myself now, hating Sandrine not because her critique had been false but because it had been so devastatingly true? "Your book has everything a great book should have, Sam," she'd told me in that sad tone of hers, "but a soul." How, in the wake of so dark and true a judgment, could I have not wanted her dead?

"In this story, it's the telltale heart that reveals the narrator's crime?" Mr. Singleton asked once Alabrandi had summarized Poe's tale. "It is the telltale heart that holds the key to his guilt?"

"Yes, sir."

"Hm," Mr. Singleton breathed softly, adding nothing else, thus careful not to suggest to the jury that a man should be convicted of murder on the basis of a literary inference. Instead, he paused a moment, then said, "All right, let's go on." He glanced at his notes. "Now, Detective Alabrandi, did you subsequently inform Mr. Madison that following the autopsy, Sandrine Madison's body would not be cremated immediately?"

"Yes, I did."

"What was his reaction?"

"There was no reaction."

"No reaction?"

"He shrugged, I think. But he didn't say anything."

This was true, and the reason for this admittedly unemotional reaction was that I'd seen another and now somewhat deeper suspicion in Alabrandi's eyes as he'd informed me that the authorities intended to hold on to Sandrine's body, a clear indication that they considered it evidence of some sort.

"Now, at this time, Detective Alabrandi, did you have a few questions for Professor Madison?"

"I did, yes, sir."

There'd been quite a few of them, actually, and as Detective Alabrandi enumerated them I found myself once again in my living room, listening closely, and perhaps guardedly, as he began to discuss what he had initially called his "concerns."

"As you probably know, Mr. Madison, in a situation like this, we have to make inquiries," he said.

"A situation like this?"

"A presumed suicide."

"Presumed?"

"Until it's proven to have been a suicide."

I sat back slightly. "I see."

"Your wife was young, and there was an initial mention of suicide, and so the fact is we have to investigate."

"You're investigating Sandrine?"

"Her death. And so, naturally, that extends to pretty much anything to do with her," Alabrandi answered. "Her situation at work, the family. What her life was like."

157

Was, I thought to myself, and in that repetition I once more affirmed that Sandrine's life must now be spoken of in the past tense.

Even on this fifth day of my trial, attending carefully as Mr. Singleton moved Detective Alabrandi step by step through our first meeting, it was hard for me to think of Sandrine as no longer alive. More to the point, it was difficult for me to accept her life as unrecoverable, to face the hard fact that nothing could be done to put it on a better track. This was the dreadful truth I could not make myself admit: that not one word of her story could be taken back, not one passage edited, not one twist added, that the last page had been written and the book was closed. Sandrine had accepted this long before I had. Deep in the remembered gloom of the bedroom in which she died, I remembered her face in soft light, her voice a whisper, the sad truth she'd unflinchingly pronounced. For most people, Sam, she'd said to me, the cavalry does not arrive.

I shook my head at the truth of this, now also understanding that it had not arrived for her.

Morty suddenly gave me a little punch in the arm.

"Hey," he whispered sharply. "You're shaking your head."

"Sorry," I told him, "Just a memory."

"Well, kill the gestures, Sam," he instructed me sternly. "The jury has no idea what you thinking about, and if you're shaking your head at a piece of testimony that strikes them as obviously true, then you've lost some credibility points with them, understand?"

"Yes," I told him. "Sorry."

"Please, Sam, just stay off memory lane and pay attention to what's being said in court."

"Right. Okay. I will."

What was being said in court was this.

"Now, Detective Alabrandi, at this time did you indicate that Professor Madison was a suspect with regard to the death of his wife?"

"No, sir," Alabrandi answered. "Because he was not actually a suspect at that time."

"But a person of interest."

"Anyone could be a person of interest when you have a death whose cause is in doubt."

"In doubt, yes," Mr. Singleton said. "And did you inform Professor Madison that the cause of his wife's death was in doubt?"

"Yes, I did."

"And what was his reaction?"

My reaction had been fear, and Alabrandi had seen it clearly, and because I'd seen in him what he'd seen in me I'd covered by immediately admitting it.

"Mr. Madison said to me, 'How strange,'" Alabrandi told the court.

"How strange that the cause of his wife's death was in doubt?" Mr. Singleton asked, though he knew better.

"No, Mr. Madison said it was strange that he'd suddenly felt what he called 'a stroke of fear.'"

"A stroke of fear?" Mr. Singleton repeated the phrase as if this were all news to him. "Did Professor Madison indicate what he was afraid of?"

"Yes, he did."

"And what was that?"

"He said that he was afraid he was about to become a character in a book," Alabrandi answered, glancing again at the notes he'd taken in his brown notebook. "Those were his words, a 'character in a book.'"

"What kind of character?"

"He said it was the type of book in which the main character suddenly discovers that life has caught up with him," Alabrandi answered.

159

"He named some Russian book that was like this. The death of someone. A Russian name." He flipped a page in the notebook. "Ivan Ilyich."

Mr. Singleton glanced toward the jury, then back to Detective Alabrandi. "Now, at a certain point, did you begin to inform Professor Madison of questions that had arisen with regard to the death of his wife?"

"Yes, I did."

And indeed he had. After that first polite exchange, Detective Alabrandi had wasted no time getting to the point. As if I were once again facing him, I saw him lean forward, his eyes quite piercing, something of a bird of prey in the way he watched me.

"Mr. Madison, you assumed your wife's death was a suicide, and you did this without examining her, is that right?" Alabrandi asked me.

"I never touched her," I told him.

Albrandi winced slightly, as if my answer had pricked him quite as palpably as the point of a knife.

"So why did you assume she committed suicide?" he asked.

"I don't know," I told him. "She was ill, and so—"

"But you described the paper found beside her bed as a suicide note," Alabrandi interrupted.

I nodded.

"Why?"

"Because at some point that day, when I'd noticed her writing in that yellow pad, she'd told me that this was her 'final word.'" I shrugged. "I hadn't interpreted that response as a suicide note, but later, after she died, I assumed that it was precisely that, her 'final word,' meaning a suicide note."

"Hm," Alabrandi said softly as he wrote this down. Then he glanced up from his notebook. "Your wife evidently hadn't mentioned to anyone that she wished to be cremated," he said.

"She mentioned it to me," I tell him.

"But no one else," Alabrandi says. "According to Officer Hill, you wanted your wife's body to be cremated right away."

"Why wait?"

Had that sounded cold? I asked myself as Detective Alabrandi recreated this same exchange for the jury. If so, my explanation must have sounded no less arctic.

"In ancient times, cremations were done soon after death," I'd told him. "Sandrine, I think, would have wanted her own to be the same. She was a historian, as I'm sure you know. Her specialty was ancient history, and she was—"

"Ancient history, yes," Alabrandi again interrupted. "In her written statement, she mentions Cleopatra."

I noticed that he'd called Sandrine's last writings a "statement," not a suicide note, and from this I'd gathered that Detective Alabrandi had already decided that I was a man who used words to confuse or conceal things.

But this had not seemed the moment to argue over what to call the yellow sheet of paper Officer Hill had earlier noticed beside Sandrine's bed, and so I'd let the matter drop.

"Cleopatra was as close as Sandrine ever came to having a passionate intellectual interest," I told Detective Alabrandi.

"So you thought she would want her body to be treated like Cleopatra's had been after death?" Detective Alabrandi asked.

Without thinking, I answered, "Something like that, yes."

"Well, I looked it up, and it turns out that Cleopatra was buried, rather than cremated," Alabrandi said. A pause, then, "In fact, she wasn't buried until several days after she died." He smiled coolly. "Your wife, of course, would have known that."

I was astonished that Alabrandi had done this sort of research, but I tried not to let him know just how surprised I was. I'd gathered by then that he had assigned me the role of suspect, and in response I was already playing the part.

"That's true," I said. I offered a slight smile that even as I made it I feared he might find snide. "I guess you're what they call a crack investigator."

Alabrandi's eyes squeezed together slightly. "I do my job," he said.

All of this part of our exchange now came into the record, every pompous, pedantic reference I'd made to the arcane rituals of the ancient world paraded before the jury until Singleton finally closed in upon the even more disastrous comment I'd later made to Alabrandi.

"Detective Alabrandi, when you pointed out that Cleopatra had not been cremated, did Mr. Madison come up with another reason why he wanted his wife cremated?"

Morty lifted his hand. "Objection to the phrase 'come up with,' Your Honor. As prejudicial."

"Sustained," Judge Rutledge ruled. He smiled pointedly. "*Come up* with a better question, Mr. Singleton," he added, and in response to which a ripple of laughed swept the gallery.

"Yes, Your Honor," Singleton responded stiffly, like a little boy scolded. "All right, Detective, did the professor express another reason for his wanting to have his wife cremated?"

"Yes, he did," Alabrandi answered. "He said they were both atheists and that neither had any use for ceremony. Funerals, rituals of that sort, that stuff was just Santa Claus for grown-ups."

Mr. Singleton suppressed a smile. "Those were his words, 'Santa Claus for grown-ups'?"

This struck me as wholly prejudicial, of course, and so I flashed a look at Morty, expecting him to object. But he only shook his head and whispered, "Too late, buddy. If I object, it'll just be repeated." He gave my wrist a gentle squeeze. "You can't unring a bell."

And so, undeterred, Detective Alabrandi tugged at yet more loose threads in the hope of unraveling what he had, by the time he first appeared at my door, no doubt conceived of as a murder plot.

"I asked Mr. Madison if there might be any other reason for wanting his wife cremated as soon as possible," he told the court.

"Did Mr. Madison provide any other reasons?" Mr. Singleton asked.

"He said he didn't want to think of her lying in a refrigerated vault," Alabrandi answered. "He said he had a very vivid imagination, and this was a picture he didn't want in his mind."

What else could I have told him at that time? I asked myself as he continued his testimony. He had come to believe that I wanted Sandrine cremated in order to get rid of evidence.

"So it is your recollection, Detective Alabrandi," Mr. Singleton continued, "it is your recollection that Professor Madison offered several quite different reasons for wanting his wife cremated as soon as possible."

"One right after the other, yes."

Mr. Singleton shot his right index finger into the air. "That somehow this would be in accordance with . . . well . . . Cleopatra?"

"Yes."

A second finger saluted the day. "That he had a vivid imagination and didn't want an image of his wife in a refrigerated vault."

"He said that too."

A third finger.

"And, finally, that rituals such as funerals were expressions of various beliefs that he regarded as . . . what were his words again, Detective?"

"Santa Claus for grown-ups," Alabrandi answered in the measured voice of a true detective.

Now Morty lifted his hand. "Your Honor, Mr. Madison gave his reasons and Detective Alabrandi has already stated them. Why go over this again?"

Mr. Singleton glanced toward the bench. "Your Honor I am . . ."

Judge Rutledge was now looking at Morty, who had by then gotten to his feet. "Yes, Mr. Salberg, is there something you want?"

To my relief, there was.

Request a Brief Recess

Morty wanted a brief recess and, though he didn't say it, I knew it was because he'd seen that I was becoming quite addled, and he'd wanted to break the relentless drumbeat of Detective Alabrandi's testimony, the way my own words were painting me as an enemy of Christ, Yahweh, Allah, or any other deity to whose ears the respective hearers of my case cared to offer up their daily prayers.

"I must come off as some kind of professional atheist," I said, once the request had been granted and Morty and I were safely ensconced in a private room a few yards from the judge's chambers. "Coburn's version of Christopher Hitchens."

Morty grinned. "I wouldn't worry about all that many members of the jury knowing who Christopher Hitchens was." He eased his enormous frame into a waiting chair. "But I wish you'd contacted me before you talked to Alabrandi or anyone else. I'd have said four little words and hoped that you remembered them: lowest common fucking denominator. You should never underestimate the capacity of human beings to be swayed by prejudice."

I slumped into a chair. "If it doesn't fit, you must acquit."

"Something like that."

I looked at him with genuine sympathy. "You're extremely bright, Morty. You must surely get tired of playing these stupid games."

His response was unexpectedly serious. "Not when I'm trying to save someone's life, Sam." He unbuttoned his jacket with a broad gesture, as if happy to reveal just how amply his stomach spilled over his belt. "Try not to get too upset. I saw you were getting worked up, which is why I asked for this five-minute recess."

"Worked up?" I offered a vaguely contemptuous snort. "I feel like Meursault in *The Stranger*."

Morty laughed. "Be sure you mention that to the press, Sam, or better yet to the jury. I'm sure they're all great fans of postwar existentialist French literature." He leaned forward, folded his huge hands, and placed them on the table. "Why did you want Sandrine cremated so quickly? Or at all? I'll be asking you that in the presence of the jury at some point. And believe me, that ancient history bullshit won't fly. Was that answer even true?"

"No," I admitted. "I made it up on the spot."

"What was the real reason?"

I felt suddenly quite heavy, the reason for my wanting Sandrine cremated quickly so cold and selfish and thoroughly reprehensible that I'd probably not recognized it myself until that very moment.

"Sandrine was beautiful," I told Morty. "And I wanted her to stay that way, or to disappear entirely."

"Is that why you later covered her face?" Morty asked. "In the bed, I mean, after the coroner left."

"How did you know that?"

"It's in the report made to the mortuary," Morty answered. "That when they arrived her face was covered. Everyone else saw her face. Hill, the coroner. So it must have been uncovered when she died."

"It was, yes."

"So why did you cover it?"

166

I shook my head and released a weary breath. "I covered her face because I couldn't bear to look at her, how beautiful she was, knowing at the same time that I would never, ever . . . hold her again . . . that she was gone." I hung my head for a moment, then lifted it. "Would the jury believe that?"

Morty sat back and waved his hand. "Who knows? Anything can go in any direction. You got a couple women on the jury who aren't exactly oil paintings. They might resent a beautiful woman. And the men? I doubt if they have women who looked like Sandrine waiting at home for them. They might not warm to a guy who did." He thought this over, then added, "But then, there are plenty of homely women who don't resent beautiful women. And every guy with an ugly wife doesn't resent the guy who has a good-looking one." He looked toward the window and seemed to see only the inscrutable nature of things. "It's a fucking crapshoot, the human heart." He glanced at the clock. "Okay, back into the ring," he said.

The Court Reminds You

"Detective Alabrandi," Judge Rutledge said, "the court reminds you that you are still under oath."

"Yes, Your Honor."

The true detective looked completely relaxed as he prepared to hammer another plank onto my scaffold. He had done this before to other such miscreants, as he perceived me to be, and the smooth way he did it showed on his face, so very dispassionate, just a man doing his job, as if he had no feelings against me personally though I knew he had plenty of them.

How did I know?

I knew because he'd returned to 237 Crescent Road about a week after our first rainy day interview, and during which time I'd recognized the tiny hint of animus that was in his eyes as he'd taken his seat once more on my living room sofa, taken out his brown notebook, and with unceremonious speed fired his first question.

"Do you know Malcolm Esterman?" he asked.

"Yes," I said. "He's teaches Greek history and mythology. He was in the same department as Sandrine. They were colleagues."

"Colleagues," Alabrandi repeated.

"Yes," I told him firmly. "Colleagues."

The look on his face caused me to lean forward slightly.

"What is this all about?" I asked. "What does Malcolm Esterman have to do with anything?"

"Your wife called him the day she died," Alabrandi said. "Several times, actually."

"I see."

"Do you have any idea why she might have done that?"

"You'd have to ask Malcolm."

"We have."

"What did he say?"

"That they were close."

"Close?" I asked quietly. "Sandrine and Malcolm weren't close." I sat back. "What does that mean, anyway? Close?"

Alabrandi shrugged. "My job is simply to look into various possibilities, Mr. Madison," he said. "When a woman the age of your wife, only forty-six, when she suddenly . . . ends up dead, we have—"

"Ends up dead?" I interrupted. "What is that supposed to mean?"

Alabrandi's gaze hardened. "What do you think it means?"

I sat back. "As you know, my wife was already dying," I told him. "And it was going to be a terrible death."

"And a long one," Alabrandi said, then, like an actor who'd inadvertently jumped ahead in the play, he added, "Her death was going to be long and very difficult for you."

"For her," I barked back. "Difficult for Sandrine."

"Too difficult for her to bear, is that what you're saying?" Alabrandi asked. "So that she began stockpiling Demerol?"

So he knows that, too, I thought.

"Yes," I answered.

To my surprise, Detective Alabrandi didn't pursue the issue that would later emerge during the fourth day of my trial, the fact that it was I, not Sandrine, who'd asked Dr. Ortins for Demerol, that it was I, not Sandrine, who'd picked up every single refill at Gerald Wayland's pharmacy.

Nor had he yet brought these facts into play during his testimony, as I noticed at that point, but rather he'd continued to follow Mr. Singleton's careful lead.

"Now, Detective Alabrandi, before the recess, we were discussing your initial interrogation of Mr. Madison," Mr. Singleton said.

"It wasn't an interrogation," Alabrandi responded. "Mr. Madison had not been arrested at that point."

"Shit," Morty whispered, "he knows I called that recess to allow the jury to forget some of what you said, and now the little bastard is going over it again."

Which was precisely what happened.

"Now, Detective Alabrandi," Mr. Singleton said. "There were various issues that you'd found troubling, is that correct?"

"Yes, sir."

"Would you tell us again what those issues were?"

As Detective Alabrandi meticulously ticked off these issues, I marveled at how few of them he'd brought up during our second conversation. He'd mentioned Malcolm Esterman, though without further elaboration and only a hint of innuendo. Throughout the interview (since, evidently, it had not been an interrogation though it had certainly felt like one) he'd been polite. No. More than polite. There'd been a cautiousness about him, so that he had seemed rather like a man forced to explore a disreputable atmosphere whose moral relativism had both surprised and embarrassed him. For that reason, he'd seemed to approach the troubling issues related to Sandrine's death quite carefully, like a computer technician who didn't actually want to know what might be on his client's computer.

170

On the witness stand, he still struck me as that technician, though now one who'd ultimately been compelled first to check out that hard drive, then reveal the dark things he found there.

"Well, there was the matter of the note Mrs. Madison left behind," he said. "Officer Hill had reported that Mr. Madison had called it a suicide note, but when we read it we found no mention of suicide in it. When I later asked Mr. Madison why he had called it a suicide note, he answered that he'd simply assumed that that's what it was."

That had been a stumble, I thought instantly, and a stupid one, since there'd been no need for me to call Sandrine's note anything at all.

"Did you gather from that statement that Mr. Madison had been aware that his wife intended to commit suicide?"

Morty rose to object that Mr. Singleton's question called for a conclusion from the witness.

Judge Rutledge sustained the objection and, just like in the movies, Mr. Singleton rephrased his question.

"Did Mr. Madison tell you why he'd assumed the statement found beside his wife's bed to be a suicide note?"

"Yes, he did," Detective Alabrandi answered. "He said that she'd called it her 'final word.' He told me that when he found her dead, he'd assumed that she'd meant this last communication to be a suicide note."

Instead, it had been her "final word" on Cleopatra, though it had ended not with the sense that she would write no more on this subject, but that she was only now beginning to explore it, a final word that had not in the least seemed final, a curious and perhaps sinister fact, which Detective Alabrandi now revealed to the jury.

"The note had nothing to do with suicide," he said. "It had to do with Cleopatra."

Mr. Singleton stepped over to the witness box and handed Sandrine's note to the witness.

"Is this the note you found beside Mrs. Madison's bed?" he asked.

"Yes."

"Would you read it to the jury, please?"

As Alabrandi read, I felt the utter strangeness of what Sandrine had written coil around me once again. Why had she written as if she'd had all the time in the world to pursue the elusive Cleopatra? Why had she indicated the nature of her future research? Why had she spoken of traveling to Egypt, walking the desert sands, and sailing up the Nile? I asked myself all these questions as Alabrandi began to read my wife's "final word."

"'More than anything, perhaps, Cleopatra's life represents a woman lost in time, the works of her chroniclers destroyed by fire or water, her own memoir unwritten, a woman all but erased, save for a likeness—or perhaps merely an imagined likeness—stamped on ancient coins.'"

The question that came toward me like a spear was the one summoned by the last line, which Alabrandi read slowly, pronouncing each word carefully so that the implication of what Sandrine had written could not be more clear.

"'Over time, my hope would be to bring this elusive woman, along with the hard-won wisdom her life bequeathed, to a larger audience than those scholars who have already dismissed her, and according to whom she was but a pawn in a man's dark game.'"

Mr. Singleton allowed the jury to absorb those final words, then, just in case they hadn't, he repeated them. "A pawn in a man's dark game." He looked at me, then back to the jury. "Yes."

I looked at the jury as Alabrandi folded the yellow paper. I looked at them and saw that they'd heard what Sandrine had written not as the final, abandon-hope-all-ye sentence of a suicide note but as the clarion call of a passionately intelligent woman who'd conceived a life's mission for herself, and who was going to pursue it as long as she had the strength to do so, a life's mission, as Sandrine's last words appeared to suggest, that had been heartlessly terminated by "a man's dark game."

I'm finished, I thought, a conclusion I labored to conceal from the jury by pretending to be deeply interested in what was currently being said in court.

"As far as your investigation has turned up, what you just read to the court is the last sentence Sandrine Allegra Madison left us, isn't it Detective Alabrandi?" Mr. Singleton asked.

"It is, yes, sir."

With that, Singleton drew the paper from Alabrandi's hand, stared at it almost lovingly, then repeated, "Over time my hope would be . . ." He looked at Detective Alabrandi. "When did Mr. Madison indicate that his wife wrote those words?"

"He said the note was written on the afternoon of November 14," Alabrandi answered.

"And when did Mrs. Madison die?"

"According to the autopsy, she died between the hours of six p.m. and midnight on November 14."

"The same day this . . . I really don't know what it is . . . but this . . . note was written?"

"Yes, sir."

Morty leaned forward, the only indication I had of just how damaging he felt all this to be.

"Did Mr. Madison indicate to you whether he'd actually read the note?" Mr. Singleton asked.

"He said that he hadn't read it."

"Did he ask you about the contents of the note?"

173

"Yes, and I told him it was more like a college essay or something of that nature."

"And what was his reaction to that?"

"He smiled."

"He smiled. Did he say anything about the note?"

"Yes. He said it was 'typical.'"

"Detective Alabrandi, did Mr. Madison ever tell you what he found 'typical' in the final communication of Sandrine Madison?"

"No," Alabrandi answered.

Which is true, though the answer would have been easy: the grace of her writing, and how heartfelt it was.

"Now, when you read this note, you noticed that Mrs. Madison made no mention of suicide, is that correct, Detective Alabrandi?" Mr. Singleton asked.

"Yes, sir."

"In fact, she only mentions herself twice, isn't that so?"

"Yes."

Singleton handed the note back to Alabrandi.

"She mentions herself in the first line," he said "Would you mind reading it again?"

Detective Alabrandi lowered his gaze to the paper and read: "'I often think of Cleopatra.'"

"That 'I' is Mrs. Madison's sole mention of herself until the last line, isn't it, Detective?"

"Yes, it is."

"Did you have occasion to mention this to Mr. Madison?"

"In our initial interview, I did, yes," Alabrandi answered. "I told him that the entire 'suicide note' was about the Egyptian queen Cleopatra."

"How did Mr. Madison respond?"

"He informed me that Cleopatra was not Egyptian."

I glanced over as Morty released a very soft sigh, then a whispered, "Shit."

"She was Greek evidently," Alabrandi added. "A Macedonian, Mr. Madison told me. He said that Cleopatra was no more Egyptian than Elizabeth Taylor."

Elizabeth Taylor.

It struck me as not at all strange that her name instantly returned me to Sandrine, a stunning young woman of twenty-one, fresh from her studies at the Sorbonne. She'd been fiery and passionate, a brightly burning blaze of a woman. Once, long into our marriage, we'd been watching Geneviève Bujold in the part of Antigone, and I'd leaned over and whispered, "That's you, Sandrine." I had expected her to be pleased. Who wouldn't have been by such a comparison? But her eyes had darkened and she said, "Only in your mind. Because it's what you want me to be."

I was jarred from this disturbing memory by the yellow paper Mr. Singleton now once again took from Alabrandi and lifted into the air, the way the jurors' eyes followed it, the grim look on their faces, as if it were a pair of bloodstained panties.

"And it was this paper that Mr. Madison described as a suicide note, wasn't it?" he asked. "This paper that makes no reference whatsoever to suicide. Isn't that true, Detective?"

Alabrandi nodded. "Yes."

It was an answer that lingered in the air as Singleton stepped toward the judge, and in the stark quiet of the room he added simply, "I'd like to offer this note in evidence, Your Honor." Then, no less quietly, he stepped away.

Exhibit A

In a movie, it would be called Exhibit A, the note Mr. Singleton called "Sandrine's last message," but I failed to notice the exact identification the court assigned to it. Clearly, save for melodramatic effect, it could not actually have been labeled "A," since a host of material had already been handed over for such labeling. But in my trial, as I had learned by then, it was the small, incremental bits of circumstantial evidence, not the "Exhibit A" of courtroom dramas, that had entangled me, little sins of both omission and commission: a cold response, a silence when I should have spoken, a question I should have asked but hadn't, these the winding fibers in the rope that could at some point hang me.

And so I watched quite impassively as the single sheet of paper moved from desk to desk, making its slow rounds until it was finally taken away by one of the court officials. Officer Hill had described the paper as yellow, but in fact the color was beige, the paper tanned and textured to resemble papyrus, my gift to Sandrine on her fortieth birthday, and not one sheet of which she'd ever used prior to penning her final . . . what?

True, I hadn't read it before Officer Hill pointed it out, then politely asked if she could take it. But since then I've read it several times, so that nothing in what Mr. Singleton began to go over in court came as a surprise.

"All right, Detective Alabrandi, after the matter of Cleopatra not being Egyptian, did you then proceed to raise another troubling issue with regard to Mrs. Madison's death?"

"I did."

"And what was that issue?"

The issue had been "various information," as Alabrandi had phrased it as we continued the second of our "interviews." I recalled the way he sat back slightly before moving to the next issue, apparently trying to relax me and probably thinking that since I was obviously the bookish type, and by definition soft, I must find him rough and a bit scary.

"According to our investigation, Mrs. Madison received her diagnosis from Dr. Ortins at just after twelve on the morning of April 12," he told me. "Do you remember when she returned home?"

"At just after six, I think. I'd just gotten back from my afternoon class when she came through the door."

"So for six hours after receiving such terrible news, she was . . . absent?"

"In the sense that she didn't come home, yes."

Alabrandi glanced at his note. "You had no classes between noon and five p.m. that day, right?"

Ah, I thought, so they have tracked down and studied my daily schedule.

"Right."

"Where were you during that time?"

"I was here. Reading."

"And your wife knew that you were here at home?"

"I suppose. I am a man of habits. She knew what those habits were."

"So she assumed that you were here, but she didn't come back home to tell you what Dr. Ortins had told her?"

"That's right."

177

"Did you ever wonder why she didn't come home to you?" Alabrandi asked.

It struck me that I had never in the least wondered why, given such devastating news, Sandrine had not come home to me.

"No," I answered softly. "But Sandrine had a certain solitary quality to her character. I suppose I just assumed that she'd gone to some place quiet and thought things over."

"Like where?"

"Oh, maybe down by the river or over to the reservoir," I said. "She liked to sit by the reservoir."

At that moment I recalled how often Sandrine had gone to the reservoir, strolled around it in her solitary way, sometimes on very cold days, with her hands deep in the pockets of her coat. With what facts had she been wrestling, I suddenly wondered, on those lonely, lonely walks?

"They can be quite lonely, married people," I said before I could stop myself.

Alabrandi watched me silently for a moment, then nodded and jotted something into his notebook.

"Sandrine did call me, though," I added hurriedly, like a man in need of proving he'd been a loving husband. "That day, I mean. The day she spoke to Dr. Ortins. She called me at around three that afternoon."

Alabrandi continued to write in his notebook. "Yes, I know," he said, as if it were a matter of course that he was by now fully aware Sandrine had called me at a particular time on a particular day.

"How do you know?" I asked.

Alabrandi looked up, and I saw something that struck me as oddly sympathetic, though to whom this sympathy was offered was impossible to know until he spoke. "We've learned a lot about Mrs. Madison," he said. Then just as quickly all signs of this sympathy vanished. "And about you."

"Me?"

As I watched Detective Alabrandi on the stand so many weeks after this exchange, I recalled the exact look in his eyes at the moment I'd said "Me?" They'd been my father's eyes when he'd caught me in some act I had fully expected to get away with. They'd seemed to say, What could you possibly have been thinking, Sammy? Just who do think you're dealing with?

He'd been a factory worker, my father, the kind of man who drank beer and watched the game and had little respect for men who didn't do the same. I'd been a perfect pussy in his eyes. He'd never shown the slightest interest in my schooling, and even less in the fact that I'd won an academic prize or landed a prestigious scholarship, least of all that I'd gotten into a well-regarded university, earned my coveted PhD. In fact, nothing I'd ever done had instilled the slightest respect for any of my achievements until I'd shown up with Sandrine glowing on my arm. Now that had gotten his attention.

I suddenly remembered how, after years of estrangement, I'd called him a couple of days after marrying Sandrine, asked if I could bring her to meet him. At the time it had seemed an ordinary thing to do, but now I wondered if the driving force behind it was my still-aching need for his approval. Had this same, sad need also encouraged me to make a little extra noise in the bedroom that same night, knowing he would hear it?

I felt Morty's hand touch my arm. "Pay attention," he whispered. "Stop drifting."

Like a schoolboy duly warned, I focused once again on Detective Alabrandi. By then he was edging toward the bombshell he had no doubt been waiting to deliver, gauging the moment, calculating the effect.

"So, Detective Alabrandi, in the course of your investigation, did you have occasion to review Mrs. Madison's cell phone records for April

12? I am speaking now of the day she had her consultation with Dr. Ortins, that is to say, the day she first received word of her diagnosis."

"Yes, I did."

"And what did you discover?"

"Well, Mr. Madison had said that his wife called him at three in the afternoon. In order to verify this statement we checked Mrs. Madison's phone records."

"And had she in fact called her husband at that time?"

"Yes."

"Mr. Madison was correct."

"Not entirely. He said that she had called him from the university library. That was not the case."

Singleton looked as if he'd never heard of any discrepancy during my long second interview with Detective Alabrandi.

"Did you subsequently discover from where that phone call had been made?"

"Yes, I did. She had made the call very near a local cell phone tower, which gave us a pretty good idea of where she'd been. What I mean is, it narrowed the search."

"But you further narrowed it, didn't you, Detective Alabrandi?" Singleton asked.

"Yes," Alabrandi answered. "We cross-referenced the coverage of the tower with the addresses of Mrs. Madison's known associates."

"And you found a known associate whose address was within the tower's coverage, correct?"

"Yes."

"What address was that, Detective?"

"4432 Devol Common. Here in Coburn."

"Is that a residence?"

"Yes, it is."

"Whose residence?"

"It is the residence of Malcolm Esterman."

Though I tried to obey Morty's instruction to keep focused on the testimony currently being offered, I found myself returning to my first meeting with Malcolm. It had been at a faculty reception, an annual affair hosted by the college president. It was the moment when our colleagues had gotten their first look at us and, sure enough, they'd been dazzled by Sandrine. She'd worn a black cocktail dress and a single strand of white pearls, and upon entering the room, which was large and crowded, she'd caught every eye in the place, particularly Cleo Billings's eye, the only man at Coburn College to whom I thought Sandrine might actually have been attracted and from whose riverside bungalow she might have telephoned me at three p.m. on the afternoon in question. In fact, when Detective Alabrandi had first raised the issue of the call, I'd felt my stomach tighten with that old familiar dread of betrayal and at that instant imagined Sandrine entwined with tall, tanned Cleo. But phone records don't lie, as Mr. Singleton clearly understood, and the stark fact was as simple and straightforward as Detective Alabrandi's demeanor when he stated it.

"So we felt that someone had been deceitful," Alabrandi said. "Either Mrs. Madison had misled her husband with regard to her actual whereabouts when making this call, or her husband, for some reason, had not wanted us to know that he had somehow been aware that Mrs. Madison had been with Mr. Esterman on this particular afternoon."

Been with.

Now there, I thought, was a euphemism that certainly deserved the name.

I looked at the members of the jury and saw that their minds were playing the same blue movie my brain had played as I'd sat in the living room and been told that Sandrine had "been with" Malcolm Esterman on

181

an afternoon when, by all rights, she should have been with me, telling me of her diagnosis, seeking love and comfort.

"How did Mr. Madison react when you informed him of the whereabouts of Mrs. Madison at three-thirty p.m. on the afternoon of April 12?" Mr. Singleton asked.

Alabrandi paused for quite some time before he gave his answer, a quest for accuracy I'd gotten used to by then.

"Disbelief," Alabrandi said. "He asked if I had any idea why his wife was with Mr. Esterman. I told him that I didn't, and asked if Mrs. Madison had ever mentioned going to Mr. Esterman's house that afternoon. He said that she had not."

It had been at that moment, yes. Despite the fact that Alabrandi had been sitting quite comfortably in my living room as if we were two frat brothers chatting about some college prank, yes, it had been at that instant that I'd felt a genuine sense of everything going dreadfully wrong from this moment on, an investigation that would dig deeper than I'd expected and that was bound to unearth possibilities I had not imagined.

It was also at this instant that the truth of something Sandrine had once said to me revealed itself. We'd come to New York from Coburn with no particular plan and so had ended up in one of those basement theaters that dotted Greenwich Village, rows of metal chairs in a windowless concrete box whose walls had been painted black. I no longer remember the play but it had surely been one of those overwrought productions that took aim at bourgeois pretentions, a huge target if ever there was one. And so, for two interminable hours, we'd watched and listened as the playwright fired his juvenile salvos, fired them over and over again so that, by the time the curtain at last fell, we'd both felt as if we had spent days in a metal drum beaten on all sides by imbecilic kids wielding iron bars.

For relief, we stopped into a local diner, ordered strong coffee, and sat, our minds ringing with the clanging foolishness of it all, lost in our own thoughts, or at least trying to become lost in them.

"The problem is that nothing is done subtly anymore," I said irritably. "Everything has to be big and loud."

Sandrine nodded, took a sip of her coffee, then let her gaze drift out the window, to where the various denizens of Village nightlife were annoying one another in the usual ways.

"I can take an actor who's over the top," I added, "but a whole play shouldn't be."

Sandrine shrugged. "It's a little problem, Sam."

"A little problem?" I asked.

Her gaze once again returned to the street and, as she did so, she released a tired breath.

This had become one of the ways she moved away from me, moved away from my trumpeted opinions, my sharpened sensibilities, my resentment of all that struck me as puerile.

"It's not a little problem, Sandrine," I said as a way to draw her back.

Sandrine continued to stare out the window.

"If you're going to write, you ought to write about something," I said angrily.

Suddenly, her eyes whipped over to me. "What would you write about now?" she demanded. "If you were still writing your book, what would it be about, Sam?"

I knew this question was offered as a challenge, and so I thought my answer through before I gave it.

"I suppose I'd write about how hard it is for excellence to overcome mediocrity," I said.

Her eyes drifted back to the window.

"And you?" I demanded.

Without hesitation she said, "Fear, I suppose."

"Fear?" I said with a soft laugh. "That's pretty general. Which one?"

"Mine."

"And what fear is that?"

She faced me then and her eyes glittered darkly. "You don't have any idea what I'm most afraid of, do you, Sam?"

"Evidently not, so please tell me."

Now her eyes glistened. "That when my life is over, all over and done with, it will all just seem like an enormous waste of time."

It was the hard thud of Judge Rutledge's gavel that brought me back from that distant evening, the animal fear I'd glimpsed in Sandrine's eyes and from which I should have understood that this deepest of all human fears was precisely her fear too.

To my surprise everyone rose and the jury filed out.

"What's going on?" I asked Morty.

He looked at me, puzzled. "You don't know, Sam?"

I shook my head. "Drifting, I guess."

Rather than scold me, Morty simply laughed. "It's just chow time, guy."

Adjournment for Lunch

During the lunch adjournment, I couldn't keep the scene with Sandrine and me in that Greenwich Village diner from replaying in my mind. But it wasn't this scene alone. For by then I'd begun to rethink not only the last weeks of Sandrine's life but all the years before that, all the classes, the student conferences, the faculty meetings, retreats, teas, all the graduations, the long drumbeat of our years together. I wondered if Sandrine had died with these same scenes playing in her mind, wondering too how thin it was, the line that had divided her life from an enormous waste of time.

Morty was having lunch with some fellow lawyers, and Alexandria had gone out to get us a couple of sandwiches, so I was alone in the room, alone with these thoughts. Had Sandrine finally come to believe that in marrying me she had made not only a grave mistake but the one great mistake of her life, the error from which all later errors flowed? And as the years passed, and without consciously being aware of it, had I grown increasingly defensive with regard to Sandrine, and was it my own pent-up disappointment that had finally exploded on that last night of her life?

This was all icily disturbing, and like a man fleeing the voices in his head I walked to the window and looked out. I could see the front grounds of the courthouse, with its squat war memorials, marble columns that erupted from the green here and there and upon which the names of the local fallen had been inscribed. There was also a statue of some regionally renowned Civil War commander who'd distinguished himself at Gettysburg . . . or was it Spotsylvania? Coburn's monuments were like Coburn, I thought, untouched by any distinction.

My gaze drifted about the grounds. The lawn was dotted with the sort of sunlight poets and bad writers inevitably call "dappled." The town traffic was moving with its usual lethargy, a pace I'd long ago labeled "sub-Saharan" and which I thought typical of the average Coburnite's failure to find anything of true moment to do.

Nothing in this Norman Rockwell tableau caught my attention until I saw Mr. Singleton and Detective Alabrandi as they moved down one of the courtyard square's concrete sidewalks. They were walking shoulder to shoulder. There they are, I thought, my twin nemeses, utterly convinced that they have seen through my plot, equally determined to make sure that I pay with my life.

I would have turned away but, just as they reached the street, a brown Ford station wagon pulled into one of the parking spaces a few feet away. It was a car I recognized, because it had always struck me as odd that a single man, as Malcolm Esterman certainly was, would buy a car that says family all over it, a car for transporting kids to school, games, lessons, for taking long in-country vacations to such faraway and exotic locales as, say, Charleston.

And yet there he was, Malcolm getting out of that very car, then walking over to Mr. Singleton and Detective Alabrandi, offering them a friendly hand. How could I have known that it would all begin to unravel with such a decidedly unthreatening man, that it'd be his gently offered confirmation of Alabrandi's initial suspicion that would keep the fire burning under the good detective and, by that means, keep his gimlet eyes on me. Watching the three of them stroll casually to a bench and sit down, I could almost imagine Alabrandi's first suggestion that there might be something fishy in Sandrine's death, Alabrandi sitting in Malcolm's musty little town house, trying out the idea on Malcolm, waiting for his response, then infinitely pleased with what he hears, though, in fact, it was little more than a hint that perhaps all had not been peachy between Sandrine and me.

A troubled marriage. Who doesn't have a troubled marriage? And yet I know now that Malcolm would not have had to say any more than that to add a wolfish pointiness to Alabrandi's ears.

The door of the room opened.

It was Alexandria with sandwiches and soda.

"Nothing for me," I told her.

"You need to eat, Dad."

She sat down at the table and began to unwrap the sandwiches.

I was still peering out the window. "You know what I miss, Alexandria? I miss the simplest things, like being able to walk around the town, go to the market."

"But you hate the market here," Alexandria reminded me. "You were always complaining that it didn't even have balsamic vinegar."

This was true. Still, only a few months before, I could at least have gone to the place without fear of being noticed, save by the occasional stray faculty member or faculty spouse of Coburn College. But since Sandrine's death I'd become a local celebrity. My picture had been in the paper and I'd been the subject of numerous local television reports. I'd even been the unidentified subject of Jesse Bloom's radio talk show, the subjunctive-deprived topic for the day having been: *If your spouse was planning to murder you, would you see the warning signs?* The show had generated a lively discussion from Bloom's phone-in audience, some of whom felt certain that they'd have been able to figure out if their spouses *were* planning to kill them, others who—rather sadly, I

187

thought—admitted they were not so sure. I remember a woman quite distinctly, the vaguely broken and self-accusatory tone in her voice, saying, My husband has deceived me so often and in so many ways I'm sure I'd be dead before I had a clue. As for me, I'd been quite certain I would have seen any sign of such a lethal intention in Sandrine. Surely she would have betrayed herself in some way, a look or word that would have tipped me off.

Yet was it not possible that I'd never really seen how much her feelings for me had changed over the years, never had the slightest inkling she might actually want me dead?

"Dad," Alexandria said, this time more sharply and with a quick nod toward the sandwiches. "We don't have a lot of time."

I joined her at the table and took a small bit of the sandwich. "Bad stuff is on the way," I said. "With Alabrandi, I mean."

"Nothing I don't already know," Alexandria said.

Ah, but there was a great deal my daughter didn't know, and on that recognition I thought of April Blankenship in her pale blue dress, Clayton's neglected wife. She'd never expected much in the way of notoriety, and she'd certainly been unprepared to be drawn into a murder case.

It was at the town park I could no longer visit that I'd had that fateful meeting with April. I'd seen her before, of course, while shopping and also at various Coburn College functions. When it came to food shopping, she was a meticulous squeezer of fruit, as I'd observed in earlier produce market encounters. Her smile was so small as to be almost invisible, and I'd instantly pegged her for one of those needy faculty wives so often caricatured in films and books, tortured by longing, but afraid of her own shadow. In all of this, as it turned out, I'd unfortunately been right.

With these thoughts, I felt myself drift back down bad-memory lane, this time to a summer day in the town park, I with the latest award-winning novel, turning the pages slowly, admiringly, wishing I'd written what I read. Leslie Stephen had once said that genius is mostly a matter of taking the trouble, but with rewrite after rewrite of "The Pull of the Earth" I'd learned that this was not exactly so. Years had passed since the last of those efforts, of course, the one Sandrine had so soundly criticized, increasingly resentful years, as I'd privately acknowledged, and which, by the time April appeared in the town park on that summer day, had caused me to ridicule my own past efforts as, well . . . an enormous waste of time.

What are you thinking?

Such had been April's question as she found herself standing before me that afternoon, her thin, faintly freckled arms holding a striped folding chair like a shield over her breast.

"I wasn't thinking much about anything," I told her. "Just reading." I nodded toward the book. "This year's NBA winner."

"Oh," April said, clearly having no idea what the initials NBA stood for.

"Is it good?"

"It's okay," I answered. "At least it got published."

"That's nice," April said. "It's important to publish, Clayton says."

Some women give off sparks and some sprout beads of mother's milk. The latter should be nuns or nurses of the old school, comforters to those wounded in the soul or on the battlefield. They are an eternal type, and they almost always attract the perfect man to use and then discard them. In love's labor, they always lose, and I had known more than one of them before April stood over me that day in the park, clutching the tiny folding chair as if it were the baby she had always wanted but never had.

In the past, I'd resisted such women, but on that day, reading that book, a man in his mid-forties whose last creative juices had long turned to dust, I'd suddenly felt a need to play a dangerous game, embrace the thrill of folly, skate, as it were, on the only stretch of thin ice that lay immediately before me, pale, wintry April.

"I guess you read all the time," she said admiringly.

"I'm sure Clayton does the same," I replied.

She nodded softly. "But his eyes are going." A tiny smile flickered briefly, then disappeared. "It happens, you know." She added shyly, "When you're old."

I knew that compared to leathery old Clayton I surely looked to April like Hercules, a middle-aged man with a straight spine and eyes that could still read the small print.

"Yes, that's part of the deal, isn't it?" I asked gently as I got to my feet and faced her.

She nodded again but said nothing.

"But it's a bad deal," I added softly. "Isn't it?"

She nodded yet again, and like a seducer in a pulp novel tugging at the button of a maiden's bodice, I drew that garishly striped lawn chair from April's arms.

"A very bad deal," I said. "For you."

She looked up and her eyes turned liquid, and right there, right then, as she pressed her face into my chest and began to sob, I thought, She's mine, and felt as heartless a surge of vanity and power as I had ever known.

Alexandria knew nothing about this, of course, so I kept silent and simply watched as she ate her sandwich in the same pleasureless way she'd been doing since her mother's death. Like me, she'd lost weight as well as a good deal of her sparkle.

"You don't have to come to court every day, you know," I told her.

She took a small bite of her sandwich. "It would make a bad impression if I weren't here. It would look like I thought you did it." She smiled but not warmly. "Don't worry, Dad. I'm loyal."

190

I couldn't help but wonder if by this profession of loyalty Alexandria was hinting at her moral superiority to me, one she has a right to feel. After all, in betraying Sandrine I'd also betrayed her. It is part of the old problem of parenthood, the need to be hypocritical, to espouse values you do not practice because not to do so will expose your children to the withering winds of moral ambiguity. And who can stand in those?

I didn't say any of this, of course, because it would open up the deep wounds that have not healed in my daughter, and probably never will. Instead I asked my usual question. "How do you think it's going so far today?"

"Okay," Alexandria answered. "Nothing Morty can't deal with when the time comes to defend you."

"That part about my calling it a suicide note, you don't think that was damaging?" I asked.

She shrugged. "It's hard to know. You were under a lot of stress. And Mom had done it, hadn't she? It was a suicide, so why wouldn't you think the last thing she wrote would have been a suicide note?"

"Of course, they're saying it wasn't a suicide," I reminded her. "That's why there is a trial in the first place. They think it was a murder."

She stared at me with unwavering eyes. "But it wasn't," she said, in a way that made it clear she had no wish to discuss it further.

And so we moved on to other subjects. I told her about an earlier exchange with Morty, how I'd mentioned the narrator of *The Stranger*, the fact that he'd then warned me away from such pedantic literary allusions. After that, we briefly fell silent, and then she talked a little about her work, first her job at the literary agency then, to supplement that income, a second job in which she churns out what she calls "content" for an online magazine devoted to celebrity mishaps and malfeasance. She has lately been following the descent of an aging female rocker, a former flower child whose Haight-Asbury antics and girl-with-the-band beddings had once been chronicled in *Rolling Stone* magazine but whose present troubles are of interest only to the invisible online readers of sleeplesseye.com. Rumor has it that either a botched plastic surgery or a reaction to some drug has emulsified her nose.

"Creepy stuff like that," Alexandria told me. "We're read mostly by insomniacs. It's not great literature."

"Don't be so sure," I said. "There is a letter from a girl who has no nose in *Miss Lonelyhearts*. And that's great literature."

She stared at me silently.

"It's by Nathanael West."

Her smile hung like a frayed string. "Just be sure you do like Morty says, Dad," she warned me, "and don't bring elitist stuff like that up when you take the stand."

"It's elitist to read Nathanael West?" I asked with a light chuckle. "Christ what a low culture we have now."

"Which is what I work for, is that what you're saying?"

"I wasn't aware of saying anything of the kind."

"Sleeplesseye, I mean," Alexandria said. "Low culture."

"Those are your words, not mine."

"No, they're your words actually."

"Perhaps, but—"

"It's okay, Dad," she interrupted sharply. "I know I'm not a tenured professor. And, you know, I'd like to find myself, okay? I'd like to discover something I really want to do, but I haven't, Dad. I haven't. I'm adrift, okay? Can we agree on that?"

"Alexandria . . ."

She waved her hand like a blade, cutting off the subject. "Really, Dad," she said, her voice now quite soft. "It's okay." She passed her fingers over the surface of the table in the way I'd once seen Sandrine pass hers over the small indentions of our copper sink, a gentle, tender probing. "So let's drop it, okay?"

I nodded. "Okay," I said, after which there was another silence, this one longer.

During that silence I found myself returning to the final day of Sandrine's life, the interval between our last heated battle and when Alexandria had returned to have her last conversation with her mother. Before, I'd avoided any discussion of what they'd talked about, but now, following some curious impulse, I wanted to know.

"That evening when you were with your mother—that last evening—the one the day she died, did she talk about us?"

"Us . . . meaning?"

"Your mother and me."

"Not specifically," Alexandria answered. "But she talked about marriage."

"What did she say?"

"She said it was like a boxing match," Alexandria answered. "Between round one and round ten, you swing at each other a lot. But you both have this hope that at some point the bell will ring, and there'll be peace, and the struggle will have been worth it. And so you stay in the ring because you want to make it to that round-ten bell."

It was as discomfiting a view of marriage as I'd ever heard, and it was hard for me to imagine that Sandrine had thought of ours in such unhappy terms, and yet, like all the evidence in my case, it offered a certain undeniable if circumstantial proof that she had thought of our life together in just that bleak and cheerless way.

"I'm sorry if any of that bothers you, Dad," Alexandria said when she caught the downcast expression on my face. "But you asked."

"Yes, I did ask," I replied softly.

There was another silence after that, this one longer than the previous two, and during which I could feel Alexandria's eyes upon me like two hot beams.

"Do you think you would have made it, you and Mom?" she asked. "To round ten, I mean, if Mom hadn't died?"

I thought of how Sandrine had often tossed and turned in bed, how she had sometimes risen in the middle of the night, tiptoed to the scriptorium to read, her gaze darkly quizzical when she glanced up to find me at her door. Once, I'd asked her what she was thinking about, expecting her to speak about the book she was reading. But she'd said only, "Our school," by which she'd no doubt meant the dream she had voiced while we were still in New York but hardly even mentioned after we'd taken our jobs at Coburn. When I'd only shrugged at this answer, she'd quietly returned to her book, though later that night she seemed particularly restless, moving about the house, reading awhile, then listening to music, then reading again.

Since her death I've found myself plagued by a similar restlessness because the question of what Sandrine sought in the middle of the night will not let me go. I think of our first days, our tour of the ancient world, those few spectacular weeks in Paris, playing the expatriate game, then our settling down here in dear old Coburn, and through all those memories Sandrine remains the same. Then, rather suddenly, she wasn't the same at all.

"Your mother changed after she got sick," I said to Alexandria.

"In what way?"

"She became more distant."

"Distant?" Alexandria asked. "Really? She didn't seem that way to me at all. Frankly, you're the one who seemed more distant."

"I did?"

"Well, what would you call it?" Alexandria asked. "You hardly ever came out to the gazebo to sit with Mom. You avoided the room where she went to read."

"The scriptorium."

Alexandria shook her head. "She hated that name for it, by the way," she informed me. "She said you gave it that name when you first moved here because you thought you were both going to write great books there."

"That's true, I did," I admitted.

"But Mom didn't want to write a book, Dad," Alexandria said. "That was your idea, not hers."

This was also true, as I now freely admitted. Sandrine had never intended to write a great book, or any book at all, for that matter. I'd tried to blame her failure to do so at the feet of her unaccountable devotion to Coburn College, those interminable private sessions with its mediocre students, more often teaching them the rudiments of literacy than anything more august. It was a lowly, remedial form of education I'd once ridiculed as "the lofty heights of subject-verb agreement," to which my firm and passionate wife had fired back, "I will be what they need me to be, Sam, not what you need me to be."

And what they'd needed her to be was a teacher, not an author, as Sandrine had fully understood.

"You're probably right, Alexandria," I said quietly. "Your mother was never ambitious in that way."

Alexandria shrugged. "Anyway, wherever Mom was, in whatever room, you didn't go there."

"That's true," I admitted. "But there was a reason for it. Your mother had gotten more difficult, more hard to read, and there was this heat coming from her."

I stopped, reluctant to go further, then felt the sharp point of a dread Morty had mentioned earlier, the fact that Alexandria might know about that last argument, which was reason enough for me now to be proactive.

"So it really didn't surprise me that last night when she just went crazy," I said.

Alexandria's gaze suddenly grew more intense and I could see something pent-up and explosive gathering in her mind. "Don't try to put the blame on Mom." She looked at me quite sternly. "Don't try to paint Mom as the mad woman in the attic, Dad, because she wasn't."

"I didn't say she was the—"

"Just so you know, Dad," she interrupted, her voice very firm, "if you and Morty come up with some way of blaming Mom, you can both go fuck yourselves."

"What are you talking about?" I said. "I'm not trying to—"

"Haven't you done enough to her," Alexandria said sharply. "Haven't you done enough to hurt her?" Her lips trembled. "She's dead, okay? Isn't that enough?"

"Enough for what?" I asked.

"Enough to leave her in peace!" Alexandria said quite loudly, then, to my immense astonishment, she leaped up like a geyser of steam. "Mom was dying, but she wanted to live!" she cried. "She wanted to live, and then, suddenly . . . suddenly . . . she was gone." She shook her head. "It doesn't make sense," she added vehemently, though now laboring quite forcefully to control herself. "It has never made any sense."

So there it was, I thought starkly. My daughter, were she a member of the jury in my case, would incontestably vote to convict me.

I looked at her helplessly. "I don't know what to say," I told her. "I don't know what to say to you."

Alexandria drew in a trembling breath. "That last day, when I left, Mom put her arms around me, and she said, 'I love you . . . Ali.'"

"Ali?" I repeated. "She never called you Ali."

"I know," Alexandria said. "But she said she had always thought I was more of an 'Ali and that to her I would always be Ali." She smiled softly. "I guess it was her way of getting closer to me at the end."

Her way of getting closer to me.

I suddenly envisioned this scene, Sandrine gazing softly at Alexandria as she called her Ali, and at that moment I heard a mental *click*, a sharp, stand-your-hair-on-end snap that turned my case on its head and brought its disparate elements into a radically new focus.

Sandrine's way of getting closer to Alexandria?

What if it had been nothing of the kind, I thought. What if that entire scene, so tender and loving, had not been designed to bring Sandrine closer to Alexandria at all.

What if, I thought grimly as the darkest conjecture I'd ever had began to take shape in my mind, what if Sandrine's speaking so sweetly to "Ali" had been her way not of getting closer to her daughter on that last evening of her life but, instead, had been her fiendishly clever way of separating Alexandria from me?

Now it was Morty's voice I heard: You have no constitutional protection against your daughter, Sam.

"My God," I whispered. "What if . . ."

Alexandria peered at me as if I were a microbe under a glass. "What?"

I couldn't tell her any part of the terrifying scenario that was at that very moment unfolding in my mind, unfolding step by step, thread by thread, so that I felt like a man in the process of seeing through and reconstructing a brilliant magician's single most brilliant trick, every angle by which the audience was distracted, every false wall and trap door, all the blue smoke and mirrors.

I thought of the deadly coil of circumstantial evidence that now entangled me, no one piece of Singleton's case enough to convict me but how, when one connected to another, together they created a lethally persuasive argument for my guilt.

Alexandria stared at me. "What are you thinking, Dad?"

My latest surmise settled over me like a winter frost. My God, I asked myself, could it be true? I thought about asking Alexandria directly if Sandrine had told her about the terrible argument we'd had on that last evening, the cup whose shattered parts had still been strewn across our bedroom floor, and which, yes, Alexandria might have seen. And what if she had seen them and asked Sandrine about them, and what if Sandrine had then told her everything about that night, ended this no doubt masterfully constructed tale with the final word she'd shouted to my retreating back: sociopath.

To open up that subject now struck me as dangerous to my case. If Alexandria had seen those incriminating fragments she'd never mentioned it. Nor, before now, had she mentioned anything about her final conversation with Sandrine. And so, given the fact that Alexandria had so far revealed nothing having to do with her last hour with her mother, I decided it was best for me to allow those lips to remain sealed. After all, what I didn't know hadn't hurt me yet.

"Nothing," I said. "Nothing at all."

In the chill of the following silence I considered all the pieces that had come together in such a way as to first engender and then steadily build a case against me: the "suicide note" that had been no such thing, a back injury of which Dr. Mortimer's autopsy had found no evidence, my subsequent call to Dr. Ortins, the way I'd always been the one who'd picked up and signed for the Demerol because Sandrine had always had a class or a meeting or some other activity that had prevented her from going to Wayland's, the coup de grâce of antihistamines in her blood, the incriminating research she'd done on my computer, claiming hers was on the blink, though a subsequent investigation had found it to be in perfect working order.

Was it possible, I asked myself, in grave wonder that such a question could ever have occurred to me at all, was it possible that fiber by clever fiber Sandrine had fashioned the hangman's noose that now dangled above my head?

With that arctic question, I found myself coldly in awe of an intrigue whose elaborations had finally formed so subtle and oddly beautiful a design, elegant in the way mathematicians use the word, a beauty "cold and austere," as Bertrand Russell once called it, a phrase often quoted by the brilliant wife I now found myself imagining as a master puppeteer, one who'd never shown her hand, each element arranged to be discovered at a slant, nothing too obvious, no bloody knife or smoking revolver, these stage props replaced by a couple of paragraphs on Cleopatra that she'd described to me as her "final word," and which I, in turn, had described as a "suicide note" when it had been nothing of the kind. After that everything—even my pedantry, that ludicrous mention of Poe's story—had fallen inexorably into place. How classically Greek, I thought, to set a trap by which a man's own flawed character would destroy him.

For a moment I thought of all the witnesses who'd testified against me in a trial that, until now, I'd thought the exclusive handiwork of Mr. Singleton, the product of his personal zeal for justice. But was it not possible that he, too, had been brilliantly manipulated, his suspicions aroused by one carefully planted piece of evidence, then subtly deepened by another and another and another, all the while believing himself at the helm of my trial when in fact, and from the beginning, he'd merely been the chief puppet in what was not now, nor ever had been, anything but Sandrine's case?

PART IV

Testimony is set to continue today in the trial of Dr. Samuel Madison, the Coburn College professor accused in the death of his wife, Sandrine Madison. Throughout the investigation and trial, Dr. Madison has professed his innocence. It is not known whether he will testify in his own defense.

Coburn Sentinel
January 20, 2011

DAY SIX

Morning Session

Throughout the following evening, as I lay on my back in the darkness of the bedroom, I increasingly came to suspect that I did, indeed, now dangle in a web cleverly spun by Sandrine. Who, after all, could have more keenly intuited my dark desires, nor had a better motive to lay a trap for me should I act upon them. Had she seen in my soulless book its soulless author, surmised that I was indeed a sociopath capable of ridding myself of a woman who would with each passing day become more of a burden? Had Sandrine suspected that I wanted her dead and, in the throes of that suspicion, devised a way to make her destruction equally my own?

I couldn't reveal so grim a prospect to Alexandria, of course. Nor could I speak of it to Morty without sounding like a man so unhinged, so paranoid, so, well, sociopathic that in order to slither out of a murder conviction he was willing to lay the charge of attempted murder on the head of his dead wife. This meant that if Sandrine had, in fact, plotted to avenge her death, she'd done it in a way that not only prevented her plot from ever being discovered but just as thoroughly prevented it from even being discussed, let alone raised in court.

Such considerations were still imposing themselves upon me during the morning session of my trial, then into the afternoon session, Detective Alabrandi still on the stand, meticulously re-creating the many interviews he'd conducted both with me and with others during his

investigation of Sandrine's death. At points during all the previous testimony, I'd sometimes found myself adrift in a grim miasma of unfathomable circumstances but, now, as Alabrandi began to offer a step-by-step
analysis of the evidence that had ultimately come his way, I no longer
felt at sea. Perhaps there was, and had always been, to employ the words
of Henry James, a "pattern in the carpet."

"Now, Detective Alabrandi, did you return to 237 Crescent Road
on December 17?" Mr. Singleton asked.

"I did, yes."

"And by then other issues had come to your attention regarding
the death of Mrs. Madison, isn't that so?"

"Yes, they had."

"And so you returned and spoke to the defendant . . . this would
be the fifth time, I believe?"

"Yes."

This time he'd come in the morning, while I was sitting in the
sunroom with my first cup of coffee, staring at the wicker chair that had
always been Sandrine's and wondering, still wondering, just how much
digging Alabrandi had done since he'd last showed up at my door, and
what he'd uncovered, a worrisome process made all the more relevant
by his first statement, one made even before he'd entered my house
that morning.

"If you don't mind, we'd like to have a look at Mrs. Madison's
computer," Alabrandi said.

"No, I don't mind," I told him. "But it's not working."

"Not working?"

"That's right," I said. "Sandrine had been using my computer during the least few weeks."

"You never thought to get it fixed?" Alabrandi asked.

"She said she'd rather just buy a new one," I answered. "But she never got around to doing that."

Alabrandi's gaze betrayed something I found quite disturbing, the sense that he found me personally repellant. "We'd like to look at your computer as well." He smiled, but it was the smile of a man who held the winning cards, and knew it. "We could get a warrant, of course, but it's easier just to have your permission."

"Take them both," I said since I'd by then surmised that a demeanor that suggested a complete confidence in my innocence would play far better than my getting a lawyer or anything of that sort, a decision Morty had later thought quite foolish.

"The office we shared was small so we just had two laptops," I added.

"Thanks," Alabrandi said. "I'll pick them up on my way out."

I nodded. "Sure."

He took out his notebook. "Would you mind describing Mrs. Madison's general attitude during the weeks that led up to her death?"

He'd said "death" rather than "suicide," but I'd gotten used to such sinister syntactical ploys, and so they no longer bothered me. I was a tenured professor of English literature, after all. I knew how to use language.

"Attitude?" I asked. "That's a very general term."

Something hardened in Alabrandi's gaze. "How she seemed, is what I mean," he said. "Her thoughts and feelings."

"That's not much better with regard to generalities."

Alabrandi shifted slightly. "Generalities are okay," he said with a hint of irritability. "Generalities are just fine, Professor. Frankly, I don't see how I can be more specific, so may we, as they say, move on?"

"Well, in general then, she had become withdrawn," I told him.

"Due to her illness?"

"Yes."

"What about that last evening?"

He knows, I thought.

As Detective Alabrandi testified to this very exchange it struck me that it had not occurred to me at that moment that Alexandria might already have borne witness against me, that even at this early stage of the investigation a police informant might be embedded in what remained of my shattered household. Even now, I couldn't be sure, so that when I glanced back toward my daughter, met her gaze with my own, I felt, for the first time in my life, unsure of absolutely everything, a man now entirely unmoored. Had that also been part of Sandrine's plan, to so thoroughly unhinge me that my life, from now on, would be no more than a long slog through ever shifting sands, rootless, uncertain, and lonely beyond words.

Alexandria nodded toward the front of the courtroom, reminding me to pay attention.

When I turned back, Alabrandi had moved a few minutes further into his narration of our fifth interview.

"I began to ask Mr. Madison about the last evening of his wife's life," he told the court.

And immediately I was back in my living room, facing him as fearlessly as I could manage.

"The last evening?" I asked hesitantly.

"Was she still withdrawn?"

"Not exactly."

"So how would you describe Mrs. Madison's demeanor that evening?"

He knows, I repeated in my mind, though I could not be sure of this. And yet, if he knows, and if I lie or even diminish what happened between Sandrine and me that night, then I'll look as if I'm hiding something . . . and I would be.

"She was angry," I said.

In fact, Sandrine had said such furiously hurtful things to me on that evening, egged me on so relentlessly that, by now, as I listened to what Alabrandi began to tell the jury about this very exchange—and given the plot I feared she might have hatched—I'd come to suspect that Sandrine's entire effort that night had been directed at forcing my hand, so that I would hesitate no longer to carry out what perhaps she had come to believe I was already plotting: her murder.

"Very angry," I added as one after another of her accusations returned to me, all she'd first admired in me—the kindness, the simplicity, the sense of service—and all she had since come to despise: my snideness, my superiority, my endless sense of grievance, the shabby gift, as she'd found opportunity to repeat, of my disillusion.

"She was in an absolute rage," I said coldly, before I could stop myself, a sudden loss of control that Sandrine would have expected, so that were souls immortal, as I suddenly imagined, she would doubtless have been smiling from on high.

"Rage?" Alabrandi repeated.

There was no going back. "Rage, yes," I said.

With that answer, Alabrandi had taken out his notebook, opened it, written something into it, then looked up and leveled his gaze upon me. "Did you and your wife ever have any physical confrontations?"

I shook my head.

"Never," I answered, then saw the cup she'd hurled at me, a white porcelain cup that had crashed on the door as I'd left and whose many jagged shards I'd quickly swept up before the calling 911.

Morty nudged me slightly. "What's going on, Sam? You look like shit."

"I'm fine," I said crisply.

"Well act it then," Morty instructed. "Don't look like you just got hit by a fucking train."

In fact, at that moment some months before, fixed in Alabrandi's glint-of-a-knife stare, I'd felt that indeed I had been hit by an idea no less powerful and destructive than a speeding locomotive, the notion that somehow Alabrandi had found out about that cup, a knowledge he'd been hinting at during the fifth interview, and upon which, now on this fifth day of my trial, Mr. Singleton was closing in.

And so I leaned forward and listened more attentively as Mr. Singleton continued his questioning of Detective Alabrandi.

"Now, Detective Alabrandi, at this time, did you inform Professor Madison of any information you had regarding the relationship between Mr. Madison and his wife?"

"No," Alabrandi answered. "Not at that time. I simply let him talk."

Yes, indeed, I thought, he'd let me talk, and talk I had. I'd described Sandrine's increasingly withdrawn behavior, her long hours in the sunroom or in the scriptorium, the way she'd listen to music for hours on end. Alabrandi had listened to all this without comment so that it was only when I'd come to the end of this recitation that he finally tossed his spear.

"Mr. Madison, that last night, when your wife, as you said, was in a rage, there was an argument, I suppose?"

"Yes, we had an argument," I answered.

Alabrandi jotted a note in that strictly by-the-book way of his, like a man simply recording a few routine details. "Can you be more specific?"

"It was around six," I went on. "Lots of Coburn students have to work, and so we have many evening classes. I had two classes that night and I didn't get home until sometime after ten."

"Do you recall what the argument was about?" Alabrandi asked.

"Lots of things, really," I said.

"Lots of things?" Alabrandi asked.

"That I was distant, that I was cold."

"Anything else?"

"There were probably other things," I admitted. "But I don't remember what they were."

"How did it end, this argument?"

"It ended with Sandrine bringing up Alexandria," I said. "She thought I'd not been a very good father to our daughter."

"In what way not a good father?"

"That I'd often made it obvious I was disappointed in her because she hadn't lived up to some idea of what our daughter should be. A writer or a scholar. Something like that." I shrugged. "I got quite defensive, of course, and she said that was typical, too, that nothing she, or anyone else, said or did could ever penetrate what she called my 'shell.' When I started to leave, she yelled at me very loudly."

"What did she yell?" Alabrandi asked.

As if I were in that darkened room again I heard Sandrine's voice split the air.

"She screamed, 'You're a sociopath,'" I said, "and that I was nothing to her. Nothing. Nothing. Nothing." I felt a shudder. "As far as I know, those were her last words."

"At least to you," Alabrandi said.

"What?" I asked.

"Well, there was a phone beside her bed," Alabrandi said.

I nodded. "Yes, there was a phone," I said, now wondering if this was something Alabrandi had intentionally planted in my brain, the idea that Sandrine might have used that phone to call for help or—could she possibly have done this?—to say just as the drugs took effect that she had been murdered?

"Anyway," Alabrandi said, "calling you a sociopath, this was said as you were leaving for your class at the college?" he asked.

"Yes."

211

"Sociopath," Alabrandi repeated as he wrote the word in his note-book. Then he looked up, his dark eyes quite intense now, so that I'd felt rather like a small animal caught in the crosshairs of a very powerful rifle.

"You knew about the argument, didn't you?" I asked him.

Alabrandi said nothing, and since at that early date I hadn't yet begun to have doubts about Alexandria, I suspected that he'd probably heard about it from Edith Whittier, our next-door neighbor, a woman divorced so early and for so long her life seemed spinsterish. It couldn't have been Carl, because he'd taken his son on a camping trip that week. None of the other houses was close enough for the people living in them to have heard voices coming from inside 237 Crescent Road. It had to have been Edith, I thought as Alabrandi wrote something else in his notebook. Even so it wasn't until I'd later seen her name on the prosecution witness list that my fears were confirmed. At the time, however, I'd surmised that if Edith had heard voices, then she'd probably heard the crash of that white porcelain cup.

"Sandrine threw a cup at me," I told Alabrandi in order to give the impression that I wasn't trying to hide anything.

The smooth movement of Alabrandi's pen stopped abruptly as he glanced up from his notebook.

"As I was leaving," I added. "She threw it at me as I was leaving. It crashed against the door. It broke into lots of pieces."

"None of the officers reported seeing a broken cup," Alabrandi said pointedly.

"That's because I cleaned it up," I told him.

"When?"

"Before anyone got there."

Alabrandi made a note of this. "Where are those pieces?" he asked.

"I threw them in the garbage, and a couple of days ago the garbage people picked it up. I suppose they're in the town dump somewhere."

Detective Alabrandi didn't appear particularly disturbed by any of this.

"You were alone in the house during this argument?" he asked. "Except for your wife, I mean."

"Yes," I answered. "Our daughter had gone out for some reason. Shopping for something, I don't remember what. She got back a few minutes before I left. She was packing her things because she was going back to Atlanta that night."

"When did you leave for your class?"

"A few minutes after Alexandria got back from whatever she'd been doing," I answered. "I went into the scriptorium and—"

"Scriptorium?"

I shuddered at how pretentious Alabrandi must take this Latinate, but I'd said it, and as Morty had later pointed out you can't unring a bell. "That little room with the books and our laptops."

Alabrandi said nothing.

"Anyway, I went there and read for a while," I told him. "I guess I was trying to calm down. Then Alexandria arrived, and we spoke briefly, and then I left for my classes."

This, too, went into Alabrandi's notebook, the same one to which he now resorted in answer to Mr. Singleton's question.

"Now, Detective Alabrandi, at that point, you had the autopsy results on Mrs. Madison, correct?" Mr. Singleton asked him.

"Yes," Alabrandi answered.

"And it was during this conversation that you revealed an important finding in the autopsy report, correct?"

"I did, yes."

As Alabrandi continued, I saw myself once again in the living room, slumped in one of its motley chairs, watching as the good detective drew a few pages of neatly folded paper from his jacket pocket.

"The autopsy report," he said as he offered it to me.

I didn't take it. "You obviously have something you want to tell me about it," I said, almost impatiently, as if the high drama of all this struck me as silly, a small town cop trying to act like some big screen cop he'd seen in the movies.

It was an attitude Sandrine no doubt would have expected me to exhibit, I thought now, as Mr. Singleton handed Detective Alabrandi those same pages, and which I knew would soon pass into evidence as Exhibit Something. She would have known my tone would seem arrogant to Alabrandi, and that surely he would start to despise me at that moment, if he hadn't already. How well and deeply she had known me, I thought, as Alabrandi glanced solemnly at the copy of Dr. Mortimer's autopsy report Mr. Singleton now handed him.

"At this time did you inform Mr. Madison of the autopsy findings?" Mr. Singleton asked.

"Yes, I did," Alabrandi answered. "I began by indicating the cause of death, the fact that Mrs. Madison had died of an overdose of Demerol mixed with alcohol."

Which is exactly what I'd expected, of course. The surprise was that antihistamines had been added to the mix.

"Do you recall your wife taking antihistamines?" Alabrandi asked.

"No."

"In some instances, they're used to prevent vomiting," Alabrandi added. "This may have been the case here."

"Well, Sandrine probably wanted to do it right," I said.

"Someone did, yes," Alabrandi added casually, with no more emphasis than he might have used to read the ingredients on a label.

Alabrandi slowly leaned forward, a movement that seemed calculated so that I'd abruptly felt like a diver deep in murky water who suddenly intuits the presence of a shark.

"Mr. Madison, when I was here last time, I asked if you knew a man named Malcolm Esterman. You said you did and that he was a colleague at Coburn College."

I nodded.

There was a long pause before Alabrandi said, "Are you aware that Mr. Esterman was the last person to see your wife alive?"

"Malcolm?" I blurted, and actually laughed at the absurdity of such a thing. "Malcolm Esterman? Why would . . ." I stopped because the look in Alabrandi's eyes was a stone wall.

"But Malcolm Esterman is just a . . ." I began, then stopped again.

"A what?" Alabrandi asked.

Because nothing else came to mind I said, "Just an associate professor, just a . . ." I stopped a third time, gathered my thoughts, then said, "How do you know this?"

"Mr. Esterman has confirmed that Mrs. Madison came to his house at just after six on the evening of November 14, which was the night she died."

I could more easily have believed Sandrine, my atheist wife, would have gone to a parish priest. So why, on the last night of her life, would she have driven to Malcolm Esterman's decidedly beige condominium?

I began to stumble. "But what . . . why . . . what would she . . ."

Alabrandi nodded toward the autopsy report. "Page four," he said.

I turned to the page, then read the one salient detail that froze my heart.

"A pale circular band is noted around the lower quadrant of the ring finger of the left hand," I read.

"Did Mrs. Madison wear a wedding ring?" Alabrandi asked.

"Yes," I said.

"When did you last see it?"

215

"I don't remember," I said, "but what does it have to do with Malcolm Esterman?"

Alabrandi took the autopsy report from me. "Mr. Esterman voluntarily came into headquarters three days after your wife died. He'd come to the conclusion that given the circumstances of her death there would no doubt be an investigation, and he thought we needed to know that he'd had a relationship with Mrs. Madison."

"A relationship," I whispered, and felt the sun and moon and all the stars fall upon me. "With Sandrine?"

At that moment, sitting in my living room, facing Alabrandi, I'd felt only the surreal nature of this revelation. Sandrine with this froggish little man who lived in a condominium that looked as if it had been built entirely from scavenged materials? Associate professor Malcolm Esterman, who taught mostly freshmen classes to Coburn's generally mindless students? I'd no way of putting this latest bombshell into perspective or any means of locating it within the fabric not only of our marriage but of everything I had ever thought about Sandrine. Still, it was then it had occurred to me that Sandrine, by some means, must have found out about April Blankenship, and thus, in a state of utter upheaval after our argument, had gone to poor, chalk-covered Malcolm and there, in a seizure of loathing and bent upon the only revenge she'd thought possible, had clamped her eyes shut and pinched her nose and clenched her teeth and done anything else she had to do to drive back her repugnance and, in that posture of revulsion, had "relations" with him.

Fatally, before I could stop myself, and with the chest-thumping bellow of a wounded primate, I blurted, "Yes, of course. To get even with me."

Alabrandi's body tensed but his voice was cool and measured. "Get even with you for what, Mr. Madison?"

216

And I thought, My God, he knows that, too, and like a soul poised on the rim of hell I hesitated, then stepped over the edge. "For what I did. For my affair."

"You had an affair?" Alabrandi asked.

"Yes."

"Did Mrs. Madison know about it?"

"I guess she must have."

"Why do say that?"

"Because of what Malcolm Esterman told you," I said. "Why would Sandrine have had a *relationship* with him except to get even with me?"

"I didn't say that Mr. Esterman's relationship with your wife was sexual," Alabrandi said.

And, of course, that was true.

Lamely, I asked, "Was it?"

"No," Alabrandi answered. "According to Mr. Esterman they had a close friendship. That's why she called on him the night of her death. She was upset, he said."

"With me?" I asked. "And so she pulled off her wedding ring and left it with Malcolm Esterman? Is that what he told you?"

Alabrandi nodded. "Mr. Esterman says that he had intended to return it to her but he never got the chance."

"I see." I drew in a deep, troubled breath and tried to regain some sense of composure. "Okay, well, let's leave it at that."

Alabrandi's face hardened. "I'm afraid I can't do that, Mr. Madison." His pen leaped to attention. "Who's the woman?"

"What woman?" I asked as if I'd entirely forgotten my blurted admission.

"Please," Alabrandi said quietly. "Just give me her name."

"I'd rather not do that," I told him.

217

Something went full metal jacket in Alabrandi's eyes, and I could see the formidable army CID man behind his polite manner. "This is a murder investigation, Mr. Madison."

"Murder?" I breathed. "Sandrine wasn't murdered. Sandrine . . ." I stopped dead. "And I'm the prime suspect, of course."

"Who was the woman, Mr. Madison?" Alabrandi repeated firmly.

I felt the floor give way beneath me, a sense of falling through space. "But she had nothing to do with—"

"Who?" Alabrandi demanded in a voice as hard as a pistol shot.

I had made only one promise to April, that under no conditions would I let pass a word of our relationship to anyone. I had sworn this secrecy again and again, but at that moment, observing the way Alabrandi remained silent, simply staring, waiting, I conveniently convinced myself that surely he must already know what I then told him.

"April Blankenship," I said.

Out-of-Body Experience

While Detective Alabrandi continued to relate all the further details of our fifth interview, I had what amounted to an out-of-body experience. Alabrandi had said April's full name in open court, even adding her middle name, which is Bernice, and I'd glanced over to see that name recorded by the court stenographer, then to my right, where several local, three regional, and two national reporters were scratching it into their notebooks, and then to the various audiotaping devices that were recording it and finally to the room's four surveillance cameras, each of which was dutifully doing the same. It was as if her name—April Bernice Blankenship—were echoing through all the hills and valleys of the republic, heard in shopping malls and elevators, in dance clubs and medical waiting rooms and sport stadiums, a name carried on quivering sound waves down hospital corridors and into the vast reaches of countless international airports: APRIL BERNICE BLANKENSHIP.

That pitiful little whore.

"That's what they'll call me, Sam," she'd said to me at the end of our final, dreary tryst, "if anyone found out."

"No one will," I told her, then glanced toward the deathly gray curtains that hung from the window of the spare little room. How in the world, I asked myself, had I come to be in such a tawdry place?

"They can't, Sam, ever." Her eyes filled with puppy dog supplication. "It would kill Clayton if he found out. And he's been good to me. He's always been kind. I shouldn't have done this. I don't know why I did it. But, Sam if he ever . . . I just couldn't, you know, live."

She'd gone on and on like that for another couple of minutes, a voice that grew more desperate and despairing as I put on first my pants, then my shirt, then my shoes. On that last day I'd even worn a tie, which I'd finished tying when her voice, small, incessant, pleading, had finally, mercifully stopped.

I drew her into my arms. She felt like a sack of sticks. "No one will ever know, April," I assured her. "I promise you that no one will ever know." I smiled. "I have a lot to lose, too, you know."

She nodded. "I guess it'll be okay then," she said weakly.

I started to kiss her on the mouth, then thought it a bad idea, and so darted to the right and gave her what amounted to little more than a peck on the cheek. "Trust me. It's all okay."

We'd mutually decided to end it that very afternoon. It had always felt makeshift and contrived, our affair, two people who should have passed in the night but who somehow had gotten hooked on to each other instead. We'd been like two pieces of lint that had randomly joined as each swirled in the summer air. We'd become attached in a momentary lapse from the usual routine, so my later analysis had run, and for that reason had ended up in bed as randomly as a couple of disconnected bits of paper might meet in the same swirling drain.

But I had to admit that I'd enjoyed the sheer conspiratorial nature of the thing, at least at the beginning. I'd rather shamelessly relished the clandestine drive to a neighboring town, waiting for April in a down-market motel room, one that had actually had a pink neon sign. In fact, it had probably been the back alley nature of the activity I'd most enjoyed about our rendezvous, the noir fiction shadowiness of it all. With April

I could play the leading man, something that had been impossible with Sandrine. In the tiny solar system of my life, beautiful, brilliant Sandrine had always been a planet in orbit alongside me, while poor, drab, abysmally needy April, however briefly, had quite comfortably assumed the lowly position of a circling moon.

April, however, had never been entirely comfortable with our affair. She had never cheated on Clayton, and she never managed to be very good at it. A gray-eyed dread hung from her like ragged clothes, and most of the time she'd been frozen by the fear of anyone finding out about us. She'd all her life been a "good girl," she said, and there were times when she expressed an almost deer-in-the-headlights wonder at finding herself in bed with a man other than Clayton. He'd been twenty years her senior and had early run out of steam, but it wasn't sex April craved; it was that old black magic love.

"I wanted to love you and maybe that you would love me back, too," she told me during the final forlorn minutes of our last drizzly afternoon at the all too aptly named Shady Arms motel. "But some things are just dreams, and if you try to make them real it doesn't work, like in movies it always does, and so they turn on you and go bad."

There is a vulnerability about the unintelligent, and April, more than anything, gave off the raw bafflement of the deeply inarticulate. As a woman she'd had little to offer but loyalty, and by being with me she'd failed even at that. In the end, it was this failure that had hurt her more, in fact far more, than our failed affair. In betraying Clayton, she had betrayed herself, as she'd made clear in the one good line I ever heard her say, and which she'd uttered on my front porch the night she came to beg me to keep quiet: I killed the little angel in me, Sam.

By then she'd heard of Sandrine's death, and the nasty fearmonger in her soul had been busy whispering all kinds of dire warnings, how there'd probably be a police investigation, that in such cases the husband is always the first to be suspected, that the authorities were bound to be looking into any motive I might have had for killing Sandrine, she, herself, being the most obvious one.

Still very much out of body, I now recalled April's face in the yellow light of the alleyway where she'd asked that I meet her, our two cars parked in a remote corner, shielded from the roadway by an enormous green Dumpster. She'd come to my car, looking thin and all but featureless, everything girlishly small, her eyes, nose, mouth, a little doll's face, though now a very frightened doll.

"What are you going to do?" she asked.

"Nothing," I said.

"I mean about us?"

"There is no 'us,' April," I reminded her. "In a way, there never was."

"But they might ask," she protested. "What if they ask you, Sam?"

"Ask me what?"

"About us?"

I moved to put my hands on her small rounded shoulders but stopped myself in time.

"Why would they ask about anything like that?" I said. "Look, April, the facts are these. Sandrine was going to die. She'd been diagnosed weeks before. She didn't want to face that kind of death." I shrugged. "It's an open-and-shut case of suicide. Nobody is going to ask me anything."

"But the paper said there was an investigation and that—"

"The cops here in Coburn are just stirring up headlines," I interrupted. "They enjoy seeing their names in the paper. That's all this is, a trumped-up investigation they'll abandon at some point. Even so, it's just routine in a suicide."

She stared at me pleadingly. "She didn't know about us, did she? Sandrine?"

"Of course not."

"I mean, she didn't . . . it wasn't . . ."

"It had nothing to do with you, April."

She glanced about, as if looking for eyes in the darkness. "I wouldn't have called you or come here but I'm so scared, Sam. I feel like it's part of a plan, you know? God's plan. Punishment, I mean."

"April, please, just go home and stop thinking about this."

"But I'm so scared."

"I know you are, but you don't need to be."

"You really don't think they're going to be asking questions about . . ." She stopped because I'd already denied the reality of "us."

"Don't worry," I said. "I have all the answers I'll ever need to get them off my back."

She glanced left and right again, as if certain she were being watched.

"I just wanted to give you my condolences," she said. "That's what you can say if someone sees us here."

"No one will see us here."

"But that's what we could say if someone did."

"Okay, sure, but I won't have to say anything, April," I assured her. "You played no part in this, and there's no reason you'll be dragged into it." I smiled quite confidently. "Don't lose any sleep over this," I told her. "Believe me, your name will never come up." I put my hand on my heart. "I give you my word. I will never say your name."

But I had given April's name, of course, and it was still ringing through the courtroom when I returned to my body.

"So Professor Madison acknowledged that he'd been unfaithful to his wife with April Blankenship, correct?" Mr. Singleton asked.

"Yes," Detective Alabrandi answered. "He said that he had carried on an affair with Mrs. Blankenship. It had lasted only a few weeks, he said, and it had ended three months before he'd learned of his wife's illness."

223

"Did you ask Professor Madison if his wife was aware of this adulterous affair with April Blankenship?"

"He said that she was not."

Had she been aware of it, I asked myself now, only half listening as Detective Alabrandi continued his testimony, whose exact content I was already well acquainted with. Was it possible at some point that Sandrine had learned about April and me? Had Clayton somehow found out and, in a seizure of anger or pain, confided April's betrayal to his best friend at Coburn College, none other than tweedy little Malcolm Esterman?

I glanced back toward the rear of the courtroom, where Malcolm sat on the back row, in his, yes, tweed jacket, staring through the bottle-bottom thickness of his hornrimmed glasses. He'd always seemed quite humble, a modest man, as Churchill once famously quipped of a political opponent, with much to be modest about. He was just the sort of man, self-effacing and seemingly without envy, to whom Clayton Blankenship might have gone in search of whatever a man seeks in the aftermath of such betrayal. But who would have told Clayton in the first place? Certainly not April. And if April had not told Clayton, then he could not have told Malcolm, and Malcolm could not have told Sandrine.

So if Sandrine had actually known about April and me, how had she known? Or had anyone told her at all? For this was Sandrine, I reminded myself, who could look through walls.

Again I went out of my body, and at the end of that unexpected journey I found myself at a faculty gathering not long after Sandrine had first learned of her illness. It had been one of those end of the academic year parties, held on the lawn of the president's house, everyone choosing between white and red wine and dining on pig-in-a-poke canapés carried on faux silver trays by mostly black servers dressed, for all the world, like plantation-era house slaves.

The president had thanked us for another splendid year, praised our excellence and commitment to the "life of the mind," then released us to wander about the grounds, forming circles of conversation. Sandrine and I had often hung pretty close together during such affairs, but on that afternoon she'd broken away, and I'd ended up alone, leaning against one of the ground's great oaks, sipping wine and nibbling at a miniature crab cake but otherwise unengaged.

It was then I'd caught April in my sight, wearing a pale blue dress that made her look almost transparent. She'd had her doll-sized hand tucked in poor, frail Clayton's crooked arm and in that pose she looked more like his nurse than his wife. For a time, they strolled haltingly among the faculty, then, rather abruptly, she was with them, my tall, elegant, porcelain-white and raven-haired Sandrine.

For a moment, I'd thought it better to keep clear, but as I watched, April had looked increasingly ill at ease, and so, by way of keeping the lid on that particular pot, I strolled over and joined them.

"Are you folks enjoying this little soiree?" I asked.

Clayton nodded. "It's always a pleasure to talk to your lovely wife, Sam," he said, the very picture of old southern charm. "You know April, of course."

"Yes, hi," I said to her. "You're not drinking. May I get you a glass?"

She shook her head but said nothing, which was not unusual for shy, birdlike April, and so I'd turned back to Clayton. "Well, I presume you had a successful academic year."

Clayton smiled, and I noticed that his teeth were quite yellow, stained by years of pipe smoking. Suddenly, I felt myself repulsed by the notion that April's pink little tongue had no doubt found itself in that repellant mouth. The thought had come to me so quickly and I'd been so unprepared for it that for an unguarded instant I must have gotten lost in the sheer horror of it, and as she and Clayton broke away I looked

225

at my little parakeet of a paramour with some impossible mixture of pity and revulsion.

I caught myself immediately, but in the way of such glances something of my true feeling was revealed, and to which April's glance responded in kind.

"April is an odd little thing," Sandrine said once Clayton and April were out of earshot.

I quickly took a sip from my glass. "She reminds me of that line of Eliot's."

"Which one is that?"

"The one about people who must prepare a face to meet the faces they meet."

Sandrine's smile was bright enough, but I sensed a certain gloom coming from her. "As do I," she said.

At the time I'd thought the shadowy darkness of this remark had had to do with her diagnosis, the death that was coming for her, and which even as it came would strip her of all her powers. She was having to prepare a face to meet the faces that would pity her once they learned the news. But now I was not so sure it was her illness that had generated her response to my Eliot reference. Perhaps, in that quick exchange of looks between April and me, she'd seen something that had forced her into a yet deeper deception, a villainous tale whose arch villain was me.

We'd stayed at the party awhile longer, then headed home, Sandrine quite pensive as she sat, watching the town go by with the sort of look one sees in very young children, as if seeing something for the first time.

"What are you thinking about?" I asked.

"How lovely it is," she answered. "Pull over."

I did as she asked. We'd gone almost to the far end of the town, where there was a little park. There were swings and monkey bars and whirligigs, but Sandrine's attention was on the shaded area at the near end of the park, where a group of teenagers had gathered.

"Remember Palermo?" she asked.

"What about it?"

"That area where the streets came together," she said.

"Four Corners."

"They were dancing that day," she continued quietly. "Those young people. The girls were in long pleated skirts, and as they danced they kicked very high, and their skirts hung down from their legs like fans."

I could find nothing to say and so I kept quiet. So did Sandrine, and for a while we sat in silence. Then she said, "Do you think it'll be this way from now on, Sam, that all my memories—no matter how sweet or beautiful—that all my memories will be heartbreaking?"

"I don't know," I answered. "I hope not."

This was, God knows, an inadequate answer, but I could find nothing better to say, and so I simply watched as Sandrine held her gaze on a group of young people who seemed quite uninspiring to me, local kids who'd eventually end up in my freshmen English class, where I'd have to remind them—repeatedly and futilely, of course—that "unique" cannot take an adjective.

"You know, Sam, the trouble with not living in the shadow of death," Sandrine said after a moment, "is that you don't notice how beautiful things are."

When I said nothing in response to this, she drew in a long breath, then released it slowly. "I've become a cliché, haven't I? The dying woman who mouths nothing but bromides."

Again, I said nothing, for it seemed to me that what she'd said was, indeed, something of a bromide, and so we sat in silence for a bit longer before Sandrine spoke again.

227

"You should get yourself another woman, Sam," she said. "After I'm gone. But not someone like me. Someone who'll make you feel important." Now her gaze slid over to me. "Someone like . . . April Blankenship."

I'd laughed out loud at this, because at the time I'd seen not a hint of incendiary sparkle in Sandrine's eyes. But was that only because I'd refused to see it, refused even to address the idea that she might have caught the look April and I had inadvertently exchanged an hour before, seen it and read it and gotten it right? Had that been the moment when I should have known that Sandrine would not go quietly to her grave, but that from then on she would begin to construct a plot whose intricate design was meant to pull me in after her?

We'd later driven in silence the rest of the way home. A pall had fallen over Sandrine. She was deep in thought, perhaps more deeply in thought than I had ever seen her. Once out of the car, she walked directly to the scriptorium, retrieved her Nano, and from there headed into the sunroom, where she put the earbuds in, leaned back in her chair, and closed her eyes.

I'd felt it best to leave her to herself for a time, but as the hours passed and night fell and she now sat in the total darkness of that no longer sunny room, I had at last made my way out to her. She stirred briefly as I entered, so I knew she'd heard me. Even so, she kept her eyes closed and the earbuds in place, waiting, I suppose, for the current song to end, and only then at last acknowledging that I was in the room.

"Sam," she said quietly.

"Yes."

Her eyes remained closed but she plucked the earbuds out and let them dangle from her long white fingers for a moment before dropping them into her lap.

"I've made a decision," she said.

"About what?"

"I don't want to wait for it," she said. "Death. I don't want to go through all those terrible stages." Her eyes opened slowly. "You understand? I want to be in control."

At the time, this had sounded entirely at one with her character, and so I made no argument against whatever decision she had made, or was in the process of making.

"Demerol," she added quite casually, as if it were merely a final item added to a grocery list. "Tell Dr. Ortins that I've fallen and hurt my back. She'll prescribe all I need."

I nodded. "Okay," I said softly.

The smile that struggled onto her lips was the saddest I had ever seen. "In the meantime," she added, "just keep doing what you've been doing, Sam."

"Been doing?" I asked cautiously.

Her smile seemed uneasily balanced, like a figure on a wire. "There'll be plenty of time for your life to change."

Judge Rutledge's gavel hammered me back to the present. I looked at the clock. My God, had so much time passed? On the stand Detective Alabrandi was gathering up his papers while Mr. Singleton turned and headed toward his chair. I looked at Morty, who was putting papers in his briefcase. When he'd packed the last of them, he glanced at me. "Okay, well, we got through some major testimony, buddy," he said. He smiled. "Have a nice weekend, Sam."

Weekend Recess

On Saturday morning, I woke up to a house whose emptiness now seemed quite familiar. Alexandria had driven me home at the end of Friday's session, then rather diplomatically she'd suggested we spend some time apart. Besides, she had a few things she had to catch up on in Atlanta, she said, although she assured me that she'd be back in Coburn in time to accompany me to the courthouse on Monday morning, when my trial was set to resume at nine a.m.

As I made my way to the kitchen to make my morning coffee, it struck me as quite strange, and very alarming, that with Alexandria gone Sandrine returned to me ever more emphatically, my mind continually calling her to the witness stand, demanding her testimony. It was as if I hungered for her accusations, deeply, deeply wished to know what she had actually thought of me.

In such a frame of mind it didn't surprise me that everywhere I looked she was there, a multitudinous ghost, her shape materializing in a chair or leaning against a bookshelf or sitting in the scriptorium as I passed it. Had I not closed that door? Probably not, but I'd begun to fall into that uncertain frame of mind where the trusted solidities of life had grown porous, the verities cracked, nothing any longer beyond the realm of possibility. Shakespeare had been right, there were, indeed, phantoms more real than their previously corporeal forms.

I made coffee but had no stomach for anything else. I felt myself growing thinner by the hour, layers of me falling away like peeling paint.

I'd never expected to be lonely but, even more certainly, I'd never expected to miss my colleagues at Coburn College. And yet, as I discovered that morning, I did miss them. How very odd and unpredictable, I thought, especially given the fact that I'd endlessly scoffed at my fellow professors. I always thought them a mediocre gaggle of academics waylaid in an inconsequential terminus at the end of the academic line. Sandrine had brought this up during that last, brutal fight. She said to me, You have always believed that you deserved better than Coburn College, Sam.

When I facetiously asked her what esteemed educational institution could possibly be better than infinitely distinguished Coburn, she'd waved her hand dismissingly then added rather cryptically, One day, you'll know.

One day I'll know.

I pondered her words as I sipped my morning coffee, parsing them for every hint of threat, studying and restudying each intonation in Sandrine's voice. Was it possible that by the time we'd engaged in that cruel battle she'd already carefully built my staircase to the gallows, this final explosion merely the last bit of business in a plot she had premeditated weeks or even months before?

I shook my head at how terrible it was, my fear that she had done just that. And if she had, it could be for only one reason: she had come to despise me, to loathe me, to hold me in utter contempt. Before finally hurling that porcelain cup, she'd accused me of every imaginable crime save the one that surely had topped them all, those ludicrous trysts with April.

But did this prove that Sandrine had never learned of my affair, or had leaving it out been part of her plan? It was a question I couldn't get

231

out of my mind, a question that was like a needle in my brain, always pressing deeper, so that finally I grabbed the phone and dialed Morty's number.

"Morty, I need to know something," I said tensely.

"Who is this?"

Morty's voice was full of sleep, which caused me to glance at the kitchen clock. Jesus, it wasn't even six o'clock.

"Oh, sorry, Morty," I said apologetically. "I thought it was later. I've been up since—"

"What do you want, Sam?"

"Well, like I said, I need to know something," I told him. "It's about Sandrine. I need to know if you ever got any hint that she might have known about April."

"You said you never told her," Morty reminded me.

"I didn't," I said. "But maybe someone else did."

Morty released a heavy breath, and I could imagine him still in bed, Rachel staring at him quizzically, wondering what in hell was going on, I no longer a harmless egghead but a deranged fruitcake who'd roused her husband from a warm bed, invaded their placid weekend, and imposed upon their private time. In my mind, I saw her shake her head and hiss, Jesus Christ! as she turned back to her pillow.

"I'm sorry, Morty," I said softly in the wake of that image. "I was just thinking about something, that's all, and so—"

"Look, Sam," Morty interrupted, a lawyer no doubt accustomed to clients afflicted with severe mental shifts. "You need to relax. That's what the weekend is for. You don't need to be wandering the house at the crack of dawn, okay?"

"Yes," I muttered and glanced outside to see that in fact the first morning light had just broken. "I'm really sorry, Morty."

"If you've come up with something new to add to the case," Morty said, "something relevant, I mean, then let's talk about it on Monday."

"Okay," I said, "Okay, Morty. Sorry to wake you. I just . . . anyway . . . my best to Rachel."

"Sure, Sam. You bet."

There was another heavy breath, and then I heard the click of the phone as Morty hung up.

It was just a click, but there was finality to it, so that for the first time during my trial I felt completely and irrevocably cut off.

I glanced about the empty kitchen, the empty yard, the empty corridor that led to the empty scriptorium and, beyond it, to my empty bed. But the greater emptiness was the terrible dread I felt at the awful possibility that Sandrine had found out about April, and that it was this and this alone that had fueled her final attack, as it might also have darkly inspired a plot to destroy me, an intrigue about which, as I had to admit, I had scant evidence but which I simply could not entirely dismiss from my mind.

But if Sandrine had learned about the bleak carryings-on at the Shady Arms, how had she learned of them? I felt certain that April had never breathed a word of it to anyone. True, as I'd earlier surmised, Sandrine might have figured it out for herself. But, even so, she would have lacked any real evidence, and would she have so meticulously plotted my destruction based solely on conjecture? I didn't think so. Sandrine, being Sandrine, would have sought evidence, that is to say, well, witnesses.

If she'd wished to confirm her darkest suspicions, to whom would she have gone? Certainly not April. But, if not April, who?

Ah, yes, I thought as I offered the only answer possible to that question, April's cuckold husband, Clayton.

233

It took me several hours to make up my mind, but in the end I decided that I had to know. Morty had previously informed me that April was no longer living with Clayton, though I had no idea whether he'd cast her out or whether she'd hung her head in shame, packed her bags, then left her husband's elegant old plantation house of her own accord. Either way, it was only Clayton I would have to confront, which seemed to me at that despairing moment the first small blessing in the long train of curses that had showered down upon my life.

The drive to Clayton's house took me back through town. It was a crisp, clear Saturday morning, and the streets were quite animated, whole families going in and out of Main Street's quaint shops. I'd rarely ventured downtown during the weekend, primarily for fear of running into someone I knew from the college, thus to be buttonholed into an inane conversation having to do with the fate of this student or that one or whether faculty pensions might be at risk to some Georgia version of Bernard Madoff.

But now, isolated as I was, I found myself quite envious of my fellow Coburnites. They could move among themselves in the easy manner of equal citizens. It would, indeed, be rather pleasant, I thought, to be regarded simply as a man who had not first betrayed then later killed his wife, a teacher, a helpful friend and colleague, a man who, above all else, was quietly and irreducibly . . . kind.

The word had come to me in Sandrine's voice, and so I felt it as an accusation, and in response to which my foot pressed down on the accelerator and the car bolted forward. Seconds later I was out of Coburn and hurtling at a dangerous speed through the green valley that led to Clayton Blankenship's picture-postcard antebellum manse.

Clayton, himself, could not have looked more surprised to find me at his door, but rather than a sudden burst of ire his eyes gave off a great weariness, and he seemed to me withered less by what April and I had done to him than by the dirty, cruel, bottom-feeding nature of life itself.

It was a look of nearly transcendental disappointment. He'd suffered a blow to the hopeful view of things he'd always maintained, as it were, against the odds, but which he no longer felt with regard to anything. The rug had been jerked from beneath his feet, and below that a trap door had opened, and he seemed, as he stared at me silently, still to be falling through black, starless space.

Facing him, all I could muster was something utterly inadequate to the destruction I'd wrought.

"I'm sorry, Clayton."

He nodded. "You probably are, Sam," he said.

"I know it doesn't matter but—"

He lifted his hand to silence me. "I have a chill. Come in."

With that Clayton eased back into the foyer and motioned me inside.

I'd never been in Clayton's house, and upon entering it my initial feeling was that I'd gone through one of time's secret portals. This was a house from the storied past, the house in which the young Clayton had once laughed and frolicked, himself perhaps a Deep South, *Gone with the Wind* version of Andy Hardy. It gave off the sort of mustiness that no amount of airing could dissipate because the air itself was seeded with the microscopic accumulation of generations of dead skin. More than anything it looked like a many-roomed coffin, draped with thick folds of curtain, its floors covered with carpets no less thick, its chairs thickly upholstered, and its tables, even the small ones, thick-legged and heavy. How light April must have seemed to the current owner of this ancestral home, how airily she must have floated through its undertow of rooms, and how, in the wake of her leaving, must the weight of everything within them now seem doubled.

"I know this must seem very strange to you, Clayton," I began once we'd taken our seats in what surely had to be called—and with a straight face—the parlor.

Clayton fingered the doilies draped over the arms of his chair. "I assume you have a reason," he said in a voice that was so gentle, so devoid of acrimony, that I found myself wondering why in the name of heaven April would have endangered her life with a man like Clayton in order to waste a moment in time with me.

"A selfish one, I'm afraid," I admitted. "A very selfish one, given the circumstances." I glanced about. There were potted plants everywhere, and in the far corner a large birdcage held two yellow and one light blue parakeets. The leaves of the plants glistened with health and the birds hopped quite happily about. In the midst of his devastation, I thought, Clayton has watered his plants and fed his birds and carried out every duty upon which some other creature's well-being depends.

"I'm embarrassed to be here," I told him. "I'm humiliated, actually. But there's something I need to know, and I have to ask you about it."

Clayton leaned forward and massaged the ache out of a bony knee.

"It's about . . . what happened," I continued cautiously, "between April and me."

Clayton eased back and the chair itself seemed to wrap its ancient arms protectively around him. It was as if he had cared for it down through the years, resisted every impulse to toss it out because it had grown old or gotten worn, lost its attractiveness, and now, in his time of need, it was repaying him for his long loyalty.

"What I need to know, Clayton," I said, "is whether Sandrine might have found out about . . ." I stopped because I couldn't bear any of the words that came to me. Instead I started again. "I know that April would never have said anything but, well, I was wondering if maybe you found out about it by some other means, some other person and then—believe me, I would understand it—if maybe you told Sandrine."

Clayton shook his head. "I would never have done that," he said. "I liked Sandrine very much. And I respected her. She was a wonderful teacher."

He shrugged, and one of his hands moved over to comfort the other. "But as far as . . . this other matter . . . I didn't know about it until later."

"Later?"

"The later revelations," Clayton said in the gently euphemistic way his great-grandfather might have called the Civil War the "late unpleasantness." "In the newspaper." He shrugged. "Even so, I didn't want April to leave," he added, "but she wouldn't hear of staying. She wouldn't take a penny either."

"Where is she?"

"Not far, I don't imagine," Clayton answered. "She still has her day in court, after all."

With that quite practical remark I once again recalled the moment I'd said her name to Detective Alabrandi, then later when I'd seen it inscribed on Mr. Singleton's witness list.

"I do wish she would have stayed," Clayton said. "I could have borne the shame more easily than I can bear the loneliness."

Watching him, I found that I could not actually fathom his pain. I could not sound the anguished depths into which April and I had so recklessly sunk his life, and it struck me that this, and this alone, should precede all other calculations, that it should be solely by this grave measure that we choose to do or not to do certain things.

He took a quick breath. "But as to your question, I should emphasize that no, I never told your wife anything because I never knew anything about you and April." He leaned forward and stared at me with great seriousness and sincerety. "But even if I had, I would have kept it to myself, Sam." His smile was as ragged as the flag of some lost cause. "I wouldn't even have told April."

"I believe you," I told him quietly, and since I'd come only to ask this one question, and now had received his answer, I rose slowly, as one in whom a deep weariness had abruptly settled, and stood before him like a disgraced knight before a noble king. "I'm sorry for disturbing you." I drew in a long breath. "I'm sorry for everything, Clayton."

With some difficulty, Clayton got to his feet, rising with so much difficulty, in fact, that I had to suppress the urge to take his arm. April had almost certainly performed this deeply human service, but she was gone now, no doubt eventually to be replaced by a hireling, a man or woman paid to lift him from his chair but who, as he weakened, would be called upon to carry out increasingly more difficult and noisome services, and who would perform all of them well and dutifully, offering him everything he would need at the end of life save love.

He escorted me to the door, then opened it.

A cold breeze swept in and I suddenly feared for the state of Clayton Blankenship's health, the irony of course being that only some years before, when April and I had had our first encounter at the Shady Arms, I'd cared nothing for the state of his soul.

"Again, Clayton," I told him, "I'm sorry to have disturbed you."

Clayton nodded but said nothing.

I started through the door, then stopped and turned back to him. "I have to tell you that I appreciate your kindness. Given the circumstances, I mean."

Clayton's smile appeared to require the last of his physical strength. "My grandfather would have shot you with one of the dueling pistols I still have," he said. Then, like a man who thought another piece of evidence was required to justify what he'd just said, he added, "But I fear I lack the courage required to defend my honor."

I started to apologize again, a gesture Clayton saw and against which, almost as a way of holding himself in check, he softly closed the door.

Sunday. Tomorrow. All Day.

On the way back home from meeting with Clayton, I turned onto Guardian Lane, in an area of Coburn known simply as the Commons. It wasn't by any means a perfect neighborhood, but the simplicity of its homes and yards and streets had appealed to Sandrine. I'd thought it too neat and orderly, however, its homes too evenly disbursed. I'd been young and full of resistance to the regulated, cookie-cutter look of the Commons, how carefully laid out it was. But now it did not strike me as so unappealing. There was a sense of proportion here, I thought, a sense of order, of rules that actually worked. Not perfectly, of course, but to some extent, rules agreed upon and which offered, however flawed in other ways they might be, some vague resistance to the chaotic sprawl into which my own life had descended, mine a desperation far from Thoreau's stoical Concord neighbors, one that had, in the end, become very noisy indeed.

By the time I reached 237 Crescent Road I'd come to feel that my decision to drop in on Clayton Blankenship had been a foolish one, but yet typical of the foolishness into which I'd often fallen since Sandrine's death. I had said foolish things at the beginning of the investigation. I'd assumed a cold perhaps even haughty demeanor from my encounter with Officer Hill onward, thus behaving in a way that had prejudiced just about everyone against me. I had needed correction but the only one who might have provided some corrective word of wisdom was Sandrine, and, as Alexandria had earlier put it with such heartbreaking simplicity, she was gone.

Even so, once back in the house, seated at the kitchen table, yet another cup of coffee growing cold in front of me, I tried to imagine what Sandrine, if she were still alive, would say to me in the present circumstances. Would it be some version of a cruel "I told you so"? Or would she relent, take pity, give me helpful counsel, be more even than a wife, be my best friend? Would she lean forward, take my hand, and say, "All right, Sam. Listen to me now. Because I know a way out of hell."

But what way was there now?

I was still pondering the question the next day when Alexandria returned from Atlanta just as night was falling. Our unpleasant exchange at the courthouse was now a couple of days behind us, and as she chatted dryly about the few things she'd gotten done in Atlanta, mailing manuscripts or dashing off something for sleeplesseye.com, I saw that she did not intend to revisit the dark pit of her own fearful suspicion that Morty and I—two men—were cooking up a plot against her dead mother.

She'd brought fresh flowers and as I watched her arrange them in a vase, her fingers delicately moving this leaf or that petal to just the right position, I recalled that, as a little girl, she'd once expressed an interest in being a florist, a sensible career choice for which I'd offered not a particle of encouragement.

Why had I done that, I wondered now. Had I read, studied, and taught the great authors, the world's great heads, only to lose respect for the work of human hands, lose it despite the beauty and usefulness of the things they made? As a young man, traveling with Sandrine, I'd stood in grateful awe at what those hands had wrought in stone and iron and stained glass. But slowly, over the years, all that had dropped away and left this harder and more intolerant man. Reading books had made the writing of them all that mattered, and because of that I'd given no support to what might have been a perfectly suitable life's work for Alexandria. Was it in order to return her daughter to that earlier more tender ambition that Sandrine had called her "Ali"?

Suddenly Sandrine's voice was in my ear, so close I could almost feel her lips. Albi, she had said, would be the moment she would forever remember. Not Venice where we'd drifted beneath the Bridge of Sighs, or anything we'd done in Paris or Athens or anywhere else on our one great tour. No, Sandrine had said, it would be Albi, where she'd turned to me and said in a tone of sweet surprise, "It's you."

Had this same woman later come to hate and despise me with such consuming passion that in her final days she might well have plotted my destruction?

In silence, as Alexandria completed the perfection of her flowers, I reconsidered all this. Live or die, the poet Anne Sexton had once said, but for God's sake don't poison everything. Then, on the hard edge of that uncompromising declaration, she had put on her mother's fur coat, removed all her jewelry, poured herself a glass of vodka, walked into the garage, and turned on the engine of her car. Perhaps I should do the same, I thought. Perhaps I should accept what I now considered the jury's inevitable verdict and carry out its sentence, thus saving the good people of Coburn any further penalty for the crime of once having welcomed me into their midst.

"There," Alexandria said. She stepped back from her arrangement. "What do you think, Dad?"

"Perfect," I said softly

She scowled, "Yeah, right," she said.

I turned away, as if rebuked, glanced toward the window, and saw Edith Whittier as she made her way to her car.

241

"Edith will probably be at the courthouse early tomorrow," I said dryly. "Eager to drive in another nail."

Alexandria shrugged. "She couldn't have much to say," she said, "She hardly knew you and Mom."

She'd lived next door to us for almost fifteen years, a divorced woman, childless, and probably friendless. She'd retired from the public school system some years before, and after that she'd spent her time beautifying her house. At Christmas the outside of 235 Crescent Road was a carnival of light, and according to Carl, who always walked his son over to see the display, the interior was much the same, with a huge tree weighted down with shiny ornaments. There were various-sized sleighs, as well, all of them filled with brightly wrapped gift boxes and overseen by a multitude of cheerful elves and chuckling Santas. According to Carl, there'd not been a single doorknob that wasn't sheathed in a knitted reindeer head, and everywhere, everywhere this lonely childless woman had put out bowls of candy and cookies and other assorted treats.

Alexandria was right. She'd hardly known Sandrine and me. So how very odd, it seemed to me, that it was Edith Whittier, of all people, who might well have heard the crash of that little cup, heard Sandrine's accusatory cry, she alone whose ears had taken in the violence of that night, and who, as tomorrow's first witness at my trial, was scheduled to tell the world exactly what she'd heard.

The curious thing was that after my talk with Clayton I no longer seemed to care what might be said of me in court, no matter how distorted the evidence might be. His moral weight had fallen upon me like a hammer, and I was now like a turtle whose shell had cracked, its moist pink innards exposed to the blazing light and blistering heat.

"There was a fight, Alexandria," I said suddenly. "Between your mother and me."

"When?"

"You'd gone into town," I told her.

"So it was that last night?"

"Yes," I answered. "And it was loud enough that Edith might have heard it."

"So you were screaming?"

"Your mother was . . . loud," I said. "And she threw a cup at me."

Alexandria stared at me in disbelief.

Because I simply had to know, I asked, "Your mother never told you about any of this?"

Alexandria shook her head. "Was it about April?" she asked.

"No."

"What was it about, then?"

"Me," I answered, which, though inadequate, was true.

I had never revealed the actual nature of Sandrine's last, furious assault, how unprecedented it had been, an attack so furious, her accusations hurled at me with such fierce resolve to wound me, that I'd finally fired back with the darkest and most cruel thing I could possible have said.

"It came out of nowhere," I added. "I mean, she'd been more or less ignoring me for weeks. She didn't want to talk to me, she didn't want me to interrupt her reading, her 'streaming.' I had gotten used to that, but nothing could have prepared me for the way she was that night."

Sandrine had often mentioned the Spartan commander who, when told that the Athenians had so many arrows that when released they would darken the sky, had starkly replied, "Then we will fight in the shade." I had wanted to be like him that night, simply take blow after blow, as it were, stoically, bravely, even nobly, and say nothing. But I had failed even at that.

"It was the cup that did it," I said. "The way she'd thrown that cup and called me a sociopath."

I could see the word sink into Alexandria's mind, though I couldn't tell whether she believed it accurate, her opinion of me as dark and unforgiving as her mother's on the night she died.

One thing was clear, however. Sandrine had told her nothing of this battle, a fact that, as I realized suddenly, had oddly urged me to confess it.

"I was going out the door and she called me by that name," I added. "Even then, I didn't turn back. That's when she threw that cup."

Alexandria's gaze darkened. "What did you do, Dad?"

"I stopped and turned around," I answered. "She was in bed, almost in the dark, with nothing but that candle burning."

Alexandria could see that I was stalling, and so she said again, "What did you do?"

"Nothing," I answered. "I didn't say or do anything. It was something I thought, something I wanted."

"What?"

"As I left the room," I stalled. "Something I wanted."

"What, Dad?"

I stared bleakly into my daughter's eyes. "For your mother to be dead when I got back."

For a moment, Alexandria stared at me in stunned silence. Then quite slowly, and deliberately, she came to her conclusion.

"Mom was right," she said. "You are a sociopath."

I nodded. "Yes," I confessed, "I suppose I am."

On that grave admission, I saw that little white cup shatter into a thousand pieces, heard at full volume Sandrine's gravest of all accusations.

Alexandria's gaze was as stern as her question. "What are you willing to do now, Dad, in order to save yourself?"

In answer I could only shrug, because at that moment I hadn't truly known.

DAY SEVEN

Call Edith Whittier

"Nothing to worry about, Sam," Morty whispered as Edith made her way to the stand.

I was not so sure because I knew just how loud Sandrine's voice had been on that last night of her life, her words exploding like cannon fire in our darkened bedroom. She'd launched all her heavy ordnance, that much I knew. Then, like a warrior who'd run out of ammunition, she'd reached for a figurative stone and cast it toward my retreating back, that porcelain cup and a final word: sociopath.

"I do," Edith said, and she brought down her hand and took her seat and looked at me squarely, as if to say, *Now you'll pay.*

She wore a dark green sweater and black skirt that came just below her knees, attire I would have described as matronly. She looked the part of a retired nanny, everything of a proper length, nothing showy. There had always been a mustiness about Edith, a sense of powders and lotions applied some years after their respective shelf lives had expired, and on this particular day she'd clearly felt no added need to spruce up.

"For the record, could you state your address, Ms. Whittier," Mr. Singleton said.

"It's 235 Crescent Road, Coburn."

"That would be directly next door to 237 Crescent Road, the home of the defendant?"

"Yes."

"How long have you lived at this address?"

"Thirty-seven years."

There followed a brief recitation of biographical details by which Mr. Singleton endeavored, but failed, to give the jury the impression that Edith Whittier had lived something other than a lonely, arid, featureless life at 235 Crescent Road, but which did succeed in moving us forward in time to a date that came quite as a surprise to me since it was many weeks before the turbulent night about which I'd expected her to be questioned.

"So, on August 17, you were tending your tomato plants, is that correct?"

"Yes."

"Now, your garden is separated from the backyard of the defendant by nothing but a small white fence, is that right?"

"Yes."

"You can see the defendant's backyard quite clearly?"

"Yes. They had recently built a gazebo back there. One of those pre-fabricated types you can buy at home improvement stores. Mrs. Madison sometimes went out there and read or listened to music. I guess it was music. She had one of those transistor radio–looking things with the wires that go up to your ears."

"And on this particular day, did you speak to Mrs. Madison?" Singleton asked.

"Yes, I did. She saw me in the garden and she came out of the gazebo and walked over to that little white fence that separates our yards."

"Could you tell the jury the substance of that conversation?" Singleton asked.

"Well, at first it was the usual things you'd expect neighbors to say over the fence. She said my tomatoes looked luscious. That was her word, luscious, and so I picked a few and gave them to her. She said she would put them in a salad."

"Now, once you were past these ordinary sorts of exchanges, did Mrs. Madison then move the conversation to more serious matters?"

"Yes, she did," Edith answered. "She said that she'd gotten some bad news recently. She had Lou Gehrig's disease. She said that in the next months and years, I would be seeing her getting weaker."

"Months and years?"

"That's right," Edith said. "She said she hoped that perhaps I'd drop in from time to time because in the future it was unlikely that she would be going out very much. She said she expected to be lonely, and though she might not be able to respond all that much, she would like to hear my stories."

"Your stories?"

"Whatever I had to tell her," Edith explained. "I guess that's what she meant."

"And did you later have occasion to go over to Mrs. Madison's house?" Singleton asked.

"Yes, I did. I waited a couple of weeks. I didn't see Mrs. Madison out much during that time, so I thought maybe she was going into one of those depressions, you know, and so I thought, well, I'll go over and bring her one of my specialties."

"And which of your specialties did you bring her?" Mr. Singleton asked with a pleasant smile.

"I made a mushroom casserole," Edith answered. "It's got broccoli and cheese and cream of mushroom soup, and I thought Mrs. Madison might like it."

"And so you made this mushroom casserole and you brought it over to Mrs. Madison's house, correct?"

"Yes. I made it in one of those tinfoil-type casserole dishes so she wouldn't have to return it."

"And did you see Mrs. Madison on that occasion?"

"No, I did not."

"She wasn't home?"

"No, she was home," Edith told the jury, "but it was her husband who came to the door."

I had entirely forgotten Edith's visit, so inconsequential it had seemed to me at the time, merely a matter of running defense for Sandrine, making sure that Edith Whittier did not intrude upon her privacy on an afternoon, like so many others during those weeks, when she'd more or less sealed herself up in the scriptorium, quite obviously preferring her music and her books to me.

"And so it was to the defendant that you spoke at that time?" Mr. Singleton asked.

"Yes."

"Can you tell the jury the gist of that conversation?"

She'd appeared quite unexpectedly at the door, steaming casserole beneath a white cloth, smiling a little stiffly but otherwise quite pleasant. It had been around three-thirty in the afternoon, and I'd been about to leave for my afternoon class. My mood had been further complicated by the persistent rain, the unseasonable chill, and finally by the fact that the door to the scriptorium remained closed as part of the wall of isolation Sandrine had erected between us.

Thus, when I opened the door to Edith Whittier it was probably with the strained look on my face she now described to the jury.

"Mr. Madison wasn't very friendly," Edith said. "He never really opened the door very wide. He just stood there and listened. I told him that Mrs. Madison had asked me to drop over. He didn't say anything really except that she was feeling indisposed. Those were his words, that she was 'feeling indisposed.' So I just gave him the casserole and he took it and said thank you and closed the door."

This was true in every detail, but it also struck me as quite irrelevant to anything, so that I glanced quizzically at Morty, who returned the same look to me, neither of us able to comprehend why this testimony had been given.

Then, quite suddenly, Edith's story took a dark turn.

"But you did have occasion to see Mrs. Madison at another time, didn't you?"

"Yes."

"When was this?"

"About three weeks later."

"Can you describe that meeting to the jury?"

She had once again been in her garden, though it was now well past the summer season, the first fall chill in the air. She had not seen Sandrine, save for quick glimpses, since their earlier encounter, but on this particular day Edith had looked up from her autumn gardening to find her standing silently by the fence, her arms folded over her chest, as if to ward off the chill.

"She was wearing an old bathrobe and she looked very sad," Edith told the jury. "Her hair wasn't combed and she just looked bedraggled . . . like a rag doll."

I had never once seen Sandrine look this way, nor could I dream that she would have walked out into the yard in a bathrobe, with her hair in disarray.

"She said hello to me," Edith went on, "and I said hello back. I couldn't think of anything else to say, so I asked her if she'd liked my casserole." She stopped, drew in a quick breath, then added, "Mrs. Madison said, 'What casserole?'" Another quick breath, then, "I told her it was

251

the casserole I'd brought over when I'd dropped by a few weeks before." With this Edith's expression turned grave. "She said she didn't know about anything I'd brought over."

I felt my lips part in sudden grave awareness of what I'd done, which was irritably to have dropped Edith's casserole into the kitchen garbage can.

"She said her husband never told her about any casserole," Edith added. "She said he probably just threw it in the garbage or something."

Sandrine had been right, that was exactly what I had done. A casserole in the garbage, I thought, trying not to glance at the jury, what a telling image to convey my indifference to Sandrine's pleasure, her enjoyment, to the simplest things that might be provided for her.

But it got worse.

"I didn't know what to say at that point," Edith told the jury. "I mean, her husband had . . . well . . . done something with that casserole. Anyway, he hadn't given it to her, so I just didn't know what to say. So I just shrugged my shoulders. Then I changed the subject and I asked how she was doing."

"What did Mrs. Madison say in response to your question?" Mr. Singleton asked.

"She smiled that sad smile and she said, 'I'm dying'."

"Was that all she said, Mrs. Whittier?"

"No," Edith answered.

Ah, here it comes, I thought, the reason Edith has taken the stand, the whole purpose of her testimony.

"No," Edith repeated. "She looked over at her house, and she said it again. She said, 'I'm dying,' and then she looked back at me and she said, 'But not fast enough for Sam.'"

If the door of the scaffold had been located just beneath my feet, I would have felt it open and myself fall through it.

"Thank you, Mrs. Whittier," Mr. Singleton said, then turned to Morty, no doubt trying not to smile, and added, "Your witness, Mr. Salberg."

Morty rose and walked to the lectern.

"Good morning, Mrs. Whittier," he said.

"Good morning," Edith replied rather stiffly.

"So you make mushroom casseroles," Morty said.

"Yes."

Morty's big smile got bigger. "I'll bet those things are quite tasty too."

"People seem to like them," Edith said, no less stiffly than before.

"Tell me, Mrs. Whittier, what are the basic ingredients to your—I believe it was a mushroom casserole?"

Edith offered a suspicious little squint. "That's right."

"All right, and is it a big secret, or could you tell the court the basic ingredients you use to make your mushroom casserole."

"Well, it's mostly broccoli, cheese, and cream of mushroom soup," Edith said. "And there's butter and breadcrumbs."

"Sounds delicious." Morty said brightly, as if he'd detected not the slightest sarcasm in Edith's response. "Now, did I hear you say that one of the ingredients is cream of mushroom soup?"

"Yes," Edith answered.

"Would you say that mushroom is a major ingredient in that soup?"

"Well, yes, I guess it is."

Morty chuckled. "I guess it would have to be seeing that the dish is called a mushroom casserole, right?"

"I guess it would be, yes."

Morty glanced at his notes, then looked up. "Have you ever heard of people being allergic to mushrooms, Mrs. Whittier?"

Edith nodded.

"Okay. Now were you aware of whether or not Mrs. Madison was allergic to mushrooms?"

Edith's face froze. "No, I wasn't aware of it."

"Well, you're aware that an allergic reaction to mushrooms can be life threatening, are you not?"

"I didn't know about life threatening," Edith squirmed.

"Well, if you were married to someone who had this allergy, you'd probably know if it was life threatening or not, wouldn't you?"

"I guess I would," Edith admitted.

"And if someone brought a casserole or anything that contained mushrooms over to your husband—or wife, if you were a man—and you knew that this casserole could be life threatening, you might decide that you didn't want to show this casserole to your wife, right?"

"I might decide that," Edith admitted with studied reluctance.

"Do you think you might get rid of it?" Morty asked. "Because what would be the point of your wife seeing a delicious mushroom casserole if she can't have any, right?"

"I suppose," Edith said.

"You might even throw that casserole in the garbage, isn't that so?"

Edith hesitated, then said, "I guess I might."

Morty nodded. "Thank you, ma'am," he said. "No more questions."

Edith stepped down. I could hardly believe Morty's cross-examination but, even so, I said nothing, and by that means tried to look as unconcerned with Edith's testimony as my lawyer clearly was.

Then, with a crooked, naughty-boy smile, Morty said, "One witness neutralized."

"But Sandrine wasn't allergic to mushrooms or anything else for that matter," I told him.

"I didn't say she was," Morty said.

He now began idly going through some papers.

"Of course you did," I insisted.

"No, I didn't," Morty replied firmly. "I'll show you the transcript. I didn't say one word about Sandrine being allergic to anything." He shrugged. "Look, Singleton could do some digging and try to find out if your wife actually had any allergies. But that would take time, and he could easily come up with nothing. Even if people have allergies they may never mention them to a doctor, right? If mushrooms make you sick, you don't eat mushrooms. End of story. So who would know if your wife had allergies, except you, Sam? And Singleton would never ask you that question on the stand because he figures you'd lie." He chuckled softly. "Life is about keeping hold of the other guy's short hairs," he added. "It's as simple as that."

My God, I thought, Morty's a sociopath too. Are we all sociopaths, I wondered, we men? Does it take a weighty complex of law and custom, one capable of imposing dire consequences for our actions, to stay our conscienceless hands? Is that what is required to keep us from doing what, without fear of such awesome consequence, we would do without a blink?

I released a long, weary sigh. "What do we do now?" I asked.

"We celebrate, because we dodged a bullet," Morty answered happily "Who knew what that old bat might say."

"I don't feel like celebrating, Morty," I said. "And actually, Mrs. Whittier is a pretty nice person."

Morty gave me grave look. "Nice? She would have handed them your balls on a silver platter."

I didn't feel like arguing the point. "So back to my earlier question. What do we do now?"

"Okay, well, in terms of the trial, we'll go on just as we have been," Morty answered. "A couple of more easy witnesses, then Singleton will go in for the kill." He smiled again, but beneath the smile I could see that he was worried. "At that point, you'll need to buckle up, because it's going to be bumpy ride."

255

Call Lydia Wilson

I'd earlier seen Lydia Wilson's name on the witness list, of course, but when Morty asked me who she was I told him the truth and said I didn't know. She was a travel agent, as it turned out, the owner of the only local agency to survive the Internet. From a later glance into the shop window of Armchair Travel, I'd gathered that it was one of those agencies that specialized in tours for the affluent elderly and which sought to make sure that no familiar creature comfort is sacrificed by the voyaging Coburnite just because he or she finds himself in a country with no running water or where the head of the losing candidate in the last election is displayed in the public square.

It was just the sort of travel Sandrine would never have undertaken, a way, as she'd always said, of seeing nothing, feeling nothing, knowing nothing, and yet, according to what Morty had learned from Mr. Singleton, my wife had strolled into the Main Street office of Armchair Travel only two weeks before her death with travel on her mind.

Until a couple of days before, when the searing possibility of Sandrine's plot had hit me, I'd have accounted for this visit by allowing that Sandrine had briefly fallen into a dreamlike unreality. In that soft state of delusion she might understandably have sauntered into Armchair Travel, perhaps drawn by the picture of one of Greece's sunny beaches, a photograph we'd glimpsed many times over the years and which had stood, more or less unchanged, in the agency's window for as long as I could recall. I could imagine that Sandrine, once inside the agency's modest storefront office and still floating in a nostalgic haze, might have mentioned to whomever she found inside that, long ago, when she was young, she'd traveled about the Mediterranean. She might even have said that she'd always hoped to do it again. But no amount of allowance for despair or delusion could account for the conversation to which Mrs. Lydia Wilson now testified under oath.

"Mrs. Madison told me that she had visited many of the countries of the Mediterranean some years ago," Mrs. Wilson told the court. "She had not been married at that time, she said."

In case the jury's attention had waned during the preceding introductory questions and answers, Mr. Singleton made a dramatic couple of steps toward the jury box before turning back to face the witness.

"At this point in your conversation, did Mrs. Madison then begin to talk to you about her husband?"

"Yes, she did."

"In regard to what?"

"In regard to that earlier trip," Mrs. Wilson answered. "The one she'd made around the Mediterranean."

"With the man she would later marry," Mr. Singleton said with a quick glance toward the jury. "The defendant, Samuel Madison."

"Yes," Mrs. Wilson said. "She mentioned their visit to Alexandria, for example."

"Why that city in particular?" Mr. Singleton asked.

"She said her daughter was named for the city, and she talked for a little while about her daughter."

"What did she say?"

"That her daughter was a very kind person," Mrs. Wilson answered. "That she was lucky to have such a daughter. She said that her daughter was very gifted."

"Gifted at what?"

"At being a human being."

When I glanced back, I saw that Alexandria was reacting to this quite emotionally. In response, I gave her a quick, sympathetic smile but she only nodded crisply then returned her attention to the courtroom.

"Did Mrs. Madison mention any other places with regard to her earlier travels?" Mr. Singleton asked.

"She mentioned a town in France," Mrs. Wilson said. "Albi. It's near Toulouse, evidently. She mentioned the cathedral there and that she and her husband had ended their trip in that town. She said that they had been very happy then."

"Happy then?" Mr. Singleton asked pointedly. "As opposed to now?"

Morty lifted his hand. "Objection, Your Honor, calls for a conclusion."

"Sustained," Judge Rutledge said.

"All right," Mr. Singleton said. "Now, at one point, did Mrs. Madison mention any feelings with regard to her own life?"

"Yes," Mrs. Wilson continued. "She mentioned a playwright. He was a Roman playwright, she said. His name was Terence. She said that he had died at twenty-five but that all his work, his plays, had survived. She said she felt lucky in that she had lived longer than Terence, and that she hoped some of her work would also survive."

"Her work?"

"As a teacher and a mother."

"And as a wife?"

"As a wife, she thought she had failed."

"Failed?" Mr. Singleton repeated with emphasis. "In what way?"

258

"She didn't say," Mrs. Wilson answered. "I could see that she was becoming quite upset. She didn't exactly cry but she was on the verge of crying. And so she got off that subject and started talking again about that earlier trip."

"And with regard to that earlier trip, did Mrs. Madison mention one place in particular."

"She mentioned several places."

"But one of those mentions you found somewhat disturbing, isn't that true, Mrs. Wilson?"

"Yes."

"What place was that?"

"Siracusa," Mrs. Wilson answered. "It's in Sicily."

"Why did Mrs. Madison's mention of that place disturb you?"

The witness's eyes cut over to me, then just as quickly away.

"Because Mrs. Madison said that Siracusa was the place where her husband had first threatened to kill her."

"Threatened to kill her . . . the first time," Mr. Singleton said with another dramatic step toward the jury.

"The first time, yes."

"Did Mrs. Madison elaborate on that threat?"

"No, she didn't," Mrs. Wilson answered.

So here it was, I thought, the moment to which Mrs. Wilson's testimony had all along been heading, Samuel Madison a husband who had perhaps many times threatened to kill his wife, Siracusa having been only the "first" time. How could the jury not think that I'd finally decided actually to do it?

Given the impression Mrs. Wilson's testimony had obviously made on the jury, it didn't surprise me that Mr. Singleton found no need to add more.

"No further questions, Your Honor," he said.

Morty rose from his chair, walked to the lectern, smiled amiably at Mrs. Wilson, then said, "During this conversation did Mrs. Madison indicate that she was intending to leave her husband?"

"No."

"Did she indicate that she was having any trouble with her marriage?"

"No."

"Did she indicate that she had an unhappy home?"

"No."

"So you had no reason to fear for Mrs. Madison's safety, did you?"

"No, I did not."

"Mrs. Wilson, are you married?"

"Yes, I am."

"So am I," Morty said with a carefully groomed downhome grin. "But some days I don't exactly get along with my wife. Is that true of you and your husband?"

"Yes, of course."

"Have you ever been really mad at your husband, Mrs. Wilson?"

"It happens."

"So your answer is yes, you have gotten mad at your husband, correct?"

"I have gotten mad at him, yes."

Morty stepped closer to the jury and scanned their faces. "Is it your experience, Mrs. Wilson, that most married people get mad at each other from time to time?"

"Yes."

"And sometimes they say things they don't mean, isn't that true?"

"I suppose they do."

Morty turned slowly toward the witness. "Mrs. Wilson, have you ever thought, when you were mad at your husband, have you ever thought, 'Boy, I could just kill that guy'?"

Briefly, Mrs. Wilson hesitated, but in the end she told the truth. "Yes."

Morty smiled. "Thank you, Mrs. Wilson," he said. "I have no further questions."

As Morty made his way to his seat, I glanced back at Alexandria, found her seat empty, and so looked farther back, toward the rear of the courtroom, my gaze still searching for her, but she was gone.

Losing My Case

We went back into the usual conference room, where I hoped to find Alexandria waiting for me, but she hadn't appeared. For that reason, I went immediately to the window, glanced out into the parking lot, and saw her standing beside our car, her back quite stiff as she leaned against it, her arms folded over her chest.

"I'm losing my case," I said quietly.

"What case?" Morty scoffed. "Singleton has no case and he knows it."

"I mean, with Alexandria," I said.

Morty came over and looked out the window. "She'll get through it," he assured me.

With a gentle movement, he nudged me from the window, then over to the table, where we took our seats, facing each other like two poker players who were still unsure of each other's games.

"Well, I don't think the little heart-to-heart your wife had with Mrs. Wilson was all that incriminating," he said. "But what the hell could have been on your wife's mind, going into that travel agency?"

"Sandrine mentioned us going on a trip," I told him.

"Really?" Morty asked. "When?"

"Not long after her diagnosis."

"You should have told me about that," Morty said.

"I'd forgotten it, I suppose," I said. "She wanted us to retrace the one we'd made when we were young."

"So it was just an idea she had?"

"Yes, and she dropped it right away, I suppose, because I never heard anything else about it." I offered a small, helpless shrug. "It never occurred to me that she'd continued to think about."

"Maybe she expected you to bring it up," Morty said.

"I suppose she did," I said quietly. "And I should have."

Morty nodded. "It's the business of you threatening your wife in that other place that was the point, of course," he said. "I couldn't find any way to counter that except to make the jury realize that people have spats, they think bad thoughts, but they don't do anything about them." He seemed still to be searching for a better way. "But I have to admit that threat business didn't play well with the jury," he added. "I could see it in their eyes. It's not evidence, exactly, but it works like evidence, because it seems like your wife was sort of crying out for help, if you know what I mean."

I shook my head. "I don't know what Sandrine was doing."

"You didn't threaten to kill her when you two were at that place?" Morty asked.

"Yes, but it was a joke," I told him "We were at the Ear of Dionysius and I whispered, 'I'm going to kill you.'"

"Jesus," Morty moaned.

"That's all it was," I said.

"That's not the way it sounds, Sam," Morty said darkly. "Not the way your wife made it sound, I mean."

I returned my gaze to the window, where Alexandria remained in place, slumped against the car, looking drained.

Morty made no effort to draw me back but I knew he was watching me closely. Finally, he said, "Sam, what's on your mind?"

I shook my head. "I can't, Morty."

He leaned toward me. "You can't what?"

"Tell you what I'm thinking."

"I think you better," Morty said firmly. "Because I can see that it's important."

"I can't."

Morty turned me to face him. "You shouldn't keep anything from me, Sam, no matter what it is."

I thought a moment, then said, "It can never leave this room."

"Okay."

"No, I mean it, Morty. What I tell you, you can never use it in court, never."

Morty's face turned solemn. "You have my word."

For the next few minutes, I laid out all the pieces that had come together in my case, the "suicide note" that had been no such thing, Sandrine's back injury, of which the autopsy had found no sign, my later call to Dr. Ortins, the way Sandrine had always had a reason for not picking up or signing for the Demerol the doctor had prescribed, the antihistamines, the sinister research, the dark mention of Siracusa, and finally that last visit to Malcolm Esterman, all of it coming together to form, fiber by clever fiber, as I said to Morty by way of conclusion, "a hangman's noose."

Morty was silent for a long time after this recitation, but I could see that his brain was turning slowly but surely, grinding toward a reluctant choice.

"If what you say is true, then we're in a different ball game here," he said gravely.

He considered all I'd just told him for a moment longer, then said, "So the bottom line is you think that Sandrine might have been out to get you?"

I nodded.

"Why would she do that?"

"To get back at me for what I did with April."

"A woman scorned," Morty said.

I shook my head. "A woman betrayed."

"It's still hell hath no fury, Sam," Morty said. He thought over what I'd just told him for a moment, then said, "Okay, to put it all together, you're saying that your wife somehow knew about you and April, and she didn't want to die without getting back at you, and so she came up with a scheme, a way of killing herself, which she wanted to do anyway because of what was going to happen to her, and she came up with a way of doing it that would take you down with her." He stopped, studied me a moment, then said, "That's what you're saying, right, Sam?"

"Yes," I answered. "And I know it's B-movie stuff, Morty, but, yes, that's what I'm saying."

I rose sharply and walked back to the window. Alexandria was still waiting for me beside the car. I could only imagine what today's testimony had done to her, how trapped between her living father and her dead mother she must feel, the horror of choosing one over the other, and of never knowing, or ever being able to know, if your choice was just.

"There's no evidence for any of it, of course," I said quietly. "And it could all be just a product of my own paranoia." I shrugged. "Not that it matters."

I watched as one of Alexandria's hands crawled slowly into the other.

"It's Alexandria I'm worried about now," I said.

Morty was now beside me, his hand on my shoulder. "Even if you were willing to use it, I doubt it would work," he said quietly. "Very iffy, a defense like that, making your wife the real criminal. It's hard to turn the tables on a dead woman. Of course, she would have known that, wouldn't she?"

"Yes."

Morty released a heavy sign. "You know a woman named Jane Forbes?"

Instantly I saw her again, standing in her red coat, watching me from the corner of the courtroom. "She teaches in the Political Science Department," I said. "I saw her once during the trial."

"Here, in court?"

"Yes."

"That all you know?"

"Yes? Why?"

"Singleton has added her to the witness list," Morty said. "Do you have any idea what she might have to say?"

"No."

Morty winked. "Maybe one of your wife's little bombs?"

I stared at him grimly. "I have no idea, Morty."

Morty released a grim chuckle. "Christ, if this was a plot she hatched, I got to say your wife was one smart cookie."

"She was brilliant," I said quietly, then saw her again sitting on the grounds of the quadrangle, surrounded by a few students, doing the best she could with them against considerable odds. "And she was kind," I added.

There seemed nothing more to say about Sandrine, and so I said nothing more.

"Well," Morty said after a moment. "Let's hope there are no more tricks in her bag."

"Yes," I said. "Let's hope."

But I had no hope and knew it. That I might ever recover from her death, such was the hope I had now abandoned. I had lost my job, my freedom to move about this little town, the respect of its townspeople, and very soon, as I could see now in the way Alexandria lifted her head and stared off into the middle distance, I would lose my daughter too. If all of this had indeed been Sandrine's plan, then she had thoroughly won her dark game.

And thus, with such grim resignation, did I confront the last days of my trial.

PART V

The state's case against Professor Samuel Madison is set to conclude this week at the Coburn County Courthouse. According to prosecuting attorney Harold Singleton, only three witnesses remain to be called, after which the defense's case will be presented by Mordecai Salberg, attorney for Mr. Madison, the Coburn College professor accused of killing his wife, Sandrine, on November 14, 2010. It is not yet known if Mr. Madison will testify in his own defense.

Coburn Sentinel
January 22, 2011

Evidence

"I had a terrible thought in court today, Dad," Alexandria said after we'd had dinner and walked into the living room for a final glass of wine. "It was while the travel agent was on the stand." She seemed reluctant to tell me what this thought had been and yet compelled to do so. "I was just sitting there, and it came to me. I guess it's the new normal for me."

Her tone was serious and confessional and so I knew she was moving toward some dark revelation.

"It just struck me that, after this, I can never fall in love with anyone," she said.

I took a sip from my glass. "I'm sorry to hear that," I said without giving the slightest hint to how devastating I found it, another consequence I hadn't counted on. "And I hope it will pass."

I could find nothing to add, and so a long silence followed, the two of us sipping our drinks, avoiding each other's eyes. It was as if Sandrine had, at last, silenced me.

"A woman named Jane Forbes has been added to Singleton's witness list," I said finally.

"Who is she?"

"She's on the faculty. The Political Science Department."

"Did you have an affair with her?" Alexandria asked without the slightest sense of it being anything other than a reasonable question.

"No," I said.

Alexandria nodded, and it occurred to me that she could absorb anything from now on. She'd faced the shocking news of her mother's diagnosis, then her death, the prospect that I had murdered her, then my affair with April. Any later revelations would be small potatoes.

"Why is she a witness?" she asked.

"I have no idea," I said. "I mean, Sandrine would sometimes meet her when she jogged around the reservoir. I've seen them running together but that's the extent of it."

"So you don't know this woman?"

"Not really." I shrugged. "I can't imagine why Sandrine would have taken her into her confidence, but I guess she did."

"She was dying, Dad," Alexandria said. "And people want someone with them when they're dying." She thought something through for a moment, then said, "Maybe that's why married people try so hard to make things work. It's not that they love each other every day, right? It's that they love each other enough to stay through the days they don't." She paused. "And so they make it to the end together. Like Mom used to say, that's the 'bottom line.'" She smiled.

She waited for me to respond to this, but it seemed so stark a truth that nothing could be added to it, no literary reference needed, nor pedantic marginalia required.

"Anyway, Mom must have gotten to know this woman pretty intimately," Alexandria said. "Otherwise, she wouldn't have any evidence."

"I suppose that's true," I said drily, then shrugged again. "Evidently this just came up, this business of Jane Forbes. Morty heard about it only at the end of court today."

Before this latest development, there'd been only two more witnesses scheduled to testify at my trial, April Blankenship and Malcolm

Esterman. I knew why they were on the list, of course, but Jane Forbes was a mystery.

"What do you know about her?" Alexandria asked.

"Nothing, really," I answered. "She may have been coming to the trial. I saw her once, early on."

I'd sometimes seen Sandrine with Jane, of course, the two of them trotting around the reservoir, though later they'd more often been sitting on one of the concrete benches beside it, Sandrine no longer in her running clothes.

"Mom never mentioned her?" Alexandria asked.

"No," I answered. "All I know is that I sometimes saw them talking at the reservoir."

Now I had no choice but to imagine that these conversations had been fiercely revealing, and that, perhaps, during one of them, Sandrine had planted some explosion she'd carefully timed to detonate toward the end of my trial.

In anticipation of just that explosion, I put down my glass and leaned forward, then stopped myself from saying what I'd wanted to say at that moment.

And what was I going to say?

Everything I'd earlier told Morty, of course, all the elements of that plot.

I'd wanted to pour all of that out, but I'd stopped myself because I knew exactly how it would sound to Alexandria. I could even imagine her staring at me distantly. What are you saying, Dad? That Mom is framing you? That she is the evil genius behind all this? That throughout this whole dismal affair it has always been Mom who was the sociopath?

I knew that there would be no defense against her questions, and with that recognition I was left with the simple fact that we are in trouble, deep, deep trouble, when we cannot reveal our deepest fears to the one we most want to hear them.

"What is it, Dad?" Alexandria asked now. "You look like something hit you."

"No, nothing," I said, then eased back into my chair.

There was some idle chatter after that, talk that seemed even emptier and more meaningless because it had to take the place of those vital things I'd wanted to tell Alexandria but never could. On that thought I saw the unforgiving and essentially adamantine nature of my position, that in order to save myself I would have to destroy Sandrine in the eyes of our daughter, turn her into the sociopath she'd accused me of being, a woman sufficiently reckless to endanger not just me but everyone connected to me, poor April and her deserving husband, Coburn College's reputation, and, of course, all this done in order to destroy me by taking away everything that held the slightest value: my profession, my daughter, my freedom, perhaps even my life.

"What were you thinking about?" Alexandria asked.

I scrambled for an answer. "Albi," I said. "It's very lovely. Your mother and I went there on our one great trip. It's where she proposed."

"Mom proposed to you?"

I nodded. "And it was a very romantic moment. We'd just come from the cathedral. Night was falling. There was a beautiful sunset, with impossible reds and purples and hints of gold. We were watching the sun go down, and she suddenly turned to me and she said, in that soft, intense voice of hers, she said, 'It's you.'"

How, from that moment, I wondered bleakly, had I reached this one?

To my astonishment I abruptly felt a great rush of emotion, one I could control then tamp down only by hurriedly moving forward through the rest of the story. "She said, 'So let's make it official,' which meant 'let's get married.' When we got back to the States we did." I smiled. "And as they say, the rest is history."

And a very unsavory history, indeed, I thought, a tale of choices that turned out to have been quite bad: Coburn, April, then that last one, that Sandrine should die.

Alexandria watched me silently for a moment, and during that silence I could almost feel the tumblers of her mind turning and turning, working to fit all the elements of life in their proper spaces. It was an effort to understand it, one more strenuous than I had ever made, so that suddenly it struck me that in some fundamental way Alexandria was, well, deeper than I was, more genuinely thoughtful when it came to the things that really matter.

I smiled. "You're going to be okay," I assured her. "You have bad thoughts now, but you're going to be okay, Alexandria."

I couldn't tell if she believed this, or even if my assurances carried weight. I had lived so unwisely, after all, been so cut off from any genuine consideration of life, that it would be perfectly reasonable for her to consider mine the last voice she should heed.

She offered her usual nod of assent, a "Sure, Dad" response that confirmed my fear of paternal disenfranchisement. Then she rose and walked into the kitchen, presumably to pour herself another round, though when she didn't return I got to my feet and joined her there.

She was sitting at the small breakfast table that looked out on the back lawn. Night had long ago fallen but I saw that her gaze was on the gazebo, Sandrine's redoubt, the place she'd gone to think and into which she'd invited the few people she'd wished to speak with during her last days, one of whom had been Alexandria.

I half expected her to wave me away when I approached, but she said nothing until I'd joined her at the table. Then she turned to me and smiled softly. "When I was a little girl Mom would read me these stories. You know, the usual fairy tales. And there was always a knight in shining armor type, some great-looking man on a white horse. And I would point to this man's picture and ask Mom, "Who is that?" and always, always, Dad, she would say that it was you."

I saw her again at Albi, radiant in that glowing air, the way her eyes had caressed me. No man had ever been more loved by a more worthy woman.

"It's you," I said softly to myself, remembering what Sandrine had said to me there.

But what had been my sword and armor then, I wondered. What had she seen in Albi, or before, that had made Sandrine choose me on that golden afternoon, choose me over so many others she might have chosen, others so much more handsome, so much more accomplished, so much richer and with such greater prospects.

"Why me, I wonder," I said. "What drew her to me? I was smart but so were lots of guys. I was just finishing up a degree, more or less broke, working at this school for retarded kids."

"You worked with retarded kids?" Alexandria asked. "You never mentioned that."

"It was only for a few months," I said. "Your mother would often meet me there, and a couple of times we took some of the kids to a little park, and she would watch while I worked with them."

Alexandria glanced toward the gazebo, so empty without Sandrine. "Maybe that was what she saw," she said. "That you were a good teacher." She turned to face me. "You should have talked to her, Dad. She shouldn't have needed that woman at the reservoir."

"I know," I told her, then thought again of the next witness, a woman I hardly knew. "But she did."

DAY EIGHT

Call Jane Forbes

She had shoulder-length hair and was dressed quite elegantly in a navy blue pantsuit, low heels, and a long necklace of azure glass beads. She walked to the witness box rather like a soldier on parade, determined, unafraid, a woman warrior. Something in her demeanor suggested that if she were suddenly discovered after having been marooned for twenty years on a deserted island she would still know exactly who she was.

Yes, I thought, however painfully and uneasily the idea came to me, it would be easy for Sandrine to talk to such a person.

"Jane Wiley Forbes," she said when asked to give her name.

For the next few minutes, Mr. Singleton took his witness through the usual biographical material. She was forty-seven years old, born in Newton, Massachusetts, educated at Sarah Lawrence, with a PhD in political science. She had taught at a few places before coming to Coburn, all of them modest affairs, a junior college in Boston, a girls' school in Atlanta. At Coburn she'd mostly taught freshmen and sophomores. Despite the modesty of these assignments, there was something formidable about Jane Forbes, something that made me both trust and dread whatever it was she'd come here to reveal.

"Now, Dr. Forbes," Mr. Singleton said. "How long have you known Sandrine Madison?"

"I met her nine years ago," Jane answered. "They have these little teas when you first come to Coburn College. Sandrine came over and introduced herself."

It had been a long time since I'd heard anyone call Sandrine by her first name. For Morty she was "your wife." For Mr. Singleton she was "Mrs. Madison." For Jenna she was "my sister." For Alexandria she was "Mom." But for Jane Forbes she had been "Sandrine," and hearing that name on her lips, spoken so softly and with a hint of loss, hit me with a strange poignancy that made me lean forward slightly, a gesture one of the juror's caught, which froze me in place. For what might this juror read in my suddenly becoming so obviously engaged? This was a question for which I had no answer but in response to which I eased myself back again and, like a good actor, prepared a face to meet the faces of the jury.

"Dr. Forbes," Mr. Singleton said, "did you have occasion to have several conversations with Mrs. Madison during the weeks prior to her death?"

She had, and she further explained.

"I had not really known Sandrine all that well, but last April, toward the end of the month, we happened to be on the reservoir together. Sandrine seemed very tired. She had always been such a presence at faculty meetings, so animated and energetic, it was unusual to find her looking so exhausted."

"Did you happen to mention Mrs. Madison's appearance to her?" Mr. Singleton asked.

"No, but she mentioned it," Jane said. "She said she was depleted. That was her word. Depleted. Then she told me about her illness. This was only a few minutes into our conversation. She was debating when she would tell her students. She didn't want them to pity her, and she wanted to keep teaching as long as she could. She had talked this over with Malcolm Esterman, she said, and now she wanted my opinion too."

And so Sandrine had discussed this most troubling of decisions with two people, not one of whom had been me.

"Did Mrs. Madison mention her husband at all during this time?" Mr. Singleton asked.

"If by 'this time,' you mean that conversation, then no, she didn't mention her husband," Jane answered.

"How about during subsequent conversations?" Mr. Singleton asked.

"During subsequent conversations, she did mention him, yes."

"Can you tell us the nature of those communications?"

They had been quite ordinary, it seemed to me, as Jane continued her testimony. During the trots around the reservoir and their sessions on the bench beside it, Sandrine had spoken of our early days together, the trip we'd taken, how much she'd loved traveling and how little we'd done of it since then. She'd described our first meeting as "interesting," though she hadn't actually found me very attractive. I was too tall and too skinny, she'd said. But later she noticed not that I was always reading but the way I read, which she described as "heartfelt," a word I found sentimental, almost schmaltzy, but which had probably been true at the time.

"She said that once she'd found him reading in a small cubicle in the library," Jane went on, "and that when he'd looked up from the book, he'd seemed so sad, so absolutely sorrowful, that she'd actually caught her breath."

She paused a moment, a dramatic pause that alerted me to the fact that something was coming, and which propelled me forward in my chair with so gentle and unassuming a force that I lost my actor's pose.

"She said it was an expression that left him after a few years," Jane added. "And that after a while she never saw it again."

"But she looked for it, didn't she?" Mr. Singleton asked.

"She said she did, yes," Jane answered.

"And on one particular occasion, she had expected to see it, hadn't she?"

"Yes, she had."

"His sorrow, I mean, that sorrowful look," Mr. Singleton said by way of emphasis.

"His sorrow, yes."

"And did Mrs. Madison tell you what that occasion was, the one when she'd genuinely expected to see this expression of sorrow on her husband's face?" Mr. Singleton asked.

"Yes, she did."

"And what was that occasion, Dr. Forbes?"

"When she told him she was dying," the witness answered. "She said that she had delayed telling him about her condition because she was actually afraid she would not see that sadness on his face. But finally she'd told him, and her fear had been justified."

I couldn't help it. No matter how much I wanted to prevent myself from reacting in any way to such a devastating answer, I couldn't help it, and so I closed my eyes and slumped backward as if pushed by an invisible hand.

After that, it was only voices coming to me from what seemed a great emptiness.

"And during these conversations, did Mrs. Madison talk about her life in general?" Mr. Singleton asked.

"Yes, she did. She mentioned a paper she'd done when she was a student at the Sorbonne. It was about the case of a woman named Blanche Monnier. She said that this woman had been imprisoned for many years by her family. She'd evidently been found locked in the attic. She'd been more or less starved, Sandrine said, and she'd lived in terrible filth. Also, the shutters had been closed and nailed shut, so this woman had lived in near total darkness. And yet when Blanche Monnier was released by the authorities she'd described this attic as her 'lovely little grotto.'"

"Her 'lovely little grotto'?" Mr. Singleton repeated.

"That was the quote Sandrine told me, yes."

"And did Mrs. Madison add anything to this story?"

"She said that in a way it was her story."

"Her story?"

"She said that for a long time she had lived in a 'lovely little grotto' that was, in fact, a cold dark place. She said she thought a lot of women lived in such places. She said it was the place where a woman inevitably lived when the core reason why she had once loved a man was no longer there."

"The core reason?" Mr. Singleton asked. "Did she say what the core reason she'd loved her husband was?"

"Yes," the witness answered. "His kindness. He had lost his kindness. His goodness. His capacity to feel sympathy. She said that he was no longer able to be tender."

My eyes remained closed but now my eyelids felt pulled down and held in place by heavy weights, eyes I could not open.

Fixed in that darkness, I thought of how I'd received Sandrine's diagnosis with little show of emotion, though I'd later made all the sweet, sympathetic motions required to demonstrate my care, not one of which had been genuine. Had she seen through all my unfeeling gestures and seen only the bloodless show they were?

"She said she knew that he had lost all these things because of something she'd seen a week or so before her diagnosis," the witness added.

Jane's voice now took on a somberness that I could hear quite clearly from the depths of my black chamber. I could also hear that she was laboring to control the tenor of her voice, as if she knew the story she was about to tell would challenge that control, loosen the strings of her own heart, break the very voice she was struggling to keep whole.

"She'd been at the home of a woman she knew, a woman who'd had breast cancer the year before and who'd just had a mammogram and was waiting for the results. Her husband came home while Sandrine was there. He'd picked up the mail, and so he had the results of her mammogram with him. He opened it and they read it together, the man and his wife. Neither of them said anything as they read, Sandrine told me, but very suddenly the man's eyes filled with tears, and he drew his wife under his arm and said, 'No cancer, no cancer.'"

"And what did Mrs. Madison make of this experience?" Mr. Singleton asked.

"That this was love," Jane Forbes answered, "that this was truly love. That when the man had heard that his wife was fine, he'd wept with joy and relief and what she called—I remember the phrase—'heartfelt thanksgiving.'"

I opened my eyes because I thought that with this it was surely over. But I was wrong.

"She added something to this," Jane Forbes continued. "She said that she could face the fact that her husband could no longer feel what she called 'the tenderness of things.' Many women did, after all, face that fact. The problem, Sandrine told me, was that she could find no way to bring him back to himself. She had wanted to do that more than anything, but she was running out of time."

"All right, and when was the last time you spoke with Mrs. Madison?" Mr. Singleton asked.

"About a week before she died," Jane answered.

"Did she speak about her condition at that time?"

"No. She talked about her daughter, how much she loved her daughter."

"Did she mention Mr. Madison?"

"No, she did not."

"Did she mention anything about suicide?"

"No. We talked for about an hour, then Sandrine said she had something to finish, a little note on Cleopatra."

"A little note?"

"Yes."

"But not a note that had anything to do with suicide?"

"No, it was just a thought she'd had about Cleopatra," Jane answered. "She had written the first part of it, about a page, she said. But there was a final paragraph she wanted to write. I fully expected to see her again, probably the very next day, but she never came back to the reservoir, and, of course, a week later I found out about her death."

"So this afternoon by the reservoir, this was the last time you saw Mrs. Madison?"

"Yes."

"But this talk about Cleopatra, this was not the last communication you had with her, was it."

"Not exactly, no."

But Sandrine had died a week later, and they'd never seen each other after that final meeting at the reservoir. How could that not have been their last communication?

"A couple of days after her death I got a letter from Sandrine," Jane Forbes said. "She'd mailed it the afternoon before her death."

Mr. Singleton then went to his table, retrieved a piece of paper, and handed it to Jane Forbes.

"Is this the letter you received?" he asked her.

"Yes, it is."

"Can you describe the contents of this letter?"

"It seems to be the final paragraph of her thought about Cleopatra," Jane answered. "I didn't think it had any relevance to this case, but when I heard Detective Alabrandi read the note Sandrine had left beside her bed as her final thought, I knew that it wasn't, and so I contacted you."

Mr. Singleton nodded toward the note. "Would you read it for us, please?"

And so she did.

Caesar was a worldling who must have enjoyed many a cynical laugh at the benighted mortals who made up the lower orders of the world. But surely it is possible that in the last days of her life Cleopatra came to understand the outcome of such vanity, that its poison numbs the heart. If this is true, then as the asp sank its fangs into her flesh, she must have feared that Caesar would continue in this folly, that without her desperate intervention, he would die as lost to tenderness as the cruelist who ever died, and that to have saved him from so drear a fate should have been the goal and triumph of her love, his redemption her final, parting gift.

Others might hear this and hear only Sandrine's thoughts on Cleopatra, I told myself, as Jane Forbes returned the letter to Mr. Singleton, then waited for Morty's cross-examination, but I could read between its heartbreaking lines, understand its devastating message, and feel the sacrificial heart that had delivered it.

Oh, my dear Sandrine, I thought, as Morty rose to question this unexpected witness at my trial. My God, what I have lost.

My Dinner with Morty

My Dinner with Andre had been one of Sandrine's favorite movies, I remembered as I drove toward Pappy's Steak and Brew, where I was to have my dinner with Morty. She'd loved the way the tables had turned in the middle of the conversation, with short, stocky, and wholly unimposing Wallace Shawn suddenly making an eloquent case for the life he'd chosen, a life that during the course of their conversation had unexpectedly emerged as quietly richer and more meaningful than that of the far more worldly Andre's.

I was still thinking of Sandrine's affection for this odd little film, one whose action I'd found predictable and whose message I'd found rather trite, when I sat down across from Morty, then glanced about the place, taking in the longhorns mounted over the bar, the plain wooden tables with their red-checked cloths.

"You probably don't like this place," Morty said. "I chose it because we're less likely to run into anyone from Coburn College."

I shrugged. "I'm past caring where I have dinner, Morty."

He looked at me closely. "I warned you that you'd be pretty worn out by the end of the state's case."

I nodded. "Well, that much is true."

Morty took a swig from the enormous glass of beer he'd ordered. "What do you make of Jane Forbes?" he asked.

Before I could answer, the waitress stepped up. Morty ordered a steak with several sides and another beer. I wanted only a salad.

"I mean, I couldn't see anything all that damaging in her testimony," Morty added. "You weren't the most approachable guy. Big deal. Your wife sometimes got blue, sometimes felt lonely. You're supposed to be hung for that?" He waved his hand. "Bullshit."

His cross-examination of Jane had been polite but to the point. He'd gone over everything she'd said in answer to Mr. Singleton's questions, then, step by step, made Jane admit that she'd heard no fear in Sandrine's tone, nor any hint that she'd had the slightest suspicion that her husband might kill her. After that, he'd gone on to ask if she'd heard anything during her conversations with Sandrine that had alarmed her such that she'd warned her friend to be watchful or advised her to contact local authorities. That is to say, the police. To this, Jane had answered with a very definite "No."

"But that note on Cleopatra," Morty added after a quick sip from that enormous mug of beer. "That could backfire on Singleton, make your wife look like an egghead." He shrugged. "Anyway, we're at the end of the state's case so I wanted us to go over the defense strategy one more time."

The food came and Morty dove in. I picked at mine, a lack of appetite he immediately noticed.

"You're wasting away," he said. "What's the problem?"

I shrugged. "A lack of will."

"To what?"

"Go on."

"Oh please," Morty said with a dismissive wave of the hand, then looked more closely and said, "You're serious, aren't you? Is it because you know more is coming? From Sandrine, I mean?"

When I didn't answer, he leaned forward and gave me his best lawyerly, fatherly expression. "She's trying to kill you, Sam. You were right about that."

Again, I said nothing.

"Which is actually something I wanted to bring up with regard to the defense," Morty added. "The fact is, I think you should reconsider your decision not to, well, bring up a few possibilities with regard to your wife."

My silence appeared to work on him like a spur.

"She is a black widow, that's the truth," he said. "A classic black widow, and she's digging your grave from the moldy depths of her own and—"

"Stop," I said softly. "Just stop, Morty."

Then I rose.

"Thanks for dinner," I said softly. "See you tomorrow."

I didn't want to go directly home. Alexandria would be there, and what I wanted was to be alone so that I could work through the many conflicting ideas that were assaulting me, all of them having to do with Sandrine, what she was or was not doing to me, and why.

But there was no place I could go to sit and think, not even the library, which was the last place I'd tried to do exactly that, only to notice Mrs. Crenshaw eyeing me from a distant row of shelves. She was the widowed wife of the man who'd first hired Sandrine and me at Coburn College. It was her kindly late husband who'd worked so hard to bring us to Coburn. She'd quickly looked away when I had caught her in my eye, and because of that I'd known exactly what she was thinking, that I'd brought shame upon her husband's reputation, as well as that of the college he had worked so tirelessly to benefit, shame upon everything that was good about this old-fashioned and genuinely upright college town.

So the library was closed to me, and the market, and the general store, places that had once welcomed me but never would again. For no matter the outcome of my trial, I had raised a great ugly noise and it would echo through my life as long as I lived here. No question about it, I thought, I would have to leave. The big red *A* was painted on my chest. There were many other Coburnites upon whom it could with equal justice have been painted, of course, but my tepid affair had come to light in the most spectacular of ways, an explosion that would reverberate with every step I took in the town park or along one of its nicely shaded sidewalks.

And so I drove around and around, circulating among the various neighborhoods. At one point I recalled one of my uncle's war stories, how American fighter planes had sunk the flower of the Japanese fleet during the Battle of Midway. He was quite amused by the fact that the Japanese pilots who had tried to return to these ships found nothing but black smoke and burning oil slicks where their home ships should have been. I suppose I'd enjoyed a dark laugh at their expense, as well, but now I felt very much like one of those doomed pilots, hopelessly searching for a refuge that had sunk beneath the waves.

The midnight hour came and went. At the stroke of one, I told myself that Alexandria would surely be asleep, and for that reason I could now drift into the driveway of 237 Crescent Road, creep into my own house, pad softly down the corridor, and finally lower myself into the bed and struggle through another sleepless night. Now, at least, I told myself, you can go to bed without further incident.

I was wrong.

She came up from behind me as I got out of my car, came up out of the shadows, like something from the deep, that shark one forever fears lurking beneath the waves. There was a slight, alerting sound, like leaves on leaves, and I turned to see her coming, quite

290

literally, from behind the wall of untrimmed shrubbery that bordered the house.

"I left my car a few blocks away," she said.

"April," I murmured.

"I had to see you."

Her slender body was wrapped in a black overcoat she'd tied at the waist, the collar up so that it spread out from her throat like small pointed wings. She'd knotted a paisley scarf around her neck, its ends tucked into the coat, and for a reason I could not fathom she was wearing black leather gloves as if this were a crime scene at which she did not wish to leave her fingerprints. But April, being April, had added a deeply incongruous pair of white sneakers.

For a moment she stood pointedly a few paces from me, like someone gauging the distance of a target on a firing range.

"I know I shouldn't be here," she whispered. Her eyes flashed to the darkened house. "Your daughter's here, right?"

"She's asleep, I'm sure."

"There was no place else to come," she said. "No place to meet."

"I know," I told her, waited for her to add something, then, when she only stood frozenly, staring at me, I said in the casual way of a clerk addressing someone who'd just strolled into a store, "What can I for do for you, April?"

The sheer and thoughtless idiocy of what I'd said tore a snarling laugh from her. "Do for me?" she snapped, a show of buried rage I'd never expected to see in her, and which, to my relief, was very quickly suppressed. "God," she breathed. "What a mess. What a mess."

"What I mean is . . . April," I sputtered. "What I mean is that if there's something you—"

"It's not me anymore," she said, her voice now quite soft, with something shattered in it. "It's Clayton. He can't take it, Sam. He can't take me going on the stand." She stared at me in that beggarly way, her shredded inner life hanging from her like flaps of skin. "He didn't deserve any of this. It was me who did it. You and me who did it."

"What we did has nothing to do with my trial," I told her weakly. "It should never have been—"

"So who's to blame, then?" April cut in with a hint of that earlier rage breaking the surface again. "The dog? The cat?"

"You know what I mean, April."

"Who's to blame for what happened to Clayton?" April demanded. "Because one thing's for sure. He had nothing to do with what we did, Sam. Or what happened after that."

She meant Sandrine's death, of course, and her reluctance to say it directly hinted that she might think it murder.

"They're going to say terrible things, Sam," she went on, now crying softly. "They're going to say we made fun of Clayton and Sandrine." She gazed at me plaintively. "Those names we picked, remember? And that story you wrote. They're going to make me read some of that, Sam!" She lowered her head and sobbed. "We're monsters," she murmured. "Everyone will think we're monsters."

"What do you want me to do, April?" I asked. "No, the question is what do you think I can do? Because it's all out of my hands. It's been out my hands for a long time." I felt a wave hit me, red and boiling, one that lifted me and rolled me and flung me down with crushing force. "I am nothing!" I said vehemently. "I have nothing!"

She lifted her head and stared at me in dark wonder, as if I'd broken apart before her eyes, as if my arms had dropped away and my legs had buckled and I'd collapsed like a building in a cloud of dust. It was as if she'd seen the external manifestation of exactly what had happened in my soul and had no idea how she might respond to it, or even if there was a way to respond at all.

Finally, she said, "I sometimes wonder if you did it."

"Don't," I said softly. "Because I didn't."

"If you did," she added in a tone that impressed me with both its directness and its honesty, "I hope they find you guilty."

"I'm sure you do, April."

I remembered something Morty had said to me early on, the fact that the classically southern way to defend a murderer was to show that the murder victim deserved being murdered and that your client—aggrieved, lied to, humiliated—was the perfect one do it.

"I'm sure you do," I repeated.

After a brief silence, she said, "I testify tomorrow."

"I know."

"Clayton's coming," she added, her eyes glistening now. "He won't let me face it alone. He told me that. It's a matter of chivalry, he said. That's the word he used. Chivalry. And he believes in it too. That's the kind of man he is."

"Go back to him," I told her.

She shook her head. "He deserves better than me."

She watched me a moment, and then, with no further word, she slowly turned and disappeared into the darkness beyond my lighted yard.

For a time, I remained outside, under the stars, listening to the soft pad of April's white sneakers on the sidewalk until they, too, had vanished. Then I turned toward the house and saw Alexandria standing at the window, motionless, but somehow moving, like the waving image of a ghostly hologram.

She was at the door by the time I reached it.

"So that's her," she said.

She'd seen pictures of April in the paper and on local television.

"She looked older," she added.

"Trouble ages you."

"And she's not very pretty."

"No, she's not very pretty," I agreed, then swept past her and moved on into the house, where I'd expected to head directly to bed. In fact, I was halfway down the corridor when Alexandria's question stopped me.

"What was it about her, Dad?" she asked.

I turned to face my daughter. "It wasn't something about April," I said. "It was something about me."

"And what was that?"

"My failure, I suppose," I said.

Alexandria's gaze grew oddly tender.

"A failure so deep I couldn't admit it, and so I put it on everybody else," I added.

On the shock of that recognition, I felt loosen and fly away the last cohering particles of me. "Now you know, Alexandria," I concluded bluntly. "And so do I."

DAY NINE

Call April Blankenship

She had taken a seat at the front of the courtroom, and there, just as he had nobly pledged, Clayton sat beside her, dressed in a fine black suit and with a small red rose in his lapel, a gentleman of the old breed, a man Sandrine had once called a chevalier, and whom she incontestably respected.

They were already seated when I came into the room, but neither of them looked at me as I took my place at the defense table. In response, I made no effort to look at them but simply pretended to busy myself with some papers Morty provided, and which he knew to be nothing more than stage props I was to use whenever I felt overwhelmed or bored. "Just pretend you're reading something," he'd told me at the beginning of my trial. "That shouldn't be hard for you."

Yet on this, the ninth day of my trial, I found the charade no longer to my liking, and so I simply straightened the papers and lifted my head and stared directly ahead until her name resounded through the crowded courtroom.

"Call April Blankenship."

I couldn't help but glance over as she rose shakily from her seat. She looked down at Clayton who reached up and very gently touched her hand, a gesture that reminded me of that dreadful moment in Oscar Wilde's life when he was being taken to prison. A single friend had found his way into the crowd that had gathered to jeer at the fallen playwright, a friend who, as

Wilde went past him, had with a great show of reverence taken off his hat. Oh evil, evil men have spent eternity in paradise, Wilde had later written, for doing less than that. And so, I thought, would Clayton Blankenship.

On the stand, April looked entirely different from when she'd appeared at my house the night before. She wore a plain blue skirt and white blouse and, in those colors, she seemed to have all the weight and substance of a floating cloud. Her white hands lay in her lap like two dead birds. Well, not quite dead, since both of them were trembling. Her nails were painted pale pink, and she'd pulled her hair back and pinned it primly so that she seemed almost spinsterish. It was hard to imagine her as the "other woman," and it struck me that, in fact, I had almost no memory of her in that role, so listless had it all been, so passionless and meaningless, along with every other "-less" that can drain the force of an otherwise substantive noun.

She would be easy pickings for Mr. Singleton, I knew, a thin sheet of paper he could effortlessly tear to ribbons and toss into the wind.

"All right now, Mrs. Blankenship," he began, his voice pointedly emphasizing that April was a married woman. "How long have you lived in Coburn?"

She had lived here for seventeen years.

"And what sort of work do you do, Mrs. Blankenship?'

She did not work, by which the jury was to gather that she lived entirely at the expense of the good, hardworking husband she had callously betrayed.

"How long have you been married, Mrs. Blankenship?"

"Twelve years."

"And you are married to Dr. Clayton Blankenship, a professor of southern history at Coburn College, isn't that right?"

"Yes."

"Where did you meet Dr. Blankenship?"

"I worked in one of the department offices at the college."

"Which department?"

"The History Department."

Ah, so she was a lowly clerk who'd caught the attention of a lonely old widower, probably by lifting her skirt to an inappropriate height, or by sidling up to him at the water cooler, or by means of some other equally whorish trick.

I stole a glance to my right and saw that all of this was also going through Clayton Blankenship's mind, as well, his expression grave, sorrowful, helpless, a classically appointed gentleman who'd first had to confront his wife's betrayal and now faced her humiliation at the hands of a very ungentlemanly public prosecutor.

"You don't have any postgraduate degrees, do you, Mrs. Blankenship?" Singleton asked.

"No."

"Or college degrees at all?"

"No."

"I see. Well, then, just how far did you get in school, Mrs. Blankenship?"

"I graduated from high school."

"High school," Mr. Singleton repeated in a sotte voce aside designed to reinforce the notion that so learned a man as Clayton Blankenship could not have been interested in poor, uneducated April save for the most obvious and lurid of reasons.

With that suggestion, Clayton all but shuddered, a moment so pitiful in its Blue Angel pathos that I turned away and focused once again on April.

She had taken a white handkerchief from one of her pockets and was frantically kneading it in her thin, birdlike fingers.

"Now, in the course of your work at Coburn College, you met another professor, didn't you?" Mr. Singleton asked. "A professor in the English Department this time, Dr. Samuel Joseph Madison?"

April nodded.

"We need a voiced response, Mrs. Blankenship," Mr. Singleton instructed sternly. "Nodding won't do."

"Yes," April said weakly.

"When did you meet Professor Madison?"

"I don't know when exactly, it could have been—"

"I don't mean for you to come up with a precise date," Mr. Singleton interrupted. "Let's put it this way, was there a time when you became involved with Dr. Madison? You know what I mean by 'involved,' don't you, Mrs. Blankenship?"

"Yes, we became . . . we . . . had . . ."

"You had an affair, correct?"

"Yes."

"And how did this affair begin?"

For the next few minutes, Singleton took an increasingly agitated April through the dreary steps by which we had finally arrived at the Shady Arms motel in nearby Raylesford, a depressed little town, with its storefront churches and abandoned textile mills, the place least likely to be visited by any of our fellow Coburnites. It was there, April said, now daubing the handkerchief at the corner of her eyes, that we'd found what she called simply "a place to meet," then, in response to yet another question, given its loaded name in little above a whisper.

"Shady Arms."

"Did you say *Shady Arms*?" Mr. Singleton asked loudly.

"Yes."

"The Shady Arms is a motel, isn't it?" Singleton asked.

"Yes."

"Could you speak up, Mrs. Blankenship," Singleton called to her. "Your words have to be recorded." He glanced at the jury as if to say, What a pathetic little whore, then returned his smoldering attention to April. "Do you remember the date?"

"No."

"Well, do you remember the name you used when you signed in at the Shady Arms?"

"Yes."

"Please, speak up."

"Yes."

"What was that name?"

I felt my body tighten. Surely, surely, I thought, there was no need for this.

"Rose," April answered.

"But your name isn't Rose, is it, Mrs. Blankenship?" Singleton demanded.

"No, it isn't."

"Did you choose a false last name too?"

"Yes."

"What was that name?"

Now April's hands were twitching birds, frantic, fluttering, as if on their backs, strings tightening around their necks.

"Loomis."

"Rose Loomis!" Mr. Singleton bawled. "That is the name you used to register at the Shady Arms motel on those occasions when you met with the defendant?"

"Yes."

"But your name isn't Rose Loomis, is it?"

"No."

"Well, where did you get that name, Mrs. Blankenship?"

301

April lowered her head.

"Mrs. Blankenship?"

Her head remained down.

"From a movie," she said. "It was Marilyn Monroe's name in a movie."

The name had been my idea, and we'd laughed about the choice because the character had been so utterly unlike April. It had been our only laugh.

"What movie?" Mr. Singleton asked.

"*Niagara.*"

"And in that movie, Rose Loomis is an adulteress, isn't she?"

"Yes."

"In fact, she wants to kill her husband, doesn't she?"

April began to cry, but through her tears she managed a faint "Yes."

"Because her husband is old and weak, isn't that right?"

"Yes."

"Old and weak and it's pretty clear in the movie that he's impotent, correct?"

April nodded.

"Please answer the question," Singleton barked. "The husband in that movie, the husband of Rose Loomis, the Marilyn Monroe character whose name you took when you signed in at the Shady Arms motel, her husband is old and weak and impotent and she has a young lover and she wants her husband dead, isn't that right, Mrs. Blankenship?"

"Yes," April said weakly.

I looked at Clayton Blankenship, his head still unbowed, but with something broken in his eyes.

"So this woman, this Rose Loomis, this adulteress whose name you chose to take during your assignations with Professor Madison, this woman wanted her husband dead, isn't that right? Wanted to be rid of him because she couldn't stand the sound of his voice, or the look on his face, or the touch of his hands?"

"Yes."

"Mrs. Blankenship, during these meetings with Professor Madison, did you discuss killing your husband?" Singleton demanded.

April's eyes widened, "No," she cried. Her eyes flashed to Clayton and filled with a desperate denial combined with a broken plea for forgiveness.

Mr. Singleton whirled around, marched to the prosecution table, snatched up a manuscript, then strode over and placed it in April's shaking hands.

"Do you recognize this story, Mrs. Blankenship?" he asked.

April nodded faintly.

"We need a spoken answer, please," Singleton said irritably.

"Yes."

"It was a story especially written for you, wasn't it?"

"Yes."

"For your eyes only."

"Yes, but it was just a . . . a . . . he called it a parody."

"Read the title please," Mr. Singleton commanded in a voice as flat and hard as a hammer hitting steel.

April's gaze fell to the title page. "The Lover's Plot."

And what a splendid literary effort that had been, I thought, as I recalled April beneath my arm, sweetly asking me to write something for her. But what could I have written for April Blankenship, I'd asked myself at the time. Certainly nothing as complicated or ambitious as any of my many failed attempts at "The Pull of the Earth." Subtlety and nuance would have been no problem for Sandrine, nor would any work dotted with obscure literary or historical references. April had been another case altogether. And so I'd penned a hothouse pulp fiction parody filled with side-of-the-mouth tough talk and imagery that was raw and violent, with character names stolen from noir films, my narrator a cynical Bible salesman named Johnny O'Clock, addicted to barbiturates, particularly Nembutal, because, as he says, "if I overdose on that, at least the morgue will smell like pears." It had all been like that, my last attempt at fiction, cold and mordant, snide and cruel, every word of it written by a writer whose vision of life could be summed up in a sneer.

Good God, I thought, as April's testimony continued, how far "The Lover's Plot" had fallen from the actual pull of the earth, from kindness, from the abiding tenderness of things.

"Now, the word 'plot,' it means a secret plan, doesn't it?" Mr. Singleton asked.

"Yes," April answered, then went on to explain. "But it's like a play on words, Sam said, because it's like the plan is the plot, yes, but it's also the plot that they end up digging in the ground. Like, a grave plot . . . and so . . . well . . . like a double meaning thing."

Singleton released a weary sign.

"In this case, we're only concerned with one meaning for the word 'plot,'" he said, then retrieved a dictionary from his desk, walked to the witness box, and thrust it toward the witness.

"Read the third definition of 'plot,' Mrs. Blankenship," Singleton demanded.

April, her voice already beginning to break, read the definition. "'A secret plan usually for an evil and unlawful end.'"

Mr. Singleton snatched the dictionary from April's shaky grasp and returned the book to his desk. Then he turned back to the witness.

"Now, in terms of the title of this story, it refers to a plot hatched by two lovers, isn't that correct?" he asked.

"Yes," April answered weakly.

"The lovers' 'evil plan' is to murder each other's spouses, correct?" Singleton demanded. "The man's wife and the woman's husband, isn't that right?"

"Yes," April muttered.

A smile slithered onto Mr. Singleton's lips. "Did you plan to murder your husband, Mrs. Blankenship?"

"No," April answered softly, then lowered her head again, the question doing exactly what Singleton wanted, so that her body suddenly began to tremble. "Oh, Clayton," she said brokenly. "Clayton, I'm so sorry."

As if beneath the weight of her husband's once illustrious but now besmirched name, April curled forward and hung her head.

In response, Singleton sprang toward the witness box.

"Who is the author of this story, Mrs. Blankenship?" Singleton asked sharply. "The author's name is on the title page. Please read that name."

April straightened slightly as her eyes again fell to the page. "Samuel Madison."

Singleton's gaze hardened, and for a moment he seemed, quite literally, to turn to stone. "Now these two lovers are going to kill their spouses, isn't that so, Mrs. Blankenship?"

"Yes," April murmured.

"What is the motive for these murders?"

"To get rid of them," April answered.

"So that they can be together, correct?"

"Yes."

"These murders are first suggested by the male lover, right?" Mr. Singleton asked.

"Yes."

"And this male lover, his wife is an invalid, isn't she?"

"Yes."

"She's in the bed most of the time, or in a wheelchair, isn't that so?"

"Yes."

"This wife is 'in the way.' Aren't those the words the man uses to describe her? She's in the way and she has to be gotten rid of, correct?"

"Yes."

"Now, Mrs. Blankenship, in what manner does the male lover in 'The Lover's Plot' plan to kill his wife?"

"He plans to poison her."

"And how does he expect to get away with it?"

"He plans to make it look like a suicide."

Mr. Singleton suddenly leaped from behind the lectern and all but hurled himself toward the witness.

"Mrs. Blankenship, did you and Samuel Madison plot the murder of Sandrine Allegra Madison?" Mr. Singleton demanded.

"No," April answered. "No." She lowered her head again, and again her body began to tremble, but this time more violently.

"Because she was in the way, isn't that right?" Singleton cried.

April pressed her face in the handkerchief as if to hide it from the world. "I never did that. Never."

"So it was just a game to you?" Singleton yelped.

"It was just . . . supposed to be funny."

"Funny?" Mr. Singleton bawled. "Funny? Well, it turned out to be anything by funny, didn't it?"

"It was just a . . ." She lifted her eyes toward the ceiling as if desperately seeking help from on high. "It was just like . . . we were in a movie."

"But it wasn't a movie, was it?" Singleton said loudly, with a lightning glance toward the jury. "It was real."

April's face now pressed again into the handkerchief, her hand trembling so violently I half expected it to tear away.

306

"It was real for Samuel Madison, wasn't it?" Singleton shouted. "A real lover's plot."

"No!" April cried. "No!"

She began to sob uncontrollably, each sob followed by a desperate intake of breath, then by something that sounded inhuman, the wail of a wounded animal. "Naaaeoooo!" Her whole body now shook wildly. Her muscles seemed to shear away from her bones, everything buckling, warping, so that she abruptly collapsed into a quivering mound of flesh, her cries now soft and childlike, the whimpering of a stricken infant.

Mr. Singleton let this go on and on, while he stood pitilessly glaring at her.

Then, like an executioner charged with the coup de grâce, he said, "Your witness, Mr. Salberg."

"Jesus Christ," Morty breathed. He turned to me. "I'll make this quick," he whispered, then rose and walked to the lectern. He paused a moment, as if to let his great weight settle, then said quite gently, "Good morning, Mrs. Blankenship."

April nodded softly.

"Are you okay?" Morty asked sweetly. "We can wait a minute, if you're not."

"No," April said softly. "Please . . . let's go on."

"All right," Morty said gently, then began.

"Mrs. Blankenship, when you were approached by the police you made no attempt to deny having had a brief relationship with the defendant, is that correct?"

"No, I didn't deny it," April said softly. Her watery, red eyes drifted over to me. "I made a mistake."

With that answer she seemed to admit two mistakes at once, that she'd betrayed her husband and that I'd been the arid soul she'd mistakenly chosen as her lover, a man she saw through now, one who'd cared nothing for her, who'd halfway mocked her even as he'd used her . . . a sociopath.

"When was the last time you saw Mr. Madison . . . in that way?" Morty asked. "It was three months before Mrs. Madison was diagnosed, isn't that right?"

"Yes."

"At that time, you and Mr. Madison were unaware of Mrs. Madison's condition?"

"We didn't know about it, no."

"Now this story Mr. Madison wrote, you said that was a parody?"

"Yes."

"Well, since we've had a few definitions offered here today, what is a parody?"

April stared at Morty blankly.

"A parody is a humorous representation, isn't it?" Morty asked.

"I guess."

"A parody is not meant to be taken seriously, is it, Mrs. Blankenship?"

"It wasn't serious, no," April answered.

"So nothing in that story had anything to do with a real wife or a real husband or a real plot to kill anybody, did it?"

"No," April said.

Morty moved closer to April. "Mrs. Blankenship, within your hearing, did Mr. Madison ever once criticize his wife?"

"No."

"Did he ever say she didn't understand him or any of the other things that men sometimes say in these situations?"

"No, he didn't."

"Did he ever indicate any displeasure of any kind with his wife?"

"No."

"Did he ever give any indication that he might wish her any harm?"

"No."

"Even jokingly?"

"No, he never said anything bad about Mrs. Madison or that he would do anything to hurt her."

Morty leaned forward slightly. "Mrs. Blankenship, you don't have any reason to protect Mr. Madison, do you?"

"No."

"You're not in love with him, are you?"

April's eyes suddenly bore into me, and in their stricken candor I saw the hardness I had added to her life.

"No," she said.

"Do you know of anything—something Mr. Madison said or anything at all—that might cause you to believe that he would ever harm his wife?"

Here was the moment, as I knew, when April could hurt me if she wished to hurt me, truly and deeply and fatally get even with me for having broken the only promise I'd made to her, the breaking of which had brought her to this public whipping post.

"No," she said, and on that word she hung her head and began to cry.

Morty let her remain in that a pose long enough for the jury to gain some sympathy for her, then he stepped back, like a man would from a good friend's coffin.

"No more questions," he said.

The Saga of Shady Arms

I watched as April struggled to compose herself, slowly and mechanically smoothing wrinkles from her skirt before she rose, still trembling, and made her way down from the witness stand. Clayton had already risen and taken a few steps toward her. When she reached him, he offered her his arm, as if escorting an elegant lady from the ballroom floor, and together they decorously made their way down the aisle, watched by a throng of locals before whom, after so public an evisceration, they must surely have felt naked.

"What's next?" I asked wearily.

"More of the same but not as dramatic," Morty answered.

By more of the same he meant various forms of corroborating evidence for my affair with April. And so Bart Lowell was next to take the stand, the owner of the squalid motel in whose bleak rooms April and I had met on those few occasions, and by whose answers to Mr. Singleton's questions the dreary saga of Shady Arms continued.

Yes, he had seen us often, seven times, as a matter of record, a number whose accuracy was demonstrated by the coffee-stained registration book he'd provided to Mr. Singleton.

Yes, we had used false names to sign that book.

In one question after another, the substance of the answers was the same. I was a liar and an adulterer and a fool. I laughed at convention and scorned all life's sacred values. I was unfaithful in love and arrogant in life and I had recklessly, wantonly, even laughingly torn to shreds the sacred fabric of the social order.

Under cross-examination, Morty made the witness admit that he had a record, two convictions for selling marijuana, and a third for postal fraud. He'd served light sentences in two cases, been put on probation for one. None of this did anything to impugn his earlier testimony, however, as Morty must have known. As he'd told me earlier, his intent here was to show that Singleton had scraped the bottom of the human barrel with regard to witnesses. There was no refuting their testimony, but they themselves could be made to look like pots calling kettles black. If jurors don't like a witness they tend not to believe him, was Morty's rule.

Willy Myers came next. He'd delivered pizza to our room at Shady Arms, during the course of which delivery he'd seen an uncorked bottle of wine on a bedside table, along with two glasses, one of which had lipstick stains. He'd also noticed a woman's slip hanging from the knob of a bathroom door and two sets of car keys in a glass ashtray. All of these Mr. Singleton shrewdly presented as visual metaphors for just the sort of back alley adultery I'd always referred to as *Butterfield 8*, and which I'd somehow distinguished from the high-toned infidelity of, say, *Anna Karenina*, though now it struck me that, in essence, adulteries, like Tolstoy's happy families, were all the same.

Morty's cross-examination attempted to paint Willy as a snoop and a gossip and, mercifully, he'd been arrested once as a Peeping Tom, though it appeared he'd been peeping into the window of the boys' shower room at his former high school rather than the hotel room of an adulterous couple.

After Willy, there were other witnesses whose testimony offered yet more seamy evidence for my crime. Phone records were presented to show a slew of calls from my cell phone to April's. There'd been e-mails, too, copies of which were waved before the jury like used condoms despite the fact that they sounded more like grocery orders than the hot-breathed exchanges of a couple carrying on a backstreet love affair.

It ended at around four in the afternoon, and after a brief conference with Morty, during which we discussed the fact that Mr. Singleton would likely rest his case the next day, I walked to the parking lot, where Alexandria was waiting for me, already behind the wheel.

"Morty says the prosecution's case is almost over," I told her as I settled into the passenger seat.

"Good," Alexandria said drily, then hit the accelerator and eased the car backward out of its place, then forward and out into Coburn's leisurely traffic.

She was silent for a long time, but I knew some dark bird was circling in her head.

"What is it?" I asked finally.

By then she'd pulled into the driveway of 237 Crescent Road.

"What?" I asked again when she didn't answer the first time.

She turned off the car and looked at me. "It's just another one of those dark thoughts," she said.

"Care to share it?"

"Not really."

"I think you should."

"Why?"

"It might give you peace."

An arid laugh burst from her. "You sound like a priest, Dad."

"A little bit, maybe," I admitted. "What's the dark thought?"

She hesitated, then came out with it. "That Mom had to have been some kind of saint . . ." She hesitated again, then added, ". . . to have lived with you."

I said nothing in response to this, but Alexandria saw how deeply she had sunk the knife.

"I'm sorry, Dad," she told me, "but you asked."

I nodded but said nothing, and in that lack of response I felt a numbness settle in, the sense that I had lost any capacity to offer anything to anyone, nothing left for my students, should I ever have any again, nothing to offer friends, should I ever have any at all, and at last nothing to offer Alexandria, not a single word of counsel nor so much as a pithy remark on how she should live.

"Dad?" Alexandria whispered, and then, when there was still no response, she reached over and touched my hand. "Let's go inside."

I got out of the car but had no desire whatsoever to go into a house that no longer held the slightest charm for me. And so, like a man looking for an avenue of escape, I glanced at the mailbox at the end of the driveway.

"I'll check the mail," I said to Alexandria, then headed for the box.

Once there, I opened it, expecting to see the usual stack of bills and junk mail, which was exactly what I found. It was the ordinary correspondence of an ordinary life, but among them was a catalog for the French chocolates Sandrine had called "original sin," and which had been her one gift to herself each month. They'd come in a beautiful red box, tied with a black ribbon, and with each month's delivery Sandrine's face became a sunburst of delight.

I'd canceled the order not long after her death and so no small red boxes had arrived after that. But with this lovely, elegant catalog they had made a final appearance, one last reminder of Sandrine.

Until then, my most vivid memory had been of our last dreadful encounter, the night she'd thrown that cup at me and in one furious statement after another delivered her smoldering *j'accuse*.

313

But now that moment seemed far way, like an ember cooling in the distance, which, in its dying, allowed room for a sweeter recollection than any I'd had since that wrenching night. It was only a few years after our arrival in Coburn. I'd come home to find Sandrine on the back porch, working with one of her students, as she often did, and so I walked into the kitchen where I found a book wrapped in a red ribbon, with a card attached, inscribed simply, *For you from me.* The book was a volume of Yeats's poetry, the favored poet of my youth, whose single-volume collection I'd taken with me on that fabled trip around the Mediterranean and which had grown tattered over the years and at last simply fallen apart. Sandrine had located the exact edition, and here it was, tied with red ribbon, and offered for no particular occasion, since it wasn't my birthday or our anniversary or any date of similar note. When I opened the card, I found Sandrine's message.

With hope that you can be aroused again.
(*No double entendre intended.*)

Suddenly, on the wave of that memory, I felt a laugh that was half a sob break from me.

(*No double entendre intended.*)

That little parenthetical wink of humor was pure Sandrine, and because of it I'd have known that the note came from her even if she hadn't signed it in that tiny script of hers.

(*No double entendre intended.*)

In the throes of that memory I suddenly felt a terrible wave of longing for Sandrine. Never in my life had I missed her more than now, as I stood, quaking, at the mailbox. Never had I mourned her more or, in the profound weakness of that moment, needed her more.

I might have collapsed, assumed a fetal position in the shadow of the mailbox and bawled like a baby or wailed like an animal, if I hadn't suddenly glimpsed Alexandria standing in the doorway.

"Are you going to stand out there all night, Dad?" she asked. She glanced at the elegant catalog that still dangled from my fingers and saw clearly that I was in distress.

"Are you coming in?" she asked.

"Yes," I said, then shoved the catalog into my pocket.

At dinner, Alexandria talked about everything but my trial. She talked a little about her work, its many dissatisfactions, although, as she said, at least she had a job.

During all of this I remained for the most part silent, a vague, enclosed figure at the end of the table, often gazing out into the backyard, where Sandrine's gazebo rested in the half-light that came from the interior of the house.

At some point I became aware that Alexandria had stopped talking, and when I looked back toward her I saw that she was staring silently at me.

"What are you thinking, Dad?" she asked.

I'd hardly been aware of what I'd been thinking until I was asked. Then it seemed quite a vivid thought.

"About your mother," I answered quietly.

"What about her?" Alexandria asked cautiously, as if afraid she might set off rather than defuse a bomb.

"She loved Terence, the Roman playwright," I said. "The one she mentioned to the travel agent. There was a line of his she often quoted."

"What's the line?" Alexandria asked.

"Terence said that he, himself, was cracked," I answered. "As a man, he was cracked and leaking from many holes."

315

There was a long silence after that, Alexandria watching me with an expression I found hard to decipher, save that it wasn't hostile.

"You've changed," she said finally and quite softly, like an ornithologist trying to decide if this was a new species of bird or one well known but oddly marked.

A few minutes later we walked into the living room and polished off the wine, just half a glass each but enough to sip at a leisurely pace.

"Where do you think you'd like to live if you could live anywhere?" she said after a moment.

I thought of her question and then of my answer for a long time.

"Here," I said finally. "In Coburn."

"But I thought you never liked it," Alexandria said.

"I never gave it a chance," I told her softly. "Everything deserves a chance."

Alexandria watched me silently, and a little fearfully, so that I knew I was cracking, leaking.

"You should go to bed now," she said, a clear sign that my daughter had no idea how she might mend the breach or plug the holes in what remained of the badly damaged vessel I'd become.

"Yes, I suppose I should," I told her.

A few minutes later I was in my room, the lights out, thinking of Sandrine, of the book she'd given me so long ago, the message inside it, and from those thoughts, moving on to others, and at last wondering what it was I'd possessed at Albi that had made her say, in that lovely, intense, come to judgment way of hers, "It's you."

We'd arrived in the town late in the afternoon, that much I remembered. We walked around for a while before going into the cathedral, where, once inside, we separated. Sandrine strolled along the right side of the church, toward where the figure of doomed Saint Cecilia lay, the three bloody cuts by which her murder had been attempted clearly visible, red and raw, on the back of her neck.

I moved down the opposite aisle toward the altar, where I stood and looked at the mural that covered the wall at the front of the church. Sandrine joined me there a few minutes later, then we turned and exited the church. By then the sun was setting and we walked along a terrace and peered out over the valley, the river below us a vein of gold, like the light around us, as softly radiant as any I'd ever seen. It was then Sandrine had said, "You're the one," with that look of surprise in her eyes. "It's you."

Such had been our single day in Albi, or at least all that I could still recall of it. We left for Toulouse the following morning and from there by train to Paris, and from Paris home, to where Coburn College's job offers awaited us and which we'd finally accepted and after which I'd lost whatever Sandrine had seen in Albi, but which I still couldn't define or locate no matter how many times I went back over my few memories of the place. And how many times was that? Fifty times during the course of the evening? Perhaps a hundred? Perhaps even more than that as night first deepened, then lightened into morning, so that I was still awake and staring at the ceiling when Alexandria tapped at my door.

"Dad," she said softly. "Time to get up."

"Do I really have to?" I asked, and truly and profoundly I meant it.

My daughter's answer was like herself, practical, matter-of-fact, deeply connected to the bottom line.

"Life goes on," she said.

DAY TEN

Call Malcolm Esterman

He gave me only the most peremptory glance as he made his way to the witness stand, a look that was hard to read, partly Malcolm being Malcolm, which meant his being somewhat shy, partly a vague dread, like a reluctant bearer of bad news.

I nodded to him casually, as I might have greeted him on the street, a friendly gesture toward the man to whom Sandrine had gone in her hour of need, and with whom she had no doubt shared quite painful intimacies.

On the stand, Malcolm raised his hand at the same slow pace that his short legs had taken him to it. He was perhaps five-foot-three, with small, rounded shoulders, and he wore thick glasses that gave him just the sort of owlish look the students of Coburn College had surely mocked. I had little doubt that he'd endured his share of such mockery, both as a boy and later. The world is rarely kind to the bookish, especially if there's nothing of the warrior-athlete-poet in the bookish boy's physique. A pipe with a gnawed stem would have completed the image but, mercifully, Malcolm had never smoked.

"I am an associate professor in the History Department at Coburn College," he said in answer to Mr. Singleton's first question.

He had been an associate professor for more than twenty years, I knew, a teacher of ancient history to students who incessantly tweeted their current location or mood swing in rapid bursts of 140 characters or less. He'd never completed his PhD thesis, and so all his life he'd lived in the all-but-dissertation backwater that is academia's eternal purgatory. I had rarely paid much attention to him, if only because he rarely made his presence known. He sat in the back at faculty meetings and almost never spoke. I'd often seen him sitting alone on the quadrangle, usually with a book, but often not reading it. Instead, he would stare off into the middle distance, his large brown eyes blinking slowly, his expression fixed in what Sandrine had once called "tragic contemplation," though she'd been referring to a bust of Marcus Aurelius rather than to Malcolm.

"Now, during the course of your time at Coburn, did you have occasion to meet Sandrine Allegra Madison?" Mr. Singleton asked.

"Yes," Malcolm answered.

"And you became friends with her, isn't that true?"

"Friends, yes." His eyes darted over to me. "Only friends," he added.

With that response, the pornographic images that had sometimes tormented me with regard to Malcolm and Sandrine immediately dissolved. Malcolm, I decided, was incapable of telling anything but the truth, a man without airs, who never hinted, however tangentially, at any experience he had not had. At Coburn, he had surely lived as a sparrow in a hawk's nest, I thought, a serene, self-contained man, at home with his own modest abilities, seeking to maintain only the few treasures he possessed, a man with no worlds he wished to conquer, nor any rival he wished to best, nor anything he needed to prove to anyone but himself, and thus, because of all that, a man so deeply grounded that Sandrine, my incandescent wife, had evidently felt the pull of his quiet gravity.

"She was interested in the women of the ancient world," Malcolm added. "Cleopatra and Hypatia." He smiled softly, then added, "She had built a home for these women in her mind."

Mr. Singleton could not have cared less for this gracious and vaguely poetic way of describing Sandrine's intellectual interests.

"Now, during the last year, you had occasion to see Mrs. Madison quite often, isn't that true?" he asked.

"Yes," Malcolm answered. "We would sometimes meet in the faculty room or in the library."

"And what did you talk about on those occasions?"

Malcolm offered his familiar, self-deprecating smile. "Well, to put it grandly, I suppose you could say that we talked about the wisdom of the ancients."

In which sacred wisdom Mr. Singleton clearly had no interest.

"But there came a time when you talked about things that were a little more down to earth, isn't that true, Dr. Esterman?"

"I don't have a doctorate," Malcolm corrected, then went on to answer the question.

"Yes, but it took a while for us to talk about these other things," he said. "At first it was just ancient history things between us. She was good at picking another person's mind, finding gems."

It was obvious that Mr. Singleton's pace was too fast for Malcolm. But it was also obvious that the witness would not be rushed.

"Sandrine was a thoughtful person," Malcolm continued pointedly. "But not in an abstract way. She thought that the purpose of philosophy was first of all to teach you how to live, and, after that, to teach you how to die."

Which surely is the bottom line, I thought.

"All right, but at some point, Mrs. Madison told you about a recent diagnosis, didn't she?" Mr. Singleton asked somewhat impatiently.

"Yes," Malcolm answered. "She said she had Lou Gehrig's disease. It was very sad, of course."

"In fact, upon receiving this diagnosis, she went directly to you, correct?"

"Evidently so," Malcolm answered. "She'd just spoken to her doctor when she came to my house that day."

I couldn't help but imagine the lonely drive Sandrine had made on that rainy afternoon. It would have taken her from Dr. Ortins's office, down Coburn's Main Street, along the edges of the college campus, and then down a quiet country lane to Malcolm's vaguely wooded condominium. She would have glimpsed the school's quadrangle as she made her way, and the library, and the little restaurant where we sometimes dined. She would have seen the college president's house, where we'd been so warmly received our first day here. The hospital in which Alexandria had been born would have appeared at the edge of town, and beyond that the reservoir where she ran, the pool where she swam, the pond along whose edges we'd sometimes strolled during our first months in Coburn and where she'd taken my hand and said, as I recalled now, "You can be happy here, Sam, if you let yourself."

But I had not, as Mr. Singleton's next question began to reveal.

"Now, after she got to your house, Mrs. Madison told you about this diagnosis, and then she expressed some concerns regarding her husband, isn't that true?"

"Yes," Malcolm answered. "She said she thought her husband felt that she had failed."

Failed?

Not once had Sandrine ever indicated such a thought to me. Yes, I had been surprised that her career had been less than meteoric, that she'd never written a great book, or any other book for that matter, that she'd made little effort to rise higher in the academic firmament. But I had blamed Coburn for that, the soporific effect it had had on both of us.

"Failed in her career aspirations?" Singleton asked.

"No," Malcolm answered. "Failed as a woman. Failed to give her husband what he most needed."

So she had known after all, I thought, known and blamed herself for my dalliance with April, blamed herself in God only knew how many foolish ways for my folly: that she was often at evening classes, that she spent too much time in the scriptorium or with her students. Sandrine, being Sandrine, could have generated a thousand reasons to blame herself when I alone had been to blame for those afternoons at Shady Arms. For that reason, it struck me that Sandrine had failed only in that she had never confronted me with regard to what she knew about April and me, and because of which her ire had simply grown hotter and hotter until it had finally exploded on that last night.

But in this, as it turned out, I was, as in so many other things, completely wrong.

"And what did she feel that her husband needed the most?" Mr. Singleton asked.

"Correction," Malcolm answered quietly.

"Correction?" Mr. Singleton asked. "What did she mean by that?"

"A correction in his course," Malcolm answered. "In his trajectory. She had failed to remind him of what he'd once been."

"Which was what?"

Malcolm's gaze drifted over to me as he answered.

"Kind," Malcolm said. "She said that he had once had a big heart. He read with his heart, and she thought that he could teach with his heart. They'd once even planned to build a school together, she said."

Now his attention returned to Mr. Singleton.

"I think that having to leave her husband was what she most regretted," he added. "Leaving him the way he was, I mean."

Mr. Singleton had by then grown weary of what he clearly considered a form of testimony that was utterly irrelevant to the larger point he now made.

"Did Mrs. Madison indicate that she thought her husband would be a good caregiver for her during her coming illness?"

"She said that he probably would not be."

"Why is that?"

Again, Malcolm's attention returned to me, almost as if he'd planned it that way, his gaze on me as quietly, and yet with the same intensity, as Sandrine's.

"She said that he had hardened over the years," he answered. "Disappointment had torn at him, she said, and it had left him with a lot of scar tissue." He paused, then added pointedly, "And scar tissue does not feel."

"Scar tissue?" Mr. Singleton said, seizing the word as if it were a bullet he could now load into his gun. "She said that her husband was without feeling, correct?"

"Yes."

"Did Mrs. Madison indicate that she thought her husband might grow impatient?"

"Impatient?" Malcolm asked, his attention now returned to Mr. Singleton, who'd begun to pace back and forth before the witness box.

"Impatient, yes," Singleton replied. "Impatient with her illness, the fact that it might take several years for her to die. Did she feel that he didn't love her, that he didn't want her to live, that he hoped she would die as quickly as possible? Did she think these things about her husband?"

I leaned forward, because surely, surely, to this question, truthful, unassuming, with no grudge against me, Malcolm could honestly say no.

"Yes," Malcolm said. "Yes, she believed all those things."

And so it had never been my affair with April—providing she'd ever even known about it—that Sandrine had accused me of on the final night of her life. Rather, it had been a far more profound betrayal, a hardness that had grown harder year by year until it had finally become a thick, interior wall, a scar tissue of dead nerves that had even separated me from Sandrine in her anguish, Sandrine in her terror, Sandrine dying.

I thought of the fear and sorrow that must have weighed down upon her. I had not offered my shoulder to any of that overwhelming weight. I should have had only one mission after that meeting in Dr. Ortins's office, to love and give comfort to the woman whose death it foretold, she who, even in her final communications with this world, had demonstrated the wit, intelligence, and fierce knowingness that had made her, too, queen of the Nile.

"She didn't want to leave him still living in this way," Malcolm added. "Alive, but dead. She wanted to change him before she died."

Mr. Singleton glanced at the jury, then stopped his pacing.

"She needed to find out who he was and so she came up with a general plan," Malcolm added.

Singleton took a step closer to the witness box. "And what was this general plan?" he asked.

"To confront him with himself," Malcolm said. "To see if it was possible to make him see himself."

"Did Mrs. Madison ever give you any idea of how she intended to do this?"

"She would try to reach him," Malcolm answered. "She would try to do this tenderly."

I thought of all the times during Sandrine's last six months when I'd come home to find her reading or listening to music, how she'd always stopped to look up from the book and turn down the music, the way she'd mentioned some little nugget from the book or the name of the song, an invitation, as I realized now, to engage her and be engaged by her, as it were, Socratically, all of which I had obliviously turned down.

"And did Mrs. Madison ever give you any idea as to her success or lack of success in this effort?" Mr. Singleton asked.

She had, of course.

"And had she had any success?"

I hardly needed to hear his answer.

"No," he said.

"Did Mrs. Madison discuss this lack of success with you, Mr. Esterman?"

"Yes, she did."

"What did she say about it?"

"She said that she was going to raise the stakes."

"In what way?"

"There would be no more of what she called 'tender traps.'"

Tender traps, I thought, how entirely Sandrine, first to try them, then discard them when they didn't work, her gaze ever fixed on the bottom line.

"Did she give you any idea of what these next attempts would be?" Mr. Singleton asked.

Malcolm shook his head. "I don't know what they were," he said, "but she said it would mean pulling away from him."

And she had done exactly that, I thought, as I recalled the days and nights of Sandrine ignoring me, barely speaking to me, no longer listening to me, days and nights of Sandrine distant, as I'd described it to Alexandria, Sandrine "streaming."

"All right, but even though Mrs. Madison never mentioned whether or not these new methods were successful, she did indicate a final effort, isn't that so?" Mr. Singleton asked.

"Yes."

"And according to Mrs. Madison, what was that final effort going to be?"

"Fury," Malcolm said. "She was going to make her husband furious."

"How was she going to do this?"

"By telling the truth," Malcolm answered. "By telling him to his face in as blunt a way as possible exactly what he had become."

"And what was that?"

A sociopath, I thought.

"She never said," Malcolm answered.

Mr. Singleton paused for a moment, his gaze sweeping over to the jury, where he kept it briefly before returning his attention to the witness.

"When did Mrs. Madison tell you that she planned to 'tell the truth' to her husband?" he asked.

"The night of November the fourteenth."

"November the fourteenth," Mr. Singleton repeated. "Which was the night Mrs. Madison . . . died?"

Malcolm nodded slowly. "Yes."

"So there were no more plans," Mr. Singleton added softly, like a man in mourning. For a moment he simply stood silently, his hands folded almost in prayer before him. At last, he said, "Mr. Esterman, did Sandrine ever indicate to you what she wanted at the end of her life?"

Ah, I thought, the moment had at last come for Mr. Singleton to demonstrate that he is now on familiar terms with my wife, free to use her first name.

"Wanted?" Malcolm asked.

"Yes."

"She wanted her husband and her daughter to find good lives," Malcolm answered. "It was as simple as that. She would like to have been able to look into the future and know that they had made good lives. But only fiction can look into the future, she told me. Only fiction

329

could, as she put it, 'crack the old verities of time and space,' and show what lies ahead." He paused a moment, then added, "But if Sandrine had been able to see a good future for her husband and daughter, then I think she would have been at rest." He smiled softly. "She even had a painting of what she thought that rest would look like."

"Did she show you this painting?"

"Yes, she did," Malcolm answered.

Mr. Singleton walked over to his desk, picked up a large book, and handed it to his witness. "Could you turn to the marked page, please?" he asked.

Malcolm did.

"Is that the painting Sandrine showed you?"

"Yes, it is."

"What did Sandrine say about this painting?" Mr. Singleton asked.

"That she had first seen it with her husband," Malcolm told the court, "In a little French town called Albi. It was by a painter named Antonio Mancini. It was called *Resting*."

Then, quite suddenly, I knew.

It had not been in the cathedral, the moment that had so seared itself into Sandrine's mind and heart, but in a small gallery off the town's central square. Not even a gallery, really, but simply a shop that sold reproductions of famous paintings. The walls had been hung with other reproductions, everything from the Dutch masters to Picasso with no sense of order as to either the era during which they'd been painted or the style in which they'd been painted, or in fact anything else that might have indicated the owner of the shop knew the slightest bit about the history of art.

Yet within all this chaos Sandrine's gaze had been drawn to *Resting,* and she'd stood before it for a long time, as I did, the two of us quite transfixed not by its technical expertise, nor by our knowing anything about the painter or his school, but simply by what hung before us on that mock canvas: a woman lying in her bed, partially covered by white sheets, her eyes open, her lips parted, a small table beside the bed, and on this table several glass jars, all of them reflecting the glow of a candle that alone illuminates the woman's face and hair and porcelain white upper body and finally the rose she holds just below her single, exposed breast.

We stood silently before this painting for a long time. Then, still ineffably moved by it, I said, "Strange, but I really care about the woman in this painting."

Sandrine nodded. "I'm sure you do, Sam."

"It makes me want to sweep into the room and lie down beside her and just . . . hold her."

"Yes," Sandrine said, then looked up at me and smiled. "That's what a knight in shining armor really is."

And that is precisely what I had failed to be in Sandrine's darkest hour, the moment when my noble, noble wife had most been in need of me.

On that recognition it struck me that if, at some moment in a man's life, he suddenly realizes just how low and selfish and, yes, sociopathic he is, then at that moment, wrenchingly and in silent anguish, he will accept the just verdict that his head should roll.

There were other questions after that, and more answers, a drone of voices, ghostly and distant, but I no longer heard what was being said until they abruptly stopped.

"The state rests, Your Honor," Mr. Singleton said.

Morty began to rise, but I grabbed his arm. "So does the defense," I told him.

Morty looked at me, stunned by what I'd just said, but not in the least doubting that I meant it.

"Rest my case," I told him resolutely. "Rest it now or you're fired."

"Sam, please."

I shook my head. "Either you do it or I will."

"Sam . . ."

"No!"

Morty nodded, then lifted himself from the chair.

"Your Honor, my client has come to a decision," he said. He paused and for a moment I thought he would stop, turn to me, argue against the choice I'd made. In fact, he did glance at me, saw that I was absolutely firm, then returned his attention to the judge. "The defense rests," he said.

And so, at last, it seemed to me, did the clearly guilty defendant in Sandrine's case.

Verdict

"Ready?" Alexandria asked as I came toward her early on what would surely be the last day of my trial. She was standing at the door and had already opened it.

I nodded. "I truly am," I told her.

"Just remember, Dad," she added. "Whatever happens, we'll deal with it."

I smiled. "Yes, we will."

During the past two days, while we'd awaited the jury's verdict, it had become clear to me that Alexandria had come to the conclusion that I wasn't guilty of the charge, that Sandrine's death had been a final, desperate effort to save my life by waking me up to what I was and would forever be if not shocked into a change.

Like a warrior prepared to charge, Alexandria said now, "Let's do it."

On the way to the courthouse we passed directly through the town, the people opening their shops, the usual traffic, a town whose quiet lanes and modest university Sandrine had accepted in lieu of that far more idealistic dream of building a school in some remote corner of the earth, one never specified but which, as a vision for us, our lives, our work, she had never entirely abandoned.

"What are you thinking, Dad?" Alexandria asked.

"It's always about your mother," I told her. "This time, it was how she could be quite a stickler for grammar and an elegant structure, the way she insisted on using phrases like 'into which' and 'about which' and 'according to whom,' because they made thoughts flow so beautifully and seamlessly, one into the other. She taught me all of that."

"She taught me that, too," Alexandria said. "And I've tried to pass it on to some of the writers at sleeplesseye.com, but they never seem that interested in learning the old lessons."

Morty stood waiting at the top of the courthouse steps, still unhappy that I'd ordered him not to defend me and now peering at me with just the sort of stern look that could, as P. G. Wodehouse had once said, open an oyster at forty feet.

"Are you sure about this?" he asked when I reached him. "There might still be some way that I could . . ."

I shook my head.

"All right, then," Morty said. "Let's go."

The members of the jury appeared quite somber as they filed into the courtroom, all of them peering either at some distant point in the room or toward the judge or in the general direction of where Mr. Singleton sat in the same suit he'd worn on the first day of my trial, though now the serpentine fold that had slithered across the back of his neck was less visible when he sat.

Once seated, the members of the jury continued to either face solemnly forward or glance at their hands or follow the dance of some imaginary light around the room, twelve citizens, good and true, who suddenly seemed exactly that to me, not the hate-filled provincials of Morty's perfervid imagination but simple, decent people with a job to do and who had done it as best they could.

"Mr. Foreman, have you reached a verdict?" Judge Rutledge asked.

"We have, Your Honor," the foreman said.

The hinge that swings us toward calamity rarely squeaks, I thought as the jury foreman rose to deliver the verdict in my case. Life should fill our ears with warnings, but it falls silent at our infant cry.

"Would you hand it to the bailiff, please," Judge Rutledge said.

He did so, then sat down and watched as the bailiff carried the jury's verdict to the court reporter.

"Would you please read the verdict," the judge instructed.

The court reporter rose and read.

"We, the jury, in the above entitled action, find the defendant, Samuel Joseph Madison, not guilty."

To my surprise, there was not a sound in the courtroom, not one ripple of discontent. A few reporters scribbled in their notebooks but, beyond those small movements, the world seemed very still.

The judge turned to the jury. "Ladies and gentlemen, thank you for rendering a service our democracy requires," he said. "You are dismissed."

Morty glanced at me and whispered, "You're one lucky bastard, Sam."

Perhaps so, I thought, or perhaps the twelve men and women of the jury had simply decided that, though I may well have murdered my wife, there was scant evidence to prove it. They had been charged by the judge to be fair and scrupulous and to adhere to the laws of evidence in my case, and that is exactly what they had done, and in response to which these people of Coburn, who no doubt still despised everything I believed and everything I was, had set me free.

Now, as they rose, I rose, too, and in that gesture of respect returned to them all I could.

Mr. Singleton came over to Morty as the last of the jurors exited the court. He smiled and offered his hand. Morty took it, smiled back, then each exchanged the sort of look that said, Well, the jury has spoken, and a good thing, too. Then, to my astonishment, Mr. Singleton offered his hand to me, and I saw that he really had believed I'd killed Sandrine, though now he seemed less sure.

"I felt the evidence compelled me to make a case," he told me. "But I knew I never had a strong one." With that, he nodded politely, turned, and left.

"What an asshole," Morty muttered.

Was he? I no longer knew. Sandrine had thought Montaigne the soul of wisdom for the simple reason that, in answer to so many conflicting matters, he had responded only with "I withhold judgment."

Which is what I now did upon Mr. Singleton, and upon all the witnesses against me, upon my colleagues at the college, too, and at last upon all the Coburnites of this world.

"So what now?" Morty asked as we made our way out of the courtroom.

"I don't know," I admitted, which was true.

At the top of the stairs, he shook my hand. "Stay in touch," he said, but I knew he didn't mean it.

"I will," I said, and didn't mean it either.

Alexandria took my arm and smiled. "You can drive us home, Dad," she said.

And so I did, back through the town, through the life I'd shared with Sandrine, back into those many memories, aware of how they seemed to sprout like flowers in every open space.

At the house, Alexandria rushed in to call Jenna and let her know the verdict. I headed for the mailbox, where I found nothing but the usual bills and advertisements. I was already halfway back to the house when I heard again footsteps behind me, though this time, when I turned, it wasn't April I found standing there.

"Clayton," I said.

He drew the pistol from his jacket, his grandfather's dueling pistol, I saw immediately, probably the very one he had mentioned to me on the afternoon I'd gone to his house.

How appropriate a weapon, I thought, with which to kill a scoundrel.

"My grandfather defended his wife's honor with this pistol," Clayton said. "I'm going to do the same."

I nodded, and for a moment I wondered why I was not afraid, why I felt it quite in keeping that I should die this way, shot by Clayton Blankenship after being freed by a Coburn jury, the fact that many of my fellow townspeople would certainly feel that no matter how much they disapproved of such vigilante justice it was, in fact, justice that had been served, and Clayton the perfect man to have served it. Morty would doubtless get him off.

"She was just a silly girl to you," Clayton said. "I'm sure that's how you thought of April, that she was just a silly girl you could toy with."

I nodded. "Yes, that's exactly how I thought of her," I told him.

Clayton pressed the pistol toward me slightly. "Don't move," he said.

"I won't," I assured him, and never had I felt more certain of anything in my life.

"I want you to know that I plan to go with you," Clayton said. "As soon as this is done."

"There's no need for that," I told him, then forced a small sad smile. "You'll be acquitted, Clayton. I myself would find you not guilty."

Something in those kind and noble eyes softened slightly. "I'm so sorry it has come to this." He drew the hammer back and it sounded with a fatal click. "Well," he said softly. "Well, then."

He hesitated, and I have no idea if he actually would have pulled the trigger. I know only that a voice came out of the dark.

"Dad?"

It was Alexandria. She was standing at the door, peering out at what must have seemed a strange tableau, Clayton and I facing each other.

"Hi, Mr. Blankenship," she said gently, sweetly, with great . . . yes . . . kindness. On that note, my eyes grew moist. Oh how like Sandrine she is, I thought, oh how like her deeply knowing mother.

Clayton immediately returned the hammer to its place and sank the pistol into his pocket.

"Do you want to come in?" Alexandria asked.

There was an edge of fear in her voice, but she acted against it and took an impossibly courageous step out onto the lawn.

"Good evening, Alexandria," Clayton said softly as he turned toward her. A smile flickered onto his lips. "I just came to tell your father . . ." He stopped and his large eyes drifted over to me. ". . . that I agree with the jury."

Alexandria took another step toward us, then another, until we formed a small tragic circle in the frigid moonlight.

"I truly admired your mother," Clayton said to Alexandria. Then he looked at me and with a decency hardly imaginable he said simply, "I hope you have a good life, Sam, the rest of it." He glanced toward Alexandria. "With your loyal, loyal daughter."

"Thank you," I told him, and with all my heart I meant it.

He turned and walked back into the darkness, in every way a knight in shining armor.

"So what do you want for dinner?" Alexandria asked.

"Popcorn," I answered softly.

She looked at me, clearly puzzled.

"Remember when you were just a little girl?" I asked. "Your mother and I would declare 'junk night' and just have popcorn for dinner, or potato chips and onion dip."

She laughed. "And a movie," she reminded me. "Always with a movie."

"Right, a movie."

"I'll go get one," she said.

"I'll make the popcorn."

I'd popped up a huge bowl of popcorn by the time she got back. I'd also melted butter and generously doused the whole mixture with a flavorful excess of salt.

"Smells good," Alexandria said as she walked into the kitchen. She held one of those generic DVD cases and I couldn't see the movie she'd chosen.

"It's an old one," she said, keeping things mysterious. "One of Mom's favorites. I remember us watching it together."

"Perfect," I said and picked up the bowl of popcorn and added it to the tray upon which I'd already placed two glasses of soda. "I guess we're ready then."

The movie was *The Chosen*, and Alexandria was right, it had been one of Sandrine's favorites. It was based on a Chaim Potok novel that I was reasonably certain she had never read, and yet something in the film had always gotten to Sandrine, perhaps its tale of two people torn apart but ceaselessly attempting to connect again. It had always struck me as a rather sentimental movie, and it still did, save for the voice-over that comes at the very end of the film relating a story from the Talmud.

Sitting in the dark with my daughter, the dregs of junk night strewn around us, I listened once again to that voice, the tale it told of two people who'd once loved each other but whose relationship had foundered and who now lived in different places. One sends a messenger to the other. "Come half the distance that divides us," the message says, "and I will meet you there." The other refuses. "I am sorry," the return message says, "but I cannot meet you halfway." The other considers this message, considers the consequences of never again seeing or being with this other person that he loves. And so he sends a second message: "Then tell me how far you can come toward me, and I will meet you there."

I recalled that Sandrine's eyes had glistened at that.

Mine hadn't, and didn't that night either. And yet I found myself quite moved by this old story, moved and wondering where it might be, this place where I could yet meet Sandrine, a woman who'd so loved language and felt that sentences should be held together by "into which" and "according to whom," held together like the fingers of a hand, as she'd told her students, so that they might bear the weight of wisdom.

"What are we going to do now, Dad?" Alexandria asked as the final credits rolled.

Suddenly I knew.

"This," I said.

Samuel Joseph Madison, the beloved founder of the Sandrine School of Kumasi, has died at the age of seventy-four. Mr. Madison founded the school in 2014, in honor of his wife, Sandrine Allegra Madison, for whom the school is named. For twenty-five years, Mr. Madison taught the children of Kumasi and its surrounding villages. Many of his students went on to obtain advanced degrees in England, Australia, and the United States, including this reporter. Mr. Madison is survived by his daughter, Ali, also a teacher at the school, and according to whom the school's doors will remain open into the indefinite future.

West African News Agency
Accra, Ghana, July 12, 2042